Wrath of Anwen
By
Gareth J Hughes

Copyright © Gareth J Hughes 2013

The Author asserts the moral right to
Be identified as the author of this work

This book is dedicated to all miners past and present.

All the characters in this book are fictitious, and any resemblance to actual persons, living or dead, is purely coincidental. The names, incidents, dialogue and opinions expressed are products of the author's imagination and are not to be construed as real. Nothing is intended or should be interpreted as expressing or representing the views of the author or anyone else living or dead.

Other Books by Gareth J Hughes

Snatchers: (ASIN: B006TJQ4VU)

Would You Believe It? (ASIN: B00945G0HO)

Content

Chapter I: The Beginning
Chapter II: November 1967
Chapter III: December 1967
Chapter IV: Christmas 1967
Chapter V: January 1968
Chapter VI: Caradog Pritchard
Chapter VII: Friday 3rd May 1968
Chapter VIII: May 1969 Plagued with water
Chapter IX: June 1970 The inquest
Chapter X: Day Two
Chapter XI: Day Three
Chapter XII: Off to the races
Chapter XIII: Christmas 1970
Chapter XIV: 1971
Chapter XV: November 1971
Chapter XVI: January 1972
Chapter XVII: Picketing power stations
Chapter XVIII: Caradog recovers
Chapter XIX: Iolo bach
Chapter XX: Christmas 1972
Chapter XXI: Fight-back
Chapter XXII: Silt
Chapter XXIII: The rescue
Chapter XXIV: Christmas 1974
Chapter XXV: Autumn 1975
Chapter XXVI: Christmas 1975
Chapter XXVII: July 1976
Chapter XXVIII: Christmas 1976
Chapter XXIX: January 1978
Chapter XXX: January 1979
Chapter XXXI: Gob heading

Synopsis: Wrath of Anwen

This is the story of a fictional coalmining village situated deep in the heart of the South Wales valleys. Cwm Derw is a small coalmining village endowed with a wealth of diverse characters. The villagers are about to experience a dramatic change as the world around them undergo an uncontrollable change.

Chapter I

The Beginning

The village of Cwm Derw nestles peacefully in the side of a windy Welsh valley, its people are mainly descendants from a bygone time when men and their families left their places of birth and travelled to the welsh valleys in search of work in the ever expanding coal and iron industries. Life was hard for those ill-fated people as they competed for work. Countless hopeful workers died of starvation brought on by paltry wages or that they were too weak to get through the tough times looking for work. Families perished in the cholera epidemics of the 19th century, and it is the descendants of the hardy survivors of the great coal rush who are among the inhabitants of Cwm Derw and other mining communities.

    Cwm Derw village was built for coal miners, rows of terraced houses stretched for a hundred yards or more, one long row behind another filling up the hillside like rows and rows of stone built dragons, puffing out smoke from the numerous coal fired chimneys.

    Life for a retired coal miner was short. It was common for him (if he had the breath) to spend his retirement days working in his small garden or he wandered about the village. Maybe he sat on the village square gossiping and laughing about days gone by when working down the coalmine. Life for the women of the village wasn't easy either; they spent their time rearing their children to a high standard of respect and decency, many existing on meagre wages and poor housing.

    When the boys of Cwm Derw left school many went to work in the Cwm Derw colliery, while others including girls went on to the few emerging industries. Very few managed to enter the Universities unless they were gifted with above average intelligence and had the benefit of opportunity.

August 1967

Monday 1pm

Colliery Overman, Iolo Pritchard's large bony knuckles gently tapped the long wooden aneroid barometer that hung on a wall by the front door. He studied the black needle as it ominously shifted indicating that there was a drop in barometric pressure. Mumbling to himself he strode to the back kitchen window. Pensively he began gazing out of the window that faced the back yard; he eyed Anwen his pretty wife. Her pearly white teeth seemed to glisten in the morning sun as she pegged up one of her husband's collarless white shirts. Her wispy blonde hair fluttered in the morning breeze. He eyed her sexiness as she slowly leaned over the laundry basket and teased out another one of his white shirts.

Iolo quickly looked at his wristwatch, his thoughts turned to the matter of what he had to do at the pit. "First see the under Manager and then visit the Blacksmith's shop. "I wonder if Dai Black Nail has finished the job I ordered," he muttered to himself.

Iolo's mind flitted from what he had to do at the Colliery to the small changes in Anwen's behaviour.

Jack Williams, under Manager, looked up from his desk and stared sternly at Iolo Pritchard over scratched half round spectacles, "Well, Iolo, I suppose you heard that water broke into your district over the weekend. There's a sorry mess down there, we've been trying all morning to get pipelines and pumps into the district. Bloody surveyors failed to tell us about standing water in the seam above, coffee stains on the plans they said!" Jack Williams was referring to Colliery safety plans.

Iolo angrily stared down over his nose at the irate under Manager; he held back his thoughts on the matter 'why wasn't he informed about the inrush of water?' He caught Bernard Thomas's eye and called to him: "Bernard, a word please!" Bernard Thomas followed the Overman 'his immediate boss' on to the Colliery yard. Iolo expressed his dire anger at the Deputy; he could have been informed about the inrush. After a heated discussion, Iolo instructed the Deputy to organise the on-going shift "We must get the water level down and get production going again," said Iolo. He then made his way to Dai Black Nail in the Blacksmith's shop. 'What's the bloody' point he muttered angrily, he turned and went in search of Bill Pumpy the pumps-man.

Bill Pumpy was sipping tea from a large enamel mug and talking to Colin Wilde, Colliery Chief Mechanic.

"I've been looking for you all over the place Bill Pumpy, I want you to do a double shift for me, we have to get the water level down and get production going again," said Iolo, he rubbed his smooth chin and waited for Bill Pumpy to answer.

"I've been on the job since early last night, called out from the Collier's Arms," explained the tired Pumps-man. "I can give you a couple of hours, and then it's up to the fitters, they'll have to watch the pumps when I'm gone," he said and then noisily drank the remains of the tea from the large enamel mug.

Colin Wilde, Colliery Mechanic looked on as Bill Pumpy picked up a heavy bag of tools from the floor and heaved it over his shoulder with a hammer pushed through the handles, and then he waddled out of the office.

"Good chap is Bill," commented the boss of all things mechanical. "I don't have to worry so much when he's on the job, works like a horse and intelligent with it," Colin remarked. Meanwhile Bernard Thomas had rounded up the men and herded them down the box- pit shouting orders at them.

Iolo Pritchard, along with the other underground bosses got on the pit-carriage ready to descend the shaft. The pit-carriage descended at a steady rate they were all laughing and joking among themselves when unexpectedly the pit-carriage picked up exceptional speed and then stopped abruptly. The steel pit-rope stretched and then recoiled you could hear a pin drop; every-one was thinking, 'this is it… my number's up!' The pit-carriage bobbed up and down on the end of the substantial steel pit-rope. After a few minutes the pit carriage began to descend the shaft once more.

Charlie Dicks the On-setter commonly called 'hitcher' raised the gate of the carriage and grinned slyly as the bosses began to leave the pit-cage white faced. "Enjoyed the ride did you boys? I hear Colin Wilde's investigating." He quipped, Charlie seemed to be always grinning, he loved his job, and nothing went up the pit or came down it without old Charlie knowing about it. It gave him an overpowering sense of authority he was in charge and he let everybody know about it.

"How long has this overwind been going on" asked Iolo, Jack Williams raced to the manhole where the pit bottom telephone was located?

"About twelve o' clock, this was the third time," stated Charlie Dicks still grinning slyly, hands in pockets and thumbs out. Iolo laughed out loud.

The roadway to the number 26 district in the Gelli Deg seam was knee deep in murky, filthy water; it stretched as far as the eye could see in the darkness and stank of excrement. Miner's cap-lamps flashed in the distance, Bill Pumpy was in charge shouting orders at the men who were suspending pipes along the water filled roadway. Iolo flicked with a piece of timber at a floating turd that had drifted from where it had lain for many weeks. Suddenly Iolo saw a small pair of red devilish eyes swimming towards him. He froze with horror as the devilish eyes got nearer. "DAGNABIT! It's a stinking rat, you'd think the bloody thing would have drowned in all this water!" he shrieked in terror, he just hated dirty, flea ridden rats. The rat swung its tail, turning, and disappeared into the gob side of the roadway much to the relief of the terrified Overman.

Iolo's large frame waded through the foul fetid water while he was chatting to Jack Williams, under Manager.

" We lost one electric motor to the water, Bernard Thomas the deputy tells me that the men have got the replacement motor to within fifty yards of the carrier road. The old motor is off and sided until we can get it out to the pit," explained Iolo. Jack Williams looked pleased, and grinned.

Iolo pushed the front gate open, stopped and examined it. "Bloody kids swinging on the bloody thing," he muttered. The gate was holding on by only one hinge and swung around in his big bony hand. As he walked the very short distance up the garden path he noticed that the house was in total darkness. Slowly he opened the door and called out "Anwen, Anwen where are you?"… There was no answer, 'she must have gone to bed with one of her headaches,' he murmured. Judy, Iolo's cocker spaniel came bounding towards him, Iolo made a fuss of her as he usually did when he came in from work. Feeling very hungry after a long and trying day at the colliery he went straight to the oven where he naturally thought food would be waiting for him. He touched the front of the oven door quickly with the back of a hand. "Stone cold," he mumbled out loud. Slowly he opened the oven door with great expectation and peered inside, Judy sat, stumpy tail wagging in anticipation, "DAGNABIT, ANWEN WHERE'S MY BLOODY SUPPER!" he bellowed and waited for a reply. "ANWEN!" he shouted at the top of his voice, "WHERE'S MY BLOODY SUPPER!

Ethel, 'her next-door' banged on the wall, loudly. Iolo's large frame bounded noisily up the stairs. He angrily opened the bedroom door, turned on the light, the bed, un-made and unoccupied. "DAGNABIT!" shouted Iolo. He then went to the spare bedroom to find that bed unoccupied! "Where can she be?" he muttered quietly. Then he heard a knock on the door, he hurriedly bounded down the stairs flinging the door wide open. He was about to give a piece of his mind but was suddenly confronted by 'her next door.'

"Every-thing all right is it? I heard you shouting and thought that there was something wrong! She gazed longingly at Iolo, he noticed something in her wide grey eyes, there was something tantalizing about them, it was many years since he saw that certain look.

"Ethel, have you seen Anwen? I've... just come in from work and there's no supper for me, not even a bloody morsel," said Iolo. Suddenly he went quiet— looking wound up and hurt. "Oh... Oh, I... I haven't seen her all day I thought it was quiet around here!" she confided. "If there's anything I can do just bang on the wall and I'll come round," she offered.

Gazing up at him she reached out and touched him, her long slender fingers caressed his manly chest and that faint look of lust in her eyes returned once more. Iolo saw it and suddenly he felt something stirring in his loins. Ethel suddenly realised what she had done and scuttled off to her house.

Iolo sat down and gave some thought as to what had happened that night. Where was Anwen his wife? "She's had some sort of accident," he muttered. "Afraid I'll lose my poise and go off the rails, probably in a hospital somewhere wondering whether to tell someone," he considered and, talking out loud. Then his mind turned to erotic thoughts of Ethel.

Thoughts of his neighbour were unexpectedly dampened, he heard someone trying a key in the front door lock; quickly he got up from his comfortable armchair and went to confront his wife. He swiftly flung open the door. Anwen stood on the doorstep in a defiant stance, her red smudged lips opening and closing. "DAGNABIT Anwen where the bloody hell have you been? I've been worried sick!" he yelled. His angry eyes raced around her beautiful but carelessly made-up face. The odour of stale alcohol wafted from between her pearly white and even teeth.

"I've... I've been to bingo, I'm late because I've been talking to friends," she said, avoiding Iolo's maddened dark blue eyes.

"You're telling me that you've been playing bingo for most of the bloody day, are you stark raving mad!"

Anwen's pale blue eyes peered out from between her mascara smudged eyelashes. She looked away, afraid that her husband might see something. "Get *out* of my way I've got to make supper," she blurted and avoided his eyes. Iolo returned to the lounge and resumed watching telly; he began thinking about the day's events. Suddenly erotic thoughts of 'her next door' began to torture him, and then he nodded off to sleep, forgetting that supper was being prepared.

"Iolo your supper's on the table! You'd better eat it now before it gets cold," Anwen yelled from the kitchen. She went to see what he was doing. Standing in the doorway she coldly stared down at her husband. "Fast asleep, well I never, after all that fuss," she mumbled. "He can have it in the morning," she said quietly and then went to bed leaving her husband fast asleep in his favourite armchair.

Maldwyn Evans, Anwen's charismatic lover sat in the pit canteen, laughing and joking with his cronies, they unconditionally guffawed loudly at his jokes and innuendos. Maureen Jones, Anwen's sister, stared at Maldwyn; large fiery eyes glowered at the bunch of half-washed coal miners. She knew what was going on between' him' and her sister. From time to time Evans would take a shifty look to where she was working behind the canteen counter. Deviously he would look at her and then lean over the tea stained table and make lurid comments about her to his cronies who were sat around. Maureen's face reddened with rage, and the more he looked at her, the more she reacted and the more Maldwyn's cronies laughed. He knew how to wind her up and he enjoyed the perverse reactions of his laughing cronies.

Maldwyn Evans worked on the coalface, he operated the power loader, the machine that cut and loaded the coal onto the coalface's armoured conveyor. He was for- ever acting up to the men who laughed at his antics.

Ianto Pugh, team captain studied the dust blackened machine operator as he crawled alongside the big and powerful power-loader. "Maldwyn keep an eye on the blutty horizon you're up and down and causing problems, the face looks like something from a blutty fairground ride?" he shouted, his coal-dust blackened face streaked with lines of dried sweat.

"Do you think he's suspicious about us?" asked Maldwyn as he stared into Anwen's light blue eyes. She stared back dreamily.
"I don't care, we don't have any kids, and he can't give me any," she sighed stroking her ash blonde hair with slender manicured fingers. Maldwyn sat back on the comfortable red velvet bench type seat and folded his slender arms across his chest. Anwen pulled out a packet of cigarettes from a small cream coloured handbag. With two long slender fingers she wheedled out a cigarette and put it between her red painted lips.

Iolo ambled up the garden path and stopped in his tracks. He stared in disbelief. "DABNABIT …! What the bloody hell is she up to?" he exclaimed loudly. Ethel next door peered round the partly opened curtains, she too must be wondering what was going on. His short temper began to take hold. Quickly he pushed the key into the door lock; he flung open the door and marched indoors. The house was in total darkness, oven stone cold, bed's unmade again. Iolo slouched in his favourite armchair holding his head in his hands, bewilderment washed over him.
"Is everything OK Iolo? Been playing bingo again, has she?" enquired Ethel,—her next door had walked in through the open door. "Why don't you come round and have a cup of tea with me, until Anwen comes home?" offered the kindly Ethel. She seemed to care about Iolo even if Anwen didn't. Ethel was ten years younger than

Iolo. They had gone to the same pit village school. Ethel's husband, Will' Probert was killed in a roof fall twenty years previously, and in all that time she rarely looked at another man, but she always admired Iolo. Will' Probert and Iolo were big friends; they worked next to each other on the coal. Iolo still had nightmares about that terrible morning 26 August 1947. Ethel placed a slender hand on Iolo's shoulder and squeezed gently. He gazed up at Ethel, her hair was long and black as coal except for flecks of grey, her striking grey eyes showed hardships and once again Iolo noticed that particular gleam in her eye.

Ethel had one daughter; she brought her up on her own and worked hard to do so. Iolo suddenly remembered his old butty Will' Probert, his mind flashed back to that fateful morning of twenty years ago.

"Will', why don't you put up a temporary support, you've gone in too far and the ground's starting to dribble," shrieked Iolo, urgency was in his voice.

"The roof's as sound as a bell," said Will'. He picked up a mandrel, and flung it up at the roof, as colliers did and listened for that bell like sound that said the roof was solid. Iolo shook his head he didn't trust the nature of geology and remembered that his grandfather was killed by a roof fall.

From time to time Iolo shouted: "For god's sake and your little kid, secure your stent or we'll be digging you out!"

"All right I know what I'm doing, I've been doing it long enough," returned Will' Probert as he began to measure for a pair of timber. He hadn't noticed that the ominous dribbling of dust from a gap in the roof was getting coarser. Iolo looked up to where Will' was measuring for an arm of timber. He threw down his shovel and dashed the 3 yards to where Will' was working; he reached out and grabbed at Will's arm, the sudden release of pressure by the stratum that had waited patiently for hundreds of millions of years suddenly pressed down with an almighty weight. A hefty stone fell knocking Iolo backwards he was sent reeling, by the time he had recovered his senses it was too late. A cloud of coarse dust had descended, colliers shouted at Iolo. "Get from there Iolo get back." again Iolo tried to save his butty, but the roof descended and knocked down roof supports like rows of skittles. He heard Will' Probert screaming, he heard others screaming as the fall of roof gathered momentum and other innocent colliers were crushed by large stones the size of kitchen tables. Men tore at coffin sized stones with their bare hands.

"Send for the ambulance man, get the under Manager here, we need more help," shouted men in desperation, they desperately tried to save their comrades. Will' Probert's pitiful cries for help screamed out from under the fallen heap of stones.

"He's still alive," shouted Iolo as he tore at large stones and pulled them to one side attempting to get at his butty.

The dust had cleared and the face deputy came scurrying up the face, *sobbing*. "What caused it, was it a crush down?" cried Bill Webster, deputy. "Get from there Iolo, or you'll be killed," screamed the deputy who has responsibility for matters of safety. Will' Probert didn't make it, 5 colliers died remembered Iolo and it could have been prevented.

"Do you still think of Will'?" asked Iolo.

"Every day I think of Will'," said Ethel, she patted Iolo fondly on the shoulder.

"What's all this? Door wide open what's going on?" screeched Anwen Pritchard trying her best not to slur her words.

"Been playing bingo again have you?" answered Iolo, sarcasm was in his voice.

"Nothing wrong in that is there, it's a free world, I'm usually here all on my own, not much to talk to," she answered with equal sarcasm. Ethel showed hurt in her grey eyes; Anwen quickly looked away and began to fumble in her handbag for her cigarettes. Ethel made an excuse and quickly left saying, "take care both."

Holding a glass tumbler to her ear and pressed to her neighbour's wall she listened to the ensuing argument between Iolo and the drunken Anwen.

"You've been potching, putting it around," shouted Iolo.

"You think more about that bloody pit than me," accused Anwen. Meanwhile Ethel's eyes raised and lowered with each accusation.

Friday afternoon

Iolo was getting ready for work and Anwen wondered whether Iolo would be working the weekend. He was always working, always challenges he would say.

"Working in the morning are you?" she asked as she neatly folded a freshly laundered towel.

"Look Anwen, people say my job is easy, but when I'm not there by god do they miss me!" said Iolo. "I make the decisions because of my mining experience the men respect me because of it!" retorted Iolo as he combed his short greying hair via the mirror that hung over the mantelpiece.

Maldwyn Evans came swaggering out of the box-pit, Iolo came out of the fitting shop and saw Maldwyn swaggering across the pit top, Iolo rubbed his wide chin he didn't trust Maldwyn Evans, a bit of a ladies man, always clowning around, he always asked about Anwen whenever they were in shouting distance. When a district ended and a new one started up he never worked on the same shift as Iolo he always managed to get on the opposite shift and Iolo wondered why?

Iolo stood listening to the haulage driver Willy Smith, cursing the journeymen. Journeymen were the men who supervised the many trams of roof supports that travelled underground roadways to the coal faces.

"Those riders want to learn how to make proper signals, I've got a boy in the house what could do better," he grumbled out loud enough for Iolo to hear him.

Return roadways were arteries or conduits for the transportation of supplies and timber used in the securing of the roof of the coalface, and the building of the roadway itself.

"I'll have a word in their ears, perhaps they may have problems, the trams may be catching the signal wires," suggested Iolo he grinned and patted Willy Smith on the shoulder saying, "Take your time don't rush, a cool head is better than a hot one."

Iolo eventually met up with the journeymen, they too had complaints, and it was about Willy Smith not driving the haulage to the signals that he should have received.

"I'll get the electrician to come and see to it, sounds like the signal box is playing up, one of you go and tell Willy Smith not to operate the haulage until the electrician has made his inspection of the signalling system," ordered Iolo.

The return road was about half a mile in length, it was hard walking. The substantial arch girders were distorted and low due to the immense pressure of the roof. Iolo moved his big frame hunched for most of the way and after a while he met Bernard Thomas who was making his statutory inspection of the district. He and Iolo had a brief discussion about the state of the district and to inform him of the situation at the face, men were complaining of the excessive airborne dust. He had ordered the coal cutting machine operator to slow down the coal-cutter.

Dust was in the air and Iolo could taste it, he spat it out onto the already dust blackened floor of the mine roadway.

He eventually reached the coalface where he could stand without stooping. All of a sudden he was met by the shouting of men, coal-face captain Dickey Watts rushed out to meet him. "Iolo, the men are complaining about the dust, they're threatening to walk out if nothing is done," said Dickey. Sweat was running down his thin features, he ran a hand over his dusty face and threw the sweat down onto the blackened floor of the mine. Iolo hurried to the coal-face telephone and demanded that the district fitter speak to him:
"Look Tommy, the men are threatening to walk off the face if you don't sort out this dust problem. Can you see to it at the gate end and I'll try and do something at this end," Iolo shouted at the phone. He borrowed some spanners and started to dismantle the water filters.

After a while Iolo had done everything to appease the men and prevented a mass walk out. He then had consultations with the colliery Manager and under Manager who seemed to be ever present always on the phone, always wanting to know the situation at the colliery as if they trusted no one.

Iolo began his usual daily crawl through the face, it was more than two hundred yards in length, the height was never more than three feet, the face consisted of a steel tunnel made up of self- advancing chocks which worked by hydraulic pressure.

Iolo stopped and chatted briefly to all of the men whom he met on his long crawl up the coalface; men would tell him of the difficulties that they had encountered while trying to win the coal from Mother Nature.

Johnny Redman the power loader operator normally called the cutter-man slowed down the coal-cutter when he saw Iolo crawling up the face. His flame- safety lamp hung from a dog collar around his thick neck, the whiff of lamp-fuel always alerted the men when an official of the mine was near, but Iolo nearly always began his inspections on the downdraught side of the men, they never sniffed the fuel fumes until he had passed them. That always kept them on their toes so to speak.

"We've been having problems with the water, the system needs flushing out, the water sprays are blocked," said Johnny Redman as he slowed the coal-cutter even more.

"Yes the bloody dust is upsetting the men, will you work in the morning with the fitters and give the system a good flushing out?" asked Iolo.

After a while Iolo reached the gate end of the coalface, it was also called the *carrier road* because this was the roadway that housed the forty-two inch wide conveyor belt.

Iolo watched as mounds of coal tipped from a powerful chain conveyor onto the wide conveyor belt almost filling the whole width of the belt. Iolo always smiled when the coal was being carried away on the conveyor.

Iolo spent most of his shift directing the operations by telephone and using the coalface speaker phone system, whereby men could communicate to anyone on the face and ten yards back into the roadway. He was a hands-on man; always willing to give someone a hand when having difficulty with a task.

Iolo looked at his watch; it was nearing the end of his shift and the split shift men were preparing to start their shift.

"I'll need to stop the face now Iolo," said Sid, a big strapping chap with a paunch hanging over his lamp belt.

"Five more minutes and it's all yours," said Iolo, smiling. Things hadn't gone so bad considering the dust problem. Granville Thomas, split shift deputy and brother to Bernard Thomas came rushing in; sweat was running down his well-worn features.

"What's the crack Iolo? Still a lot of water out there, puddles everywhere," exclaimed Granville looking down at his soaking-wet boots.

"Bill Pumpy, will be working between shifts and all over the weekend," explained Iolo. He then handed responsibility to Granville after briefing the deputy about the work going on between shifts.

At the pithead baths, Iolo wondered whether he had time for a pint of beer, he looked at his wristwatch, "I might just make it to the Collier's Arms." he muttered.

"Yes I'll have a pint with you, I haven't had a pint all week!" said Bernard, smiling at the prospect of a nice pint of beer with a lovely frothy head. It was only a five minute walk from the pithead baths to the Collier's Arms pub.

Iolo and Bernard walked into the bar of the pub and ordered a pint each, Iolo raised the glass of beer and studied it briefly. He slowly put the foaming glass to his lips and drank from it greedily, five seconds and the glass was empty. Iolo slammed the empty glass onto the bar, Kath the barmaid remarked, "Good god, you needed that one Iolo, another one is it?"

"Aye and one for Bernard please, Kath," said Iolo as he looked around to see who was in the bar. Maldwyn Evans was sat in a corner as usual with his cronies. Iolo watched him lean over and say something to one of his cronies. They both sat bolt upright and laughed out loud. Iolo heard the name Anwen and guessed that the laughter was aimed at him. His suspicions grew stronger and he was convinced that Maldwyn and Anwen were carrying on together; all he had to do was prove it. Bernard Thomas deliberately looked the other way as if he knew something but didn't want to get involved. Iolo guessed that Anwen was at home and his supper would be in the oven, the beds would be made and the house spick and span. Iolo made his excuse and left Bernard to his own devices, and as he went through the bar room door he heard Maldwyn Evans and his cronies, still laughing noisily.

Iolo walked up the garden path and stopped suddenly, the front bedroom light went out; the house was now in darkness. He gingerly opened the front door, the rowdy laughter from the pub still ringing in his ears. The house was warmer than usual and a glow lit up the lounge from a glowing coal fire. Judy the cocker spaniel came and met him as usual and then quickly retreated to the warmth of the glowing coal fire, watching with one eye from beneath a floppy ear. Iolo went to the oven and felt it quickly with the back of a hand, "I've got supper," he said to himself quietly and smiled. He opened the door and peered into the oven, on the middle shelf was a large plate of food. Iolo got a tea towel and gently pulled out the hot meal carrying it to the kitchen table. He ate the meal greedily, he almost forgave Anwen but the sound of the men laughing in the pub made him quickly forget any idea of forgiveness. Time for bed, he remembered he was to work in the morning overseeing the extensive work that resulted from the inrush of water that had flooded his district. Quietly he trod on the stairs trying not to make a sound but the stairs creaked anyway. Carefully, he opened the bedroom door. Anwen was sound asleep or so it seemed.
Iolo lay awake, the heady scent of Anwen's perfume, filled the bedroom. Her warm soft body momentarily affected her husband's inner sexual needs. He began wondering about Maldwyn and Anwen.... was he seeing things that weren't there? Was it his imagination? Everything seemed to add up, but he had to catch them together and then sort it from there. What would he do, he thought? What would be the outcome and then murderous thoughts began to take over his mind as he started to plot the demise of his unfaithful wife.

Saturday Morning

Iolo sat on a makeshift seat at the lamp station alongside Bernard Thomas, the men sat around waiting for him to enter their names in the time-book which he had to do by law. Iolo momentarily sat and stared angrily at Maldwyn Evans, he stared back grinning arrogantly.
Bernard shouted to him for his registration number so as he could enter it in the time-book and Iolo gave Maldwyn his orders, his voice

changed into one of stifled anger. He didn't want the men to know that he was ruffled by the presence of his adversary. Bernard Thomas showed in his eyes that the situation was not to his liking but he could do nothing about it.

After the men had left the lamp station, Bernard opened up to Iolo. He was not just a work colleague but a friend also. "There was murder in the Colliers pub after you left last night, there's a lot of men who don't like Maldwyn Evans, don't think that we don't know about him and Anwen. The majority respect you, but that swine has his cronies and they too are scum, birds of a feather spring to mind," said Bernard as he took off his dusty glasses and cleaned them with an old piece of cloth.

Iolo decided to change tactics he would travel the carrier road as there were no journey men working in the return road that morning. Bill Pumpy was busily leaning over a four inch compressed air operated pump, swearing at it as he usually did when things failed to work properly. His young assistant stood to one side hands on hips, waiting for Bill to give him an order.

"You're getting rid of this nuisance water, bit by bit, it'll be nice to walk into the district without getting your feet wet, Bill Pumpy," said Iolo, smiling, Bill Pumpy's young assistant eyed Iolo cautiously and tried to weigh him up, what made bosses tick said the look in his young eyes.

Iolo steadily made his way down through the steel tunnel made of self-advancing hydraulic chocks. He looked down alongside the coalface chain conveyor, beams of light from the cap lamps of the few men that were on the coalface panned around like miniature search lights. Iolo started to crawl down the coal face his flame safety lamp hung from the dog collar that was fastened around his neck. One of the men was making his way up the coalface. Iolo could see it was Maldwyn Evans. Evans looked up, Iolo saw fear in his eyes; he quickly got between two chocks and escaped onto the face chain conveyor promptly scuttling up the face and away from the angry Iolo. "I'll get you Evans!" he hissed, angrily.

Iolo sat on a plank in the return roadway writing in his notebook. From time to time he would go to the face speaker-phone and ask for the team captain. He liked to be kept up to date with progress regarding the work that was being carried out, then inform the under Manager of progress to date. Iolo couldn't help thinking of Maldwyn and Anwen. He began to think of ingenious, murderous schemes. But how could it be done in a small mining village without anyone finding out?

Chapter II

November 1967

Many long weeks had passed; autumn leaves were plentiful and lay deep in the hollows that formed beneath trees. The winds blew lazily sweeping up golden carpets of fallen leaves fit to cover bodies of unsuspecting lovers.

Iolo had spent many hours idly planning the demise of his wife and her lover, piece by piece the hate consumed him, every day he endured the sniggering, the loud laughter, and knowing looks by the cronies and others whom Maldwyn Evans called friends.

Saturday morning

The back bedroom felt incredibly cold as Iolo reached into the tallboy and grabbed the shotgun that had lain there for many months untouched; on the top shelf were a half box of shells. He put half a dozen in his overcoat pocket and began to whistle merrily. Anwen eyed him cautiously as he cheerfully whistled his way down the stairs. "Off shooting and taking the dog are you?" she asked and nervously rubbed her hands.

"Aye, me and Judy haven't been rabbiting for months," said Iolo. Judy jumped up at Iolo whining eagerly, she inquisitively sniffed at the gun. Anwen looked anxiously out of the window as Iolo and the dog disappeared round the back of the houses.

The morning was cold as a light wind blew whipping up fallen leaves that had lain in the roadside. In the lane that led to the colliery slag-heap, ragged looking sheep were busily browsing in the hedgerow for anything that resembled nourishment. Judy swept by them ignoring their startled gazes and carried on sniffing, zigzagging as she went. Iolo whistled orders at her like a sheep farmer directing his flock. Further down the lane a five bar gate opened onto a track that the machines used to get around the slag-heap. Iolo heaved the gate open, squeezing between a small gap before heaving the heavy gate back into the closed position. Iolo took the shotgun out of its khaki coloured sheath and slung it over his shoulder; he then carefully inserted a shiny red cartridge into the breach of the gun barrel and snapped the two halves together. He raised the shotgun to his shoulder and began aiming at an imaginary target; Judy stopped and tilted her head inquisitively. She began sniffing for the scent of a rabbit's trail. Iolo stopped and watched Judy working among the brown lifeless bracken that adorned the foothills of the mighty slagheap.

He strained his eyes for anything that moved among the bracken. He saw something move; a small white bob of a tail was just visible between clusters of brown fronds. Judy jumped up and yelped, this was her signal to Iolo that a rabbit was about to rise. Sure enough the rabbit bolted across a clearing. Iolo quickly raised the shotgun and aimed just in front of the rabbit's path; he pulled the trigger and the shotgun went off with a loud echoing bang, the rabbit ran into the deadly buckshot killing it stone dead. Judy duly emerged from the bracken with the dead rabbit in her mouth, her stubby tail wagging energetically with pride as she allowed Iolo to take her quarry from her soft mouth.

"Good girl Judy, well done," he said, patting her on her side. Iolo took out his penknife and made a slit between the tibia and fibula bones of the rabbit's leg, he expertly inserted one of the rabbit's feet through the two bones of the other leg and threaded the legs with his stout leather belt and then put the belt around his waist, that was the way his father had done it and Iolo had carried on the tradition.

Iolo listened to the sound of a machine working somewhere in the distance. He looked up at the overhead slag buckets hanging mysteriously from steel ropes. They were unmoving and silent; crows cawed and glided around them in the morning sunshine.

"There must be a Bulldozer working somewhere," uttered Iolo. He followed the track that the machines used to navigate around the slagheap; the track rose uphill and was deeply rutted with pools of thick black slurry. On reaching the summit of the hideous black mountain he stopped and watched as a Bulldozer worked moving slag into heaps beneath where the flight buckets emptied their loads of mined rubbish. The Bulldozer backed off from where it was working and stopped. The driver got out and stretched away the stiffness from his legs. "Hello there, can I help you?" he asked, smiling.

"Just watching you working the machine," replied Iolo.

"I know you! I've seen you on top of the pit," said the dozer driver. "You're one of the underground bosses aren't you?" he said, grinning broadly. "What can I do for you?" He pulled a packet of cigarettes out of a shirt pocket as he waited for a reply.

Iolo had an idea but he was unsure how to put it to the driver, he didn't know him sufficiently.

"Is there anyone else around here, do you work on your own?" asked Iolo, naively.

"I'm usually on my own on weekends, the foreman visits me from time to time, have you seen a land rover around here?" asked the driver.

"No I haven't, what times does he makes his visits?" asked Iolo

"I can't usually tell, he comes when he feels like it," the driver replied. Iolo wondered whether he should give him a leading question.

"Looks like a good place to bury a load of old junk or something," said Iolo.

"Some people bring their junk here for me to bury it, some scrapyards charge for taking away clapped out cars," he said, he eyed Iolo with some suspicion; he knew he wasn't working because he had a shotgun and a dog with him.

"My missus has got an old banger, I'm always paying out for it, I'm buggered if I'm going to give it to some scruffy scrap-monger," said Iolo, wondering if he has said the right thing.

"Can it be driven?" the driver asked.

"I can just about get it here, which is the best way to get it here considering the state of the track?" asked Iolo.

"The best way is to drive in through the bottom gate and go for about a hundred yards which will be out of sight of the lane, no police come in here it's too rough," he said and he winked at Iolo. It'll cost you some rolling tobacco is that all right? By the way you can call me Jim," he said and he winked again.

"Cheap at the price considering what I fork out for it," said Iolo lying through his teeth.

"How do I get the tobacco to you?" he asked.

"Just leave it on the front seat and I'll pick it up from there. Is that all right? "Iolo winked in acknowledgement. They worked out the best time for him to bring the vehicle to the slag-heap; Iolo's plan was beginning to work.

Iolo knew that Maldwyn Evans would be working the afternoon shift. This was the week that Anwen never went out, only to the local shops. Iolo began his plan for the coming week it was now or never! As the week slowly passed he was more determined than ever, Maldwyn Evans and Anwen Pritchard were soon to meet their maker.

Friday evening

Iolo had worked a week of day shifts' and he knew that Maldwyn would be working late shifts. He also made sure that Maldwyn would not have permission for a change of shift on the coming Friday,
Six o'clock, it was dark and raining heavily, but Iolo could not delay his dreadful plan. He put on his old overcoat, the one he used when he went shooting rabbits.

Soggy yellowy leaves filled the roadside gutters. Iolo held down his head as the wind drove the heavy rain into his scrunched up face. Steadily he tramped on to the colliery car park determined to see this fateful scheme through to its final conclusion. Maldwyn Evans's car would be parked up. Furtively he looked all around, no one in sight and the heavy rain was keeping the car park free of wandering people. Iolo was soaked to the skin but he had to press on with his plan. Then he spotted the car in a corner of the car park.
"DAGNABIT, THE BLOODY CAR'S LOCKED," he shrieked, he had forgotten about getting into the car and starting it up.
 Hurriedly he looked for something to smash the driver's side window. Luckily he found a stone hefty enough to break a side window. With a mighty thrust he heaved the stone through the window and quickly managed to open the door.
 His heart sunk as he noticed the door lock button was in the up position. 'SOD IT!' he shrieked over the rumble of thunder, torrential rain hammered down relentlessly. Quickly he removed broken glass

and squeezed himself into the driver's seat, feverishly he fumbled for the ignition harness 'Ah found it,' he said as he pulled out several wires and touched them together hoping that the car would start.

By now Iolo was breathing heavily, his hands trembled uncontrollably. Sweat mixed with rain ran down his forehead and into his eyes. He feverishly tried to start the car by hot wiring the ignition leads. He heard the starter motor slowly turn and the car lurched backwards it was in reverse gear. He fumbled with the clutch and gear shift, he managed to put it into neutral gear. Again he tried touching the wires. The starter motor turned and the engine burst into life. He smiled for the first time in a while.

The car door slammed shut, and Iolo began driving it out of the car park and towards the colliery slag-heap.

Rain blew hard through the smashed side window drenching Iolo even more. He drove the car up to the gate that opened onto the track below the slag-heap. Quickly he heaved the heavy gate open then got into the car for the last time.

The car drove the up the track and out of sight. Iolo reached into a pocket of his old overcoat and pulled out the tobacco that he had promised Jim. He placed the tobacco pouch onto the driver's seat. Iolo wondered about the smashed window and the wiring harness. What would Jim think, would he think that the car was stolen? Iolo was soaked to the skin but he had more to do. He had to somehow murder Maldwyn Evans.

Iolo was feeling exhausted but he had to carry on regardless. He studied his wristwatch; the afternoon shift would soon be ending their stint. There was little time, and so much to do.

Maldwyn Evans would soon be searching for his car. Iolo had to put the next stage of his plan into operation. As fast as his legs could carry him he raced to his house, he had to use his own car; he wondered whether he was going the right way around this stage of the operation. Breathing heavily he reached his house, the Ford Anglia car waited patiently on the kerbside. He feverishly searched the deep pocket of his overcoat for his car-keys then he opened the boot of the car and checked for the shotgun and a short roll of brattice cloth that he had pinched a week earlier from the colliery stores. Iolo smiled faintly, he quickly glanced at the house to see if Anwen would be looking out of the lounge window, 'good she's watching telly,' he said to himself quietly.

Iolo drove his car down to the colliery car park and waited for Maldwyn. Men came and drove away but Iolo worried beyond belief, how could he murder Maldwyn without anyone witnessing anything? The night was very dark owing to the black storm clouds overhead; still no sign of Maldwyn Evans, 'Where could he be?' hissed Iolo. Suddenly the heavens opened, the car park was partly obliterated by the heavy rain. Iolo watched as a hunched figure came running towards him, he wondered if it could be his intended victim, he looked like Maldwyn Evans, but he could not be sure.

The running figure stopped dead in his tracks, Iolo heard him screaming obscenities as he ran around looking for his car. 'It's him!' said Iolo. He quickly got out of the car and raced around to the car's boot he reached in and grabbed his shotgun. The rain fell heavily, small pools of rainwater quickly appeared inside the boot of the car. The shotgun was already loaded; Iolo put it under his soaking wet overcoat, and went over to Maldwyn. "Need any help, Mal!" shouted Iolo with a touch of sarcasm in his voice.

"Some bastards pinched my car," he shouted, his wet hair fell over his face in a wet tangled mess. He was very angry, water sloshed inside his shoes as he vainly tottered around searching for the elusive vehicle.

Maldwyn turned to face Iolo, anger filled his whole being; Iolo raised the shot gun and aimed it at his victim's chest, at point blank range he could not possibly miss. The look on Maldwyn's face turned to one of abject fear.

"Take it easy Iolo you could go down for this, put the shot gun away don't be so silly," shouted Maldwyn as he reached out to snatch the shotgun away from Iolo. Slowly Iolo teased the trigger until he felt pressure on his fore finger and then with a short lug the shotgun went off, Maldwyn Evans stared at Iolo disbelievingly as he was shoved backwards by the force of the buckshot that tore into his fragile chest. Iolo momentarily stared down at Maldwyn's sorry carcass.

Quickly Iolo recovered his senses, he dragged his victim's bleeding body and bundled it into the boot of the waiting car. Iolo had previously arranged the half roll of brattice cloth so that it could be wrapped around the lifeless body. The heavens were still tipping it down; the car's windscreen wipers could hardly cope with the torrent of rain that battered them relentlessly.

Iolo had previously identified the spot where Maldwyn's body would be hidden until Anwen's demise and the next stage of his plan.

The car trundled along a narrow track near to the edge of a quarry and below was the colliery supply yard where various types of roof supports were stacked.

Iolo hauled the body of Maldwyn Evans out of the boot of the car and rolled it a couple of yards down a slope towards the edge of the quarry. He dug a trench using the heel of his foot in a hollow filled with yellowy soggy leaves, deep and long enough to conceal the corpse.

He rolled the corpse into the hollow and covered it with a piece of brattice cloth cut from the roll. He dragged the excavated leaves over it with his foot until it could be seen no more. Iolo had one more task, his wife Anwen. This he had already planned, but he wondered whether he might get away with it, he had the neighbours to consider.

Iolo drove his car around to the back of the house and reversed it onto the concrete patch that he called *'my drive'* and opened the back door. Anwen was waiting wringing her hands in anticipation. "Where've you been? You've been out all day and look at you soaked to the skin!" she shouted at him.

"What do you care, I've been walking around trying to clear my head," said Iolo, he looked at his pretty wife, his eyes gleamed, and she saw the madness in them. Iolo took off his overcoat, Anwen saw blood on it.

"Isn't that blood?" She yelled, "Where have you been? How did you get blood on your coat?" she began to sob.

"Rabbit's blood," replied Iolo.

"Like bloody hell it is!" cried Anwen, tearfully. She feared the worst; somehow she sensed that something was drastically wrong. She had an idea but dared not say it in front of her husband. Iolo then said something out of the blue.

"The blood belongs to..." he paused for a moment and then he said it.

"The blood belongs to Maldwyn Evans your lover, he's no longer with us he's with his maker the devil himself!" uttered Iolo. He stared into Anwen's beautiful but horrified, frightened eyes then he closed his own tired eyes.

He reached out and grabbed Anwen by her smooth and slender neck; with both hands he squeezed with all his strength. She made no attempt to stave off his sickening attack. Her once beautiful eyes bulged and hands hung limply at her side, as if she had no will to live, her lover was dead and she wanted to be with him.

Iolo watched the light go out of Anwen's dying eyes; he knew he had killed her. He let her drop to the floor and then stared down at her lifeless beautiful body, he fought back tears and for a moment he was sorry, he sobbed uncontrollably and fell to his knees. He kissed her tender lifeless lips and begged for forgiveness but there was no one to hear him save for Judy his faithful Cocker Spaniel.

Iolo had no time to waste despite the blinding tears that were now rolling down his reddened cheeks.

Quickly he looked out of the kitchen window, watery eyes blurred his vision, sobbing he checked for anyone who might be innocently passing by, Judy the Cocker Spaniel howled pitifully as Iolo put his big arms around Anwen's slim waist and hauled her out of the door and towards the waiting car; the engine was still idling.

Unknown to Iolo, Ethel his nosey but kindly neighbour peeked from behind her curtains, her grey eyes widened as she witnessed the macabre spectacle that was being carried out before her very eyes.

Anwen's lifeless eyes stared out at her ghoulish husband. He closed the lid of the car's boot and a cold shudder ran down his spine.

Iolo got into the car and slowly drove away struggling to see through the car's windscreen, the storm hammered down relentlessly. Slowly but surely he drove the car to the very edge of the quarry.

Painfully he hauled Anwen's lifeless body out of the boot of the car, his muscles ached and he was exhausted. He struggled to roll her corpse to where Maldwyn Evans's body lay waiting then he carefully laid them back to back and covered them with brattice cloth and the abundant autumn leaves that were shed by the spreading giant oak tree that would stand as a silent witness to this terrible deed.

Iolo still had more to do, but he needed time and prayed that his victim's bodies would not be discovered. One week would pass before he could carry out the next stage of events he needed to covertly transport the corpses to their final resting place. Then the perfect murders would have been carried out.

Chapter III

December 1967

Monday afternoon

Iolo stood in the bathroom staring blankly into his shaving mirror, his mind flashed to that terrible Friday night, repeatedly he visualised Maldwyn Evans reeling backwards his blood splattered chest redder than a Christmas Robin's breast. Iolo was slowly becoming aware of someone tapping at his kitchen window. He quickly finished shaving and went to see who it was, Ethel Probert's nose almost pressed at the window pane looking into the kitchen, she strained to see if there was anyone at home. Iolo smartly rushed to open the door. "What is it Ethel? I'm just about to go to work," he said, he could see a mischievous look in her eye.
　"Is Anwen... in?" she asked hesitantly.
　"No, she's not in, I haven't seen her since Friday night," he answered innocently.
　"Are you sure she's not in?" she asked, the look on her face said she knew what was going on.
　"Yes Ethel I'm sure," he said and he said it with confidence.
　"Ok then, I'll keep an eye open for her, I'll talk to her when she gets home, have a nice shift and I'll see you tomorrow," she said and then gave a funny sort of smile that worried Iolo, did she know something?

　Jack Williams under Manager came darting out of the Manager's office "Iolo, Iolo," he called just as his Overman came out of the pithead baths.
　"Hello there Mr Williams, we've got challenges have we?" said Iolo, managing a grin.
　"Wait till you here this," said the under Manager, frowning. "Twenty-six' district has had a massive fall of ground, thirty yards

long and it's gone up twenty feet or more," explained the under Manager.

"It's one thing after another, one week we have an inrush of water and now we have a fall of ground. I trust that the men have been feeding the sheep properly," said Iolo, joking and trying to make light of the situation.

"Very funny, Iolo, but I need a meeting with you and the other officials of the district," he said. They briefly discussed the situation as they walked to the officials-lodge together.

Iolo gave the men at the coal face time to settle down and take stock of what was to be done to secure the fall area; the day shift men had already started work on the project.

Iolo knelt on the chain conveyor at the edge of the fall area and shone the beam of his cap lamp up into the cavity in a vain attempt to see where the roof above the fall might be. Men had already begun dismantling the face chain conveyor because the weight of stone over thirty yards of the conveyor was a hundred tons or more, too much weight for the already powerful electric motors that hauled the continuous chain around the two hundred and twenty yard conveyor; the conveyor had to be shortened and the fallen stone painstakingly removed by hand, the conveyor then lengthened as necessary. The edge of the roof of the fall must be captured and supported; the roof cavity filled where possible so as to protect the men working below, this work would take a week to carry out working around the clock. Iolo retreated to the gate road and reported to the under Manager and Manager by telephone.

Iolo sat on a makeshift seat and took out his notebook and began to write in it, it was warmer than usual he was perspiring, a drop of perspiration hung from his nose he wiped it away with the back of a dusty hand. The ventilation was being slowed by the obstruction of the fall of ground on the coalface.

Many tons of timber supports would be needed to secure the fall area. This situation was to be useful to Iolo as his plan for the final disposal of the bodies of Anwen Pritchard and Maldwyn Evans was to transport them down the mine buried inside a tram of timber supplies, then re-bury them in the waste area on the edge of the coalface.

Timing was imperative and there was to be no witnesses to this terrible deed.

Bernard Thomas called on the face speaker phone system.
"*Iolo can you come to the return road, I need a hand with the ventilation, there's nothing to worry about, it's a bit sluggish,*" Iolo returned the call.

"I'll be right with you Bern'; give me a couple of minutes," said Iolo who was expecting trouble due to a sluggish flow of air around the district, this situation can cause methane layering because of reduced air pressure.

From time to time the Friday night murders haunted the normally unflappable Iolo Pritchard and he worried about the corpses resting silently on the edge of a quarry above the colliery supplies yard.

Friday afternoon

The work on the fall area of twenty six district was ninety per cent completed the conveyor was now running in its full length, work would continue into the weekend and Iolo could start the final stage of the journey of the corpses.

At the end of his shift and when he was satisfied that he wouldn't be discovered Iolo made his way on foot still in his working clothes to the edge of the quarry where Anwen and Maldwyn were buried under the fallen autumn leaves.

Iolo scratched around trying to find the exact spot where the lovers were buried, he began to worry, he had difficulty finding them, he felt something hard he scratched further and uncovered one of Maldwyn's shoes. 'Huh, huh, he uttered to himself, Iolo completely uncovered the corpses and rolled them to the very edge of the quarry, he looked down onto the floor of the supply yard it looked about thirty feet or so down and he worried that the drop would dismember the bodies on impact. However, he had to carry out the next stage or he would be found out and therefore a lifetime in jail.

With a mighty push of his working boot he shoved the body of Maldwyn Evans over the edge of the precipice and he watched as the body fell through space taking what seemed an age to crash onto the ground below. Anwen's pale and lifeless eyes hauntingly stared up at

Iolo, and for a brief moment he thought he saw her bluish lips quiver as if to say something. He stared at her for a moment and then shoved her lifeless body over the precipice; he turned away as she plummeted, tumbling in the cold night air to the ground below.

Iolo hurried in the darkness to the supply yard hoping that he would not meet anyone; he found the bone shattered corpses at the bottom of the quarry his once beautiful wife now blue and grey stared at him. He carried Anwen's corpse to an empty tram and lifted her into it, he felt her soft decaying breasts as he eased her dead body into the tram. Then Maldwyn Evans' finally covering the bodies with timber roof supports. He then marked the tram with the number 26 and the word URGENT in large chalked characters and he drew asterisks on each corner of the tram so that he could identify it when it finally reached 26 district. Iolo now depended totally on luck as the tram had to be supervised throughout its entire journey through the mine by various unsuspecting miners.

Saturday Morning shift

Iolo Pritchard was a big wide shouldered man but the coalface held no difficulties for him, he never needed to rush through the coalface, he preferred to take his time and have short chats with the men as he met them on his journey through the moveable steel tunnel that ran the length of the coalface, they respected him for his short informal chats. "The face line is looking good," said Iolo to team captain Dickey Watts. "Aye... the men worked hard, we've got good teams here on 26 but we've still a bit to do," replied Dickey Watts. Iolo was thinking that he must use the situation to his advantage.

Iolo looked at his wristwatch it was almost time to call it a day, he was satisfied that all the work that the men set out to do was completed adequately. He went to the speaker phone. "Ok lads you can all come off the face," he grinned as he said it. The men as expected crawled out of the coalface, Dickey Watts approached Iolo: "Iolo would it be possible to give the men half an hour off?...considering, what they have done for the Management of this colliery," Iolo eyed the team captain, and pretended that he had no intentions he was not going to give the men any time off. Dickey Watts stood with hands on hips and waited for a response, the men began to huddle round each other when Iolo announced,

"Alright, fifteen minutes and not a second more," the men began to shout and got agitated. "Ok, half an hour," said Iolo, reluctantly. Most of the men patted Iolo on the back as they passed.

Most had to crawl the two hundred and twenty yards up the coalface and then travel the carrier road.

Iolo waited until the men were well out of sight, then he began to search the supply trams that he had marked with chalked asterisks, he shone the beam of his cap-lamp along the length of the trams that were standing in the in-bye parting. Iolo peered into each of the trams as he passed them, suddenly he began shrieking.

"DAGNABIT, I TOLD THOSE RIDERS NOT TO UNLOAD THIS BLOODY JOURNEY, "Iolo began to panic every tram was empty except for the very last two trams, he breathed a sigh of relief as he saw that the last tram had those chalked asterisks marked on it, they still hadn't been unloaded. Iolo heard the magneto type pit phone ring four times, Iolo ran to answer it.

"Hello, who's that now?" he shouted at the phone.

"It's me, Bernard, how much longer will you be?"

"I'M ON MY WAY, I'LL CATCH YOU UP," shouted Iolo into the phone that hung on an arch girder on the side of the roadway. He replaced the earpiece onto its clip and returned to the waiting tram that contained the two corpses. Iolo quickly threw out the heavy timbers that had covered the corpses of Anwen and Maldwyn. One by one he carried the decaying, mucky and reeking bodies; he retched noisily as the stench hit him. He struggled to the waste side of the coalface taking his life into his own hands by doing so.

Stones the size of kitchen buckets began to fall as Iolo tried desperately to haul the bodies as far as possible into the waste and alongside the roadside pack area; one stone caught Iolo on the foot he yelped with pain luckily his steel toe-capped boots absorbed most of the impact. Iolo limped into the roadway and searched for bags of stone dust.

Dust was used to dilute any coal dust that accumulated on the roof, floor, and sides of mine roadways thus stopping any coal-dust that was raised into the mine atmosphere from exploding. This dust also hid a multitude of sins and Iolo was now using it to hide the bodies of Anwen Pritchard and Maldwyn Evans, lovers.

Iolo painfully limped out of number 26 district and was met by Bernard Thomas.

"Iolo what have you done to your foot?"

"I dropped a hydraulic prop on my foot, I should have left it lying in the middle of the bloody roadway," said Iolo lying through his teeth.

"We'll have to fill in an accident report form when we get to the surface," said Bernard, he frowned. "It's getting late and pit bottom hitcher will be wondering where we are," he retorted.

Bernard Thomas phoned pit bottom and informed the hitcher what had happened, he was not very happy as he could not leave his place of work while men were still down the mine.

Monday morning

Iolo limped into work he was using his probe stick as a walking stick, a probe stick is a kind of walking stick used by mine officials to take samples of mine air from cavities and high places, this sampling worked by fitting an aspirator bulb to an adapter, the adapter fitted on the ferruled end of the probe stick, the official raised the stick to a solid part of a cavity or high place and pressed it against the solid part, the adapter valve opened and let air and methane into the pre evacuated aspirator bulb. The official then inserted the injector end of the aspirator bulb into a hole at the base of his special flame safety lamp; with his cap lamp turned off he slowly squeezed the bulb, the captured air was then fed to the lowered lamp wick called a testing flame. The official read the size and shape of the pale blue flame called a '*cap*' the official was trained to read off the different possible shapes and sizes in percentages of methane.

"How's the foot this morning, Iolo?" asked Bernard Thomas.

"Still giving me gyp, I'll be ok as long as I keep taking pain killers," replied Iolo wincing every time he made a move.

Jack Williams eyed Iolo as he hobbled around the officials-lodge.

"Will you be alright Iolo, you have a lot of walking to do, you may not make it to your district?" said the under Manager showing unusual concern.

"Let me try, if I fail, I fail," said Iolo as he glowered at the under Manager who was showing unusual concern for him. Iolo had to spend some time at the district; he had to make sure that the bodies of the unfortunate lovers were not accidently discovered.

Iolo had managed to hobble the mile walk from pit bottom to number 26 district; He could not wait to get a look along-side the waste area in the return road.

He shone his lamp along-side the gob wall of the road side pack area. The roof had fallen and had completely covered the corpses there was now no hope of anyone accidently discovering the bodies of Anwen Pritchard and her lover Maldwyn Evans.
Iolo marked the date in chalk on the arch girder nearest the coal face as pit officials did to prove that they had made an inspection on that date.

"There's a terrible stink coming from the gob," said young Dai Roberts, the youngest member of the team at nineteen years of age who worked on the ripping lip. The ripping- lip is an area behind the coal face where miners build the roadway ready for the transport system and ventilation, the gob was pit-speak for the waste area of the coalface behind the coalface chain conveyor.
"Aye, it must be that stinking water from that inrush we had; it's hanging about a bit," said Iolo making an excuse for he knew it was the deathly smell of the corpses resting for evermore in the gob half a mile below the green rolling hills way above number26 district.

Iolo was happy, the bodies would never be discovered and people would think that the lovers had run away together. Everybody knew about their affair so it would come as no surprise to the pit village community.
Iolo had returned to the surface saying that he was suffering too much pain, it was too much! Jack Williams under Manager gave Iolo the rest of the week off as the district was in good hands. Iolo was sent to hospital for an x-ray.

Iolo rested in his favourite armchair, injured foot supported on a footstool, telly switched on and the football results were being announced. Iolo heard the back door being opened. "Coo-ee it's only me!" shouted Ethel,' her-next door.'

"What do you want Ethel?" said Iolo as she poked her head around the lounge door.

"Have you heard from Anwen, yet?" She said in a soft almost whispery voice. "There's rumours' going around the village... she's run off with someone," she said again in that whispery voice. Iolo noticed that Ethel had smartened herself up, she had her hair done in a new and more modern style, she pulled up a chair and sat beside him, Iolo sniffed at her perfume, it suddenly made him notice her just like the other week when Anwen had come home late and intoxicated. Ethel beamed at Iolo with knowing eyes she showed a confidence never seen before. Did she know anything thought Iolo, did she unwittingly witness anything? Iolo began to wonder and then she said it.

"I know what happened to Anwen, I saw you bundle her into the boot of your car!" she blurted." I'm glad she's gone, I never liked her she was too full of herself," remarked Ethel. Iolo's heart sank he had been found out.

"You saw it then?" said Iolo; he gazed into Ethel's wide grey eyes.

"Yes I heard and saw it all!" she said and put an arm around Iolo's shoulder she leaned forward and kissed him full on the lips and said: "You're all mine now!" Then Ethel grinned and confessed: "I know you have always wanted me, your eyes have undressed me many, many, times." Iolo was suddenly taken aback, she had surprised him, and he began to respond to her advances.

"Take me, take me now! I must have you" she said in loud gasping whispers. Iolo stared at her heaving breasts she had undone some buttons her cleavage milky white and inviting. Iolo ignored the painful foot; he pulled open her half undone blouse and cupped a hand under a lovely, full and heaving breast. "Take me," she gasped as her long skirt fell to the floor, Iolo's fingers clenched Ethel's firm lovely buttocks, quickly she pulled off his shirt tearing off some buttons he looked startled but then it didn't matter. Their naked bodies entwined, they kissed, and caressed. He lay Ethel down on the soft warm couch. She raised a long naked leg and then poured out long lasting gasps as Iolo entered her soft, wet, hot, and grateful vagina. Iolo had now realised his sexual fantasies and for a while all thoughts of Anwen disappeared into the ether.

"So, how are you going to tackle Anwen's disappearance?" asked Ethel staring into his eyes, she kissed him again, gently placing a slender hand in-between his ample and naked thighs. Iolo became aroused once more and he pulled her to him and again they were in heaven. But Anwen was resting deep in the bowels below.

One week had passed and still the rumours persisted, people had begun noticing the change in Ethel, but they had not yet seen Iolo and his mistress together.

"What will the villagers make of us when they find out that we are lovers?" questioned Ethel as she stared into Iolo's blue eyes; she stared intently, her eyes searched for an answer.

"It'll be very interesting; Maldwyn Evans's cronies are already giving me problems trying to undermine my authority, they haven't the brain to suss out that their butty won't be coming back, or that they are playing with fire," said Iolo, grinning.

Chapter IV

Christmas 1967

It was generally accepted that Iolo Pritchard, Overman and Ethel Probert *'her next door'* were now an item but not yet living in *tally* as people in Cwm Derw called it, but Maldwyn Evans's cronies would not lie down, they insisted that all was not right with the disappearance of their butty, he never confided that he was to run away with anybody yet alone with the wife of a colliery official.

It was Christmas day in the Probert's household Ethel had invited her family around for Christmas lunch and to mark the occasion with the announcement of her and Iolo's engagement. "I knew there was something going on, Mam, the minute I saw you with your new hairdo, I said to myself, Mam's got a fancy man and about time too," said Bethan Morgan, Ethel's daughter a tall strapping woman with her father's looks. David Morgan sat quietly in a chair by the fire and from time to time he would put his hands to the flames rubbing them vigorously.

Iolo tried to make conversation with young David. "Still working in the washery, David?" asked Iolo.

"Aye, still there, still trying to make ends meet, still working for a living," he said while staring into the flames of the glowing coal fire.

"Why don't you see the training officer, and get yourself some training, you could come and work for me after you have completed your training? I could pull some strings for you if you like," explained Iolo sounding very polite. David looked up from where he was sitting his face lit by the glow of the open coal fire. Bethan stared down at her husband; she bit and chewed at her bottom lip, and then glanced at her mother.

"You two, can do whatever you like, but the fact remains; that colliery took away your father's life, and the same thing could happen all over again," said Ethel, she then stared at Iolo, her mouth quivered, her argument lost, she could easily lose Iolo.

"Please yourselves!" she said and moved to the window and stared out at the cold, rain soaked day.

The day went unmarked by the morning's differences regarding whether David Morgan, son-in-law to Ethel should take up the proposal made by Iolo Pritchard

Iolo used his persuasive charms on Ethel and explained that coal mines were a lot safer than they used to be, Will' Probert her late husband was killed in different circumstances. Ethel eventually agreed that things were different and that she had lost the argument since Iolo was a miner too.

Christmas evening and the Collier's Arms pub was quiet except for the usual rabble of misfits. Maldwyn Evans's cronies sat at their customary table in the bay window of the public bar. Iolo and Ethel used the *best bar* as the locals called it. It was always a penny dearer but usually free of youngsters and very little hassle. Iolo went to the bar to buy drinks it was possible to look into the public bar area. Dewi Brice chief trouble maker after Maldwyn Evans, spotted Iolo standing at the bar waiting for the barmaid to serve him. Quickly he walked around to the best bar. "Well, Pritchard... it didn't take you long to find another woman, did it?" Said Brice standing at the door arms folded across his chest. Iolo decided to ignore him,

Brice began to get agitated, Iolo took no notice, Kath the barmaid began to worry; she knew Brice might cause trouble and pressed a button situated under the bar, this button alerted the landlord when needed he lived upstairs in the living quarters. Brice walked up to Iolo and stood face to face with him, Iolo brushed him aside spilling his drinks. Brice grabbed him by the shoulder with one hand.

Iolo put down his drinks on a table near-by, and swung a punch at him, Iolo had missed his target but Brice came back with a blow to the solar plexus, Iolo went down on his knees he was severely winded, Ethel hurried to his aid and comforted him. "That's for Mal Evans; I'll get to the bottom of why he disappeared without telling his butties, run off with a woman... my arse!" shouted Brice.

Howell Davies, Landlord, came darting in he stared down at Iolo who was still on his knees being comforted by Ethel Probert.

"You all right Iolo? I've had enough of this idiot and his cronies. You Brice and your cronies are barred until you learn that you do not

42

do what you like in a public house, my public house!" shouted Howell Davies, Landlord, being very assertive "You can enjoy the rest of your Christmas somewhere else, now take your cronies with you!" said Howell offering a helping hand to Iolo.

"Thanks for that but there was no need, Howell," said Iolo trying to recover his breath.

Iolo and Ethel eventually settled down, well-wishers came and offered sympathy as they all had dealings of a kind with Brice and his cronies. After closing time Iolo and Ethel slowly walked home and from time to time he would look over his shoulder wondering whether Brice and company would follow and make some kind of attack on him. Eventually they reached their houses and Ethel suggested that he stayed with her until morning.

Brice did not make himself a nuisance nothing happened overnight and Iolo wondered, what would happen next, he agonised on whether he should go to the police. "I think it would be best if the police didn't know about last night," said Ethel looking anxious she wrung her long slender fingers, worrying. "I don't want them poking their noses into our business, you never know what they might uncover, them… forensic people are quite clever, I've seen them on the telly scratching and searching for evidence,' said Ethel, and Iolo began to worry also.

"Yes, I think we had better put our heads together, just in case Dewi Brice gets clever and tell the police about the disappearance of Maldwyn Evans," said Iolo, quietly. "Any case, what about Maldwyn's wife, what about her?" said Iolo, suddenly raising his voice.

"There was no love lost there, they were always arguing, she was probably glad to get rid of him," said Ethel she gave a little laugh.

"Well that's in our favour, I think I'd better go and see her, and put her mind at rest, who knows it could work out for the better, we could start divorce proceedings," said Iolo, grinning.

Boxing morning was bright and fresh; a gust of wind blew lazily as Iolo walked up the garden path of Mr Maldwyn Evans— deceased. He rang the door-bell a blonde woman pulled back the heavy looking curtains she stared at Iolo through dark, brown, tired looking eyes. In a matter of seconds she was standing on the doorstep. "Should I know you?" she asked as Iolo was about to speak.

"You may remember me from our schooldays, I was a year above you," answered Iolo, he hadn't realised until then that the woman he was speaking to was not only Maldwyn Evans's wife but a girl from his past.

Iolo agonised as to how he could steer the conversation to her wayward husband. "I've come to see you about your husband, I believe he's run away with my wife, Anwen...Anwen Pritchard," said Iolo shyly.

"You had better come in," said Mrs Evans as she beckoned him into a shabby neglected lounge, he sat in an old looking armchair a mongrel dog came up to him and sniffed at him vigorously and then sat wagging it's stumpy tail staring intently. "Well what do you have to say? I've been waiting for something like this to happen," she said, her dark, brown eyes stared at Iolo. "You haven't changed much in all these years, I thought I recognised you when I saw you walking up the garden path, but your name escapes my memory."

"Iolo... Iolo Pritchard," he answered.

"I'm Ruth...I was Braithwaite before I married that swine of a so called husband," she said and she looked around the shabby neglected room, shame was in her eyes, and Iolo could see it.

"You suspected that Maldwyn and my wife were secret lovers," said Iolo, nervously.

"Yes it was going on for some time, so I'm told, every-one in the village knew about it... except me. People didn't want to tell me, they didn't want to get involved, just gossip!" she hissed.

"Same here, I wondered when people started whispering, men were laughing at me behind their hands. What plans do you have now? I'm thinking of starting divorce proceedings," said Iolo, feeling quite confident.

"Yes, my sister is pushing me in that direction— she said... I should have divorced him years ago, I could have done better she said." Mrs Evans' worn face looked down at the dingy brown carpet, she bit at her lower lip.

"Well I'd better be off; I've got a lot of thinking to do, take care now, I'll see myself out," offered Iolo.

"Yes, and thank you for calling, maybe I can get my life back together now that the waster has gone," said Mrs Evans, looking a little pleased.

Iolo strolled home thinking about Dewi Brice's threats, was it time to start a bonfire? Or would bonfires stir people's imagination. Iolo decided that the only way to destroy evidence was to take it down the mine and lose it in the gob area where it would be lost for ever. First things first, get rid of the old blood stained overcoat he wore when he shot Maldwyn Evans; the shotgun was licensed so it was to be thoroughly cleaned in case it was examined by the police. Iolo had to consider scrapping his old car; evidence was in the boot in the form of bloodstains.

Chapter V

January 1968

Iolo had his old Ford Anglia car scrapped, he was glad to see the back of it; he also managed to bury his blood-stained dismembered overcoat deep underground in number 26 district. He and Ethel considered getting married She talked about giving up her coal board house when Iolo's divorce came through. Everyone seemed to accept that Anwen Pritchard and Maldwyn Evans had indeed run away together to start a new life somewhere else in the country. Dewi Brice continued to harass Iolo and Ethel.

February 5th, Monday morning

The day's morning was cold, the wind blew in short gusts; an empty crisp packet rose in the air falling majestically in wave like movements. Iolo shuddered as a cold shiver ran up his spine it foretold that something gruesome might happen. In the distant a figure of a man wearing a flat cap crossed the road diagonally, he slowed menacingly, Iolo suddenly recognised the sauntering figure, it was Dewi Brice he had just ended his night shift and he was early, he must have guessed that Iolo would be making his way to the pit at that time and had sought time off from his supervising deputy. "Well... well; Iolo Pritchard we meet again; put me in the picture! What happened to Maldwyn Evans... and your missus?" uttered Brice menacingly. Iolo thought quickly.

"I knocked them on the head took them down the pit and buried them in the gob," said Iolo, grinning broadly.

"Very funny, I'm watching you, Pritchard, I'm thinking of going to the police, let's see what they dig up!" said Brice, frowning with frustration. Iolo walked on and left Brice dumbfounded he did not expect that kind of an answer, little did he know Iolo was almost telling the whole truth.

Jack Williams stood at the door of the official's lodge staring and listening at a group of men who were shouting.

"That was one of the worst Christmases me and my family have ever had, it's about time we had parity pay with the English coalfields," shouted a young disgruntled miner.

"Aye, we pay our union dues, and what do we get?" shouted Billy Parfit.

"Sod all, they shut our pits and pay us peanuts," shouted Bill Pumpy. More men were gathering around, listening and agreeing with the ensuing argument. Jack Williams pulled out his pocket watch and stared at it briefly. "Come on you lot, down the pit, the hooter will be sounding soon and the box-pit will be stopped for materials," shouted the angry under-Manager.

"We are not going down the pit until we see the lodge, we've had enough!" shouted Billy Parfit in reply. Parfit marched smartly towards the NUM's office, followed by most of the morning shift. Harry Carter the lodge chairman came rushing out of the little hut called the NUM lodge office.

"What's the matter boys?" shouted Harry Carter looking at his pocket watch and then up at the motionless wheels high up on the pit head gear.

Parfit stood on the buffers of a tram filled with muck from a gob heading. "Look here Harry Carter, me and my family struggled to enjoy a Christmas dinner last year, and many of the boys here suffered the same," Shouted Parfit. "HERE— HERE!" shouted the morning shift.

"You can come down from that tram of muck, nobody talks down to me!" shouted Harry Carter, he quickly climbed five of the steps that went up one leg of the pit headgear backstay. He looked over the heads of the men who were shouting "Parity, Parity".

"Ok boys, I know we lag behind the English coalfields, but all I can do is bring the matter up at conference," shouted Harry over the heads of the amassing crowd, surface men had now joined the shouting and Harry had trouble getting his words across. Eventually he managed to appease the maddened crowd, most of the men went down the pit, some of the men, however, vowed never to go down the pit again and went home.

Iolo belatedly stepped onto the pit cage followed by Jack Williams and the senior pit engineers. "What did you think of that?" Said Jack

Williams staring wide eyed at his Overman. Iolo thought long and hard.

"Well, the governments' of the past have had it pretty easy, considering that the NUM haven't struck since nineteen-twenty-six, but history will repeat its self you can be sure of that, the old ones have all but gone now, and these youngsters of today have itchy feet they'll up sticks and emigrate or move onto other emerging industries,' said Iolo who had seen the morning's trouble coming some time ago.

Jack Williams remembered—"My father was an old miner, and I remember him telling me of the terrible poverty in the mining communities, the soup kitchens, truck shops, and the like... Looks like they may be coming back," said the under-Manager, "I hear that other pits are experiencing wildcat strikes, the natives are indeed restless," he said, he didn't look happy and Iolo went into deep thought until he felt the pit cage shudder as it touched the landing at pit bottom. The pit bottom smelled like an old and discarded damp dishcloth, it reminded Iolo of the smell given off by the inrush water experienced in the year previous.

Charlie Dicks, hitcher, raised the gate that had held the riders in the cage. "Good morning gentlemen, nice to see some smiling faces," he said sarcastically and grinned to himself.

Iolo and the under-Manager made their way to number 26 district; talking generally and discussing what was being planned for the district, they stopped from time to time and spoke to the various men who were working doing vital jobs. Philip Jones, Bill Pumpy's young assistant came walking briskly to meet them. "You'll have to go around the other way, the pump had stopped between shifts and we have two foot of water, the men are refusing to walk around or walk through it," reported young Philip. Iolo and the under-Manager were incensed,

"Why hadn't someone told me about this?" shouted the under-Manager as he made his way to where the men were sitting waiting for the water to recede. Bill Parfit, ring leader, took up the challenge.

"Look here Mr Williams, we didn't know this body of water was here when we came down the pit, as far as we are concerned, there should have been a safe clear walk-way into the districts, if the deputy had done his job right, the danger would have been fenced off and we would have been directed around to the intake side," Said Bill Parfit, who knew more about mining law than he knew about his own job as conveyor belt charge-hand.

"Ok gentlemen, If you'd like to follow me, we can all walk around the intake side where it's nice and cold and a bit further to walk," said the under-Manager grinning away to himself. The men had no alternative but to follow the under-Manager onto the intake side of the airway that served the west side of the mine.

"How deep is the water, Bill Pumpy?" asked Iolo as he eyed the stretch of water that seemed to go on forever.

"It's not as bad as it looks, deepest is about a foot, the worst has gone," said the Pumpy, eyeing the expanse of foul smelling water. "You'll be getting a new pumps-man, I've been offered a job in the steel works, young Philip here is going too, when his father can fix him up with a job," said the disgruntled pumps-man.

"Why is that?" asked Iolo innocently.

"I would have thought it would have been obvious, if it wasn't for the overtime that I put in every week, my missus and the kids would not get a decent holiday and we'd have a lousy Christmas," stated Bill Pumpy. Iolo had to agree with him, wages were the lowest for many years, the English coalfield were enjoying a different power-loading agreement fought for by the same union as the welsh miners. What had gone wrong?

Iolo decided that time was getting on, he had to get to the number 26 district and make sure that the men would not waste time arguing among themselves, Bernard Thomas had waded through the water, it went over the tops of his boots, Iolo followed walking gingerly behind as the floor of the mine could not be seen, the water smelled of old engine oils and dampness as it had seeped through old workings and brought the old filth with it.

Iolo reached the lamp station ahead of most of the men, Bernard Thomas was duty bound by law to make an inspection of the district as the time limit from last inspection to the first man arriving at the district was exceeded due to the mass meeting at the surface. The men waited, sitting around discussing union politics, things were getting heated as Bill Parfit stirred up more trouble.

At last Bernard Thomas had completed his pre shift inspection of number 26 district and the men's names and numbers were recorded in the time-book as required by law. Bernard took off his safety spectacles to wipe them, after replacing them he showed Iolo the overtime recorded in the time-book. "Look Iolo, the men are not working the overtime that they used to work, management have cut it right down to bare minimum," said Bernard shaking his head wondering what was going on.

"I should know, I dish out the overtime, I can only work to the critical jobs that the management give me, I'm given an overtime budget and I have to stick to it," said Iolo wishing he could solve the impending pay dispute.

Jack Williams closed one of a set of heavy ventilation doors that separated the two airways, walking smartly up to Iolo he asked: "How much coaling time have we lost, Iolo?"

"About an hour, this could go on for some time; Bill Parfit seems hell bent on stirring things up.

"Aye, my cousin works down the valley, and he told me that the colliers there are playing up, it's only a matter of time before the whole thing blows up in everybody's faces," informed Bernard.

"The overtime has been cut drastically no wonder the men are pleading poverty," stated Iolo, he stared at the under-Manager's long tortured features, Jack Williams had worked his way up, he knew the men, and had a good understanding of the pit's geological difficulties.

"No pit is safe, we all have the pit's economy at heart but we must plod on regardless," said the under-Manager, frowning. Iolo and Bernard shrugged their shoulders and wondered about the future of their colliery.

The magneto type telephone rang three times, "that's for us by the sound of it," said Bernard he walked up to the telephone unit that was bolted to an arch girder and picked up the ear piece and listened intently. "Ok then, get him out, use the men on the ripping lip as bearers, we'll meet you," said Bernard, frowning at the news. "Bill Parfit has had an accident; first aider said, he's fractured his leg, a lump of coal came over and caught him," said Bernard stifling a grin.

Jack Williams angrily threw down his canvas gloves onto the dusty floor of the mine. "Bloody hell, this man's a walking catastrophe, come on let's meet the stretcher party, some men will try any excuse to put their point across," he shouted angrily.

The three officials of the mine hurriedly made their way into the district in order to meet the stretcher-party. In the distance they could see the many flashes of lamp light and men shouting amongst themselves. Clive Pugh, district first aider came ahead and met them. "Parfit won't be working for a bit, he's got a compound fracture of the Tibia, the bone's sticking through his skin," said the first aider. The under-Manager stopped the stretcher party and spoke to Bill Parfit.

"What happened bill?" asked the now slightly anguished under Manager.

"I was ripping the loose face with a mandrel and a big piece of coal came out unexpectedly, it caught me unawares," uttered Parfit, pain etched on his face.

"Where were you working when *this* coal-slip fell on you, Bill?" asked the under-Manager sounding serious and concerned. "In front of the road, making room for the stage loader extension," replied Bill Parfit wincing with pain. The under-Manager thought for a moment, you could see the wheels working behind his eyes; he didn't quite believe the troublesome miner, it was early in the shift and Parfit was a belt charge-hand and not a collier.

"Have you administered morphine, first aider?" asked the under-Manager looking around for an answer from the first aider. "Aye, but it hasn't taken effect yet,"

Chapter VI

Caradog Pritchard

Caradog Pritchard is an elder brother to Iolo by twenty years, now sixty-six and retired from the darkness of the pit, he spends his time between visiting the workmen's club the allotments and sitting in his favourite armchair smoking twist which is chewing tobacco cut up into flakes and burned in the briar. He warms his hands by the open coal fire, and from time to time he would tap his briar violently on an old tin ashtray perched precariously on a bony knee. He dismembered the briar and proceeded to poke a blackened and twisted pipe cleaner through one section pushing and pulling vigorously until bits of hardened soot fell onto his corduroy trousers.

"Caradog come and have a look at this," shouted Rowena his wife.

"I'll be there in a second my love," answered Caradog as he began to bang the briar on the old tin ashtray pinched from the workingmen's club.

"I want you now! This second," screamed Rowena. Caradog stiffly got out of his armchair and went to see what his wife wanted. "Look at them kids," she said staring into the distant.

"What kids?"

"Those kids in that tree over there," she said, pointing to a large spreading oak tree.

"So what do you want me to do about it?" said Caradog hand on aching hip.

"Go and tell them to get out of that tree before one of them falls out and breaks their neck," she squealed.

"Ok, I'll go and tell them now," he said and painfully made his way to the noisy children who were playing.

"You kids get down from that tree, before you fall out," demanded Caradog.

"We're ok Mr Pritchard, we won't fall out we've climbed this tree hundreds of times," answered a tall ginger haired boy.

"Get out of that tree this minute, before I get your father to you," demanded the frail aging man. The ginger haired youngster duly obliged followed by the rest of the group including a young denim clad girl. Caradog eyed the ginger boy, he knew his father as he had trained him when a young miner not much older than the boy who stood before him.

"You're Jimmy James's boy, aren't you?" asked Caradog. The boy studied the old man's craggy looking features; he could see that years of hard work had made their mark; he knew old shopkeepers and they didn't look half as old as Mr Pritchard.

"My granddad worked with you, didn't he?" asked the inquisitive youngster.

"Aye and I trained your father when he wasn't much older than yourself, your father's a good conscientious worker, what's he doing now lad?" asked Caradog,

"He finished in the pit he's working in the steelworks now!" replied the ginger haired youngster.

Friday March 1st Saint David's day

Iolo and Jack Williams watched as the afternoon shift men shouted and argued amongst them-selves, again low pay continued to plague the welsh mining workforce. Harry Carter lodge chairman did his best to cool things down; he was almost in tears as he desperately tried to explain the politics of unionism. Bill Parfit was not to be blamed for this disruption as he was still on the injured list. Thomas Thomas, known as Tommy twice-er, held his water-jack up high, and let the drinking water flood out in long streams splashing onto the concrete floor out-side of the officials-lodge. Then everyone else did the same.

"Come on boys let's make our voices heard," shouted Tommy twice-er turning towards the pithead baths. Most of the men followed; the lowest paid tended not to respond and made their way to the box pit. Jack Williams felt helpless as he watched the coalface workers scurrying towards the steep steps that led to the pithead baths.

3pm Cwm Derw workingmen's club

Caradog Pritchard sat in his usual place in the bay window; the March sunshine shone brightly and warmed his narrowing shoulders.

'Your deal,' said Caradog as he raked in the playing cards. His broad hands scarred with blue marks fumbled as he desperately tried to control the movement of his thick fingers, he slowly bundled the cards together and passed them to Fred, his butty.

"It looks like there's trouble down at the pit" bellowed Lil the club's stewardess. The door opened and a little narrow shouldered man walked in followed by ten other miners. Lil, club's stewardess beamed a big smile as she pulled pints for the striking miners. The miners sat around discussing the politics of strikes. Little Cliff Warrender sat on a chair his short stubby legs swung to and fro and he seemed to be in charge as Tommy twice-er did not make an appearance. Little Cliff's flat cloth cap rotated around his head in increments with each pint of bitter that he had drank.

Lil's head turned towards the door as it slowly opened. Ray Chapman the club's burly chairman slowly and cautiously stepped through the open door. "What's this all about?" he said as he recognised some of the strikers who were from up the valley. Little Cliff Warrender stood up and welcomed the chairman into his own club.

"Gentlemen, please be upstanding and give a warm welcome to Cwm Derw's resident virtuoso Mister Raymond Chapman." Everyone in the club stood and raised their pints and began chanting 'song' 'song'.

Ray Chapman club chairman got onto the stage and without any music or beer in his belly began to sing: 'Pa ham mae dicter, O Myfanwy' Yn llenwi'th lygaid duon ddi? Which translates as 'Why is it anger, O Myfanwy,' that fills your eyes so dark and clear?

Caradog had his entertainment catered for as the miners sang their songs and the club made some more money.

Monday 4ʳᵈ March, day shift

Jack Williams, under-Manager sat at his desk in the officials'-lodge; on his desk lay many thick dusty diaries of the records of the mine, he read out one entry to Iolo. "Friday March first. 26 district afternoon report. District delayed due to collier's wild cat strike, manpower reduced by seventy percent. Shift's production stopped insufficient men to man coalfaces. Men transferred to cleaning spillage from around trunk conveyors three hundred yards cleaned, twenty trams filled with clean coal," he read aloud. "We don't need many shifts like this; the Manager was pulling his hair out, he had demanded the names of all of the men who went home last Friday, they should have a nice polite letter with their lamps this morning," he said, a wry smile lit up his lined face.

"Iolo we need to carry out some maintenance, get the men to spend the first hour doing essential jobs like changing the picks on the power loader and changing oils. I want you to breathe the hot breath of Satan on their necks," growled the irate under-Manager. However it was the colliery custom to use the night shift labour to make up for short comings like breakdowns and wild cat strikes.

Number 26 District Return Road

Iolo sat on a makeshift seat writing in his diary when he was approached by one of the journey men. "Iolo come down by here, there's a terrible evil smell coming from the waste side of the road," said big Bob the leading hand of the journeymen, the men called him Preacher because of the way he spoke just like an old time Welsh preacher. Many men refused to work with him as they never knew which way to talk to him except for little Mervyn Coles who didn't care a damn anyway.

Iolo knew what had caused the smell, the ventilation was pulling foul air from the waste it could only be the stench of rotting flesh, the flesh of Anwen Pritchard and her lover. Iolo looked for the tell-tale chalk mark the one he had marked onto an arch girder the day he had dragged the corpses into the waste in December 1967.

"It must be a dead rat!" said Iolo trying to put the blame on an ill-fated rodent.

"A gigantic evil one at that, judging by the smell issuing from the waste," said big Bob.

"I'll order some disinfectant from the stores, maybe that'll disguise the rotting smell," said Iolo trying to allay big Bob's dislike of rotting flesh. Iolo began to worry that if the incident regarding the disgusting smell wasn't resolved it might result in management ordering the digging out of the offending area of the waste, and that situation was not what Iolo wanted, he had to act fast before the whole district rebelled they didn't need much of a push regarding the wage disputes.

Iolo had ordered the approved non- flammable and non- toxic disinfectant from the pit stores the head stores-man had assured Iolo that he would organise the immediate transportation of the order and Iolo sent big Bob to meet the man carrying the disinfectant from the stores.

Big Bob met his opposite number on the outside parting which is where full and empty supply journeys are exchanged. The big can of disinfectant was getting very heavy as he arrived at the offending spot, but not far away Bob observed a beam of a cap-lamp coming from inside the district, Iolo was coming to meet the big man who carried the stuff that would hopefully mask the smell of rotting flesh. "What kept you Bob?" demanded Iolo, he stared at the big man his face streaming with sweat, Big Bob reached for his water-jack he had left it hanging on the side of the roadway. Bob raised the four-pint jack of warm water to his dry lips and drank from it greedily, he then offered the half-drunk jack of water to Iolo, he politely refused, Bob had a greater need of the water than Iolo, Overman of the district.

Iolo stood on pit bottom waiting for the pit carriage to descend the shaft, Charlie Dicks, Onsetter more commonly called the Hitcher stared at Iolo and grinned slyly, Iolo often wondered why this keeper of bottom of the shaft was not liked, he was always grinning, the men gave him a hard time and he did his very best to be awkward in return.

The carriage duly arrived, Charlie Dicks raised the carriage gate and motioned with a gloved hand that Iolo and others should get into the awaiting carriage. Iolo listened to banter between the men and the Hitcher. And as the carriage began to ascend the shaft they all began to sing, 'Charlie is a bastard' Charlie Dicks was incensed but there was nothing he could do, it was illegal to stop the carriage when it was in motion unless there was an emergency.

In the officials'-lodge Iolo wrote his reports for management; the smell of rotting flesh lingered in his nostrils, no matter what he did to rid himself of that terrible stench he failed miserably.

In the pit head baths Iolo began to scrub away at the day's filth, most of the men had finished showering and had gone home, some lived well away from Cwm Derw and had buses to catch others used the luxury of their own transport. Iolo was busily scrubbing away at his finger nails when someone tapped him on a bare shoulder. "Give my back a rub please butty," asked a voice. Iolo turned to see who it was. Dewi Brice stood before him naked except for an old and soaped flannel.
"Well... well Bricey," exclaimed Iolo as he held out an empty hand; Dewi Brice slapped the soapy flannel onto Iolo's open hand. Neither of the two men expected this situation to happen as Dewi Brice had changed shifts. Nothing happened as there were still some men showering near-by.

Meanwhile in the Cwm Derw working men's club Caradog Pritchard was enjoying his retirement he liked to while away the hours playing cribbage with his lifelong butty, Fred Morgan. "Fifteen two... fifteen four... and the rest won't go," said Caradog as he moved the pegs along the cribbage board, his large fingers dwarfed the small wire-like pegs.
From time to time a club member would call in for a quick pint before dinner as was the custom amongst many miners, especially if they were retired, or miners who were on the sick list. As Caradog and Fred Morgan played their card game, miners began to talk about the pit.
"How's the dust on number twenty-six district? Our Georgie said it was so thick the lamp of the man next to you was just an orange glow," said Billy Parfit sat on chair with his leg in plaster and resting on another chair.
"I heard that the water-pipes were blocked with rust, and the fitters had to strip the dust suppression system right down," shouted Fred

Morgan who was listening intently to the mining discussion that was going on.

"Our kid's the Overman down on number twenty-six, some of the men there, should get the boot, not worth a cup of cold water, luckily they're on the other shift," said Caradog smiling as he began to count the number of holes that he had scored. Billy Parfit studied Caradog for a moment he eased his backside into a more comfortable position and then began to stir up trouble.

"The trouble with nacods is they are living off the backs of the workers," remarked Billy Parfit, a gleam was in his eye. Nacods is an acronym for National Association of Colliery Overmen Deputies and Shotfirers. Billy Parfit had a dislike of bosses and let everybody know of it. Caradog stopped and placed his hand of cards on the table he stood up and faced the stirrer 'Parfit' pointing a finger at him.

"How did you break your leg, Parfit, fell of your grub box did you?" said Caradog, grinning with a wide cheeky toothless grin.

"A bye-law of this club says Communists are not allowed to become members— Parfit, you should show some respect and take your foot of the furniture," said Fred Morgan who happened to be the club's vice chairman.

"I'm not a communist, and never have been," said Billy Parfit showing signs of uneasiness. Fred Morgan and Caradog Pritchard resumed their game of cards.

Iolo strolled home alone from the colliery and from time to time he would turn and look back towards the pit wondering whether Dewi Brice would be following. The day was bright and windy, he shuddered as a gust of icy wind filled his overcoat but he only had a short walk home and Ethel would have his dinner ready and a warm smile always greeted him.

"Did you have a good shift love?" asked Ethel as she eased the heavy overcoat away from Iolo's broad shoulders and hung it neatly over the banister at the bottom of the stairs. Ethel looked horrified as Iolo told her of the smell coming from the waste side of the roadway in number 26 district.

"Will they find out, what will happen if the smell doesn't go away?" said Ethel, her eyes filled with worry.

"It's only a matter of time before the bodies dry out and then the smell will stop," said Iolo hoping his reasoning would allay her fears.

Iolo and Ethel sat at the dinner table she uneasily chewed at her food as she remembered the description Iolo had given her of Anwen and Maldwyn, rotting half a mile below in the gob of twenty six'.

Chapter VII

Friday 3rd May 1968

The smell of rotting flesh had disappeared from the waste side of the return roadway in number 26 district. Dewi Brice had accepted that his butty Maldwyn Evans had run away with the wife of Iolo Pritchard, Overman of Cwm Derw colliery. The good people of the small pit village also accepted that fate had thrown Ethel Probert and Iolo Pritchard together and they were happy except for the memory of that Friday night in December 1967.

All was quiet in the pit village; Billy Parfit had started back to work and was busying himself trying to stir up trouble and the colliery workforce wondered whether he belonged to the communist party as he never missed an opportunity to stir up problems where none had existed before.

Friday afternoon

Jack Williams had that feeling of dé·jà vu something said he had seen it before and it was about to happen again. Billy Parfit was shouting the odds as he always did and some of the less well-read men listened intently. "For the last four years this government has shut down one pit every week, and what does our so called union do about it? SOD all! that's what. At the rate they are going there won't be a pit left in the land before too long!" he shouted, but this time most of the men walked by as the Miner's holidays were looming and no one wanted to be on holiday with no money in their pockets, every penny counted because the wages were low. Jack Williams called to Billy Parfit but he walked away pretending not to hear the under-Manager calling his name.

Iolo, along with some of the other Overmen were talking about Billy Parfit, most of them agreed with what he was saying but wildcat strikes only made the miners' poorer. "If they were to stand united against a labour government they could win any argument," commented one official, another said "The NUM were bending over backwards for the government, they were blind to what was happening."

Iolo looked down over the gate of the pit carriage as it travelled downwards, the sound of the guide ropes hummed as they rubbed loosely inside the heavily greased brass boxes that were fitted to the sides of the pit cage. As the cage slowed and the pitch of the hum changed Iolo could hear Charlie Dicks the Hitcher shouting to someone. "Get back from the Penthouse, stay behind the sign that says *no unauthorised men to pass this point*". Some men had worked beyond their normal hours and were behaving badly.

As the officials ducked under the gate that was being held by Charlie Dicks, men shouted abuse, but the man just grinned slyly as he always did. The officials made their way to their respective districts.

Iolo stopped and pulled out his pocket diary he thumbed through the dusty pages and studied one page in particular. "Time to make an inspection of the main intake airway," he mumbled to himself.

He walked, stooping, and from time to time his pit helmet touched the bent and twisted arch girders that supported the roof and sides of the mine. The trunk conveyor which is the main conveyor on which two districts tipped their productivity was in a poor condition, he was horrified to see that coal spillage was not being cleaned up, the conveyor belt rubbed against its steel structure. Litter blew in the brisk ventilating air of the mine; coal dust was thick and covered the sides as well as the floor of the roadway.

Iolo shuddered at the thought of something terrible happening. At the first opportunity Iolo made a point of informing Jack Williams of the terrible conditions he had encountered on making an Overman's inspection. Iolo shook his head in disbelief as he replaced the earpiece of the pit telephone.

Eventually Iolo arrived at the coalface he travelled via the return road and by now he had made it a habit off sniffing as he passed the final resting place of his late wife and her lover.

Bernard Thomas crawled out of the coalface his dusty expression streaked with dried sweat. "I've had a phone call from the surface, the barometer is falling sharply, it was reading six hundred and ninety millimetres of mercury at two o'clock this afternoon— it is now six hundred and seventy… as we speak and the lowest I have ever experienced," informed the deputy.

"Yes," said Iolo. I am aware of the barometer readings, and I'm also aware of the condition of our main trunk conveyor. I phoned Jack

Williams and all I got was, 'I'm aware of the problem but because of the manpower shortages, it'll have to wait until tonight".

"I was going to mention it to you, as I travel that roadway once a week and did make a report of it and so did the deputy responsible for that area," said Bernard Thomas as he took off his safety specs and wiped the dust off them.

"Come with me, we need to take some gas readings along the roof and sides and monitor the general body of air in the roadway," ordered Iolo showing concern.

"I did an inspection fifteen minutes ago, general body was nought point eight per cent CH_4, and considerable layering for two hundred yards from the ripping lip," informed the deputy.

Iolo went back in the roadway and adjusted his flame safety lamp he turned off his cap lamp and so did the deputy, they studied the properties of the methane cap that burned above the testing flame inside the lamp. "I make that... one and a quarter per cent," said Iolo he grimaced as he said it.

"Yep, I make it one and a quarter per cent CH_4, too," said the deputy. "I'll go to the gate road and take some readings there, and I'll contact the district electrician and inform him that all power to the tail road must be isolated. If I get adverse readings in the gate road I'll evacuate the men".

"Ok, I'll make my way to the mouth, isolate the power in the crosscut, but first I'll contact all officials out-bye of the return airway and inform them of the situation," informed Iolo. His face took on a worried expression.

Bernard Thomas made his examination of the general body of air in the gate road. "Bloody hell," he exclaimed as he studied the gas-cap inside the lamp. "Nearly two per cent, I must tell the under-Manager and get the men out now!" he muttered loudly as all men must be withdrawn from a place in the mine where the general body of air has reached two per centCH_4 by volume.

 Bernard was wondering about the gas content in the tail road it must be more than two per cent he reasoned.

The men made their escape from the gassy district travelling towards the downcast shaft, Bernard waited for Iolo to return and meet him in the gate road.

The pair of officials were last to leave, they made quick inspections of the ventilation using an electronic CH_4 gas detector as they went.

"It's up to five per cent shouted Bernard," sweat ran from his chin, Iolo stopped and briefly studied the electronic gas detector. He wiped away the sweat from his brow with a dusty hand.

"Come on, we'll have to go faster than this," shouted Iolo. He was now very worried as the percentage of gas was now on the borderline of an explosive mixture. Bernard stopped and took another reading of the gas detector. The district transfer point was not far away they had to make for pit bottom.

Meanwhile on the surface of the colliery the weather turned foul, rain lashed and the wind blew, the heavens lit up as a bolt of lightning hurtled to earth and struck the lightning conductor that was supposed to protect the ventilating fan of the mine. Within seconds another bolt of lightning struck the unprotected fan house then everything stopped, all lighting and machinery stopped. Dai Thomas senior Overman came rushing out of the officials'-lodge and ran across to the powerhouse to see what he could do, he knew the lightning had caused the loss of power but at that moment he had no idea of the carnage it would cause. Dai Thomas studied the damaged switchgear the duty shift-charge electrician stared in bewilderment at the damage that threatened the lives of two hundred miners.

"I've alerted the mines rescue— colliery Managers, unit- electrical and mechanical engineers, the ventilation officer is already on the premises,' said Percy Higgins who manned the powerhouse, he had been following procedure. Fitters and electricians came from everywhere; many were called to the colliery as an emergency measure. The management had a duty to get the ventilating fan going and see that all men were taken to the surface using the emergency measures such as counterbalance water tanks designed so that men could be evacuated from the mine in the event of an emergency but the system was never tested under an actual crisis. It would be a long and laborious task in raising to the surface something like two hundred men.

Mouth of 26s district

"Five and a half per cent and rising fast!" shouted Bernard he ran after Iolo stumbling in his haste. Then suddenly, Iolo fell over and

Bernard fell on top of him. They felt a hot blast of air and then a faint banging that sounded like ventilation doors opening and closing.

"Quick get in that manhole!" screamed Iolo. The two officials dived into a transfer point manhole which was always larger than usual. The air got hotter the dust almost choked them; all they could do was to stay in the manhole and wait.

It seemed ages as they waited for the dust to settle, they listened for sounds of other men who may have evaded the gas explosion, they heard faint voices not too far away, Iolo recognised one voice it was that of young Philip Jones, Bill Pumpy's young assistant, and then he heard the voice of Bill Pumpy himself.

On seeing the light from the officials cap-lamps Bill Pumpy came walking up smartly and peered into the man hole. "It's you two, is it?" Said the pumps-man, there's a fall of ground fifty yards out-bye we can't get by it.

"How bad is it, any sign of fire?" asked Iolo, anxiously.

"The force of the explosion knocked out a few of the posts that were underpinning the broken arches, and then the whole area caved in," said Bill Pumpy. "What makes it worse is that this whole area was saturated with water about thirty years ago, this water made the above ground very friable and could fall like aggregates if the ground was disturbed," he added with an air of authority.

"Did you hear the second explosion?" asked Bernard Thomas.

"Aye, I think it came from up there," he pointed in the direction of the old in-bye workings. "But before we move from here can I suggest that we try the pit telephone?" said Bill staring at Iolo then at Bernard.

"There may be an outside chance that the pit telephone may be still connected," said Iolo as he picked up the earpiece and rotated the magneto handle. "Dead as a doornail," remarked Iolo disappointment showed on his sweat streaked dusty face.

"Come on, let's have a look in-bye, there may be a chance of getting to the return side through the crosscut doors and then into the intake side," suggested Bernard, meanwhile young Philip Jones stayed silent fear gripped him as he tried to say something. Iolo noticed the fear in the young miner's eyes, his bottom lip quivered uncontrollably, Iolo reassured him by putting an arm around him.

"We'll get out of this, you'll see," said Iolo. "Anyhow how did you two escape the blast?" asked Iolo staring at Bill Pumpy, amazed.

"We were working in the snicket road, working on the four inch Evans' pump, the blast bypassed us, I think it was a bloody miracle," exclaimed Bill Pumpy.

"Just our sodden bad luck! The underpinning has been knocked out there, as well," gasped Iolo, abject disappointment showed in his eyes. The ground from above was still trickling from the massive hole; way above the frightened men. We can't go back through the face because the district is full of gas, god I have never felt so frightened in all my life!" admitted Iolo, the others stared at him, and they too were very frightened.

"Ok, we'll have to admit we are trapped, we need to survive, it may be some time before the rescue brigade get to us, We'll have to make our- selves as comfortable as possible, let's get back to the transfer point man hole," ordered Iolo who was the most senior man among them.

Iolo ordered that only one cap-lamp and one flame -safety lamp was to be lit at any one time, and they were to try the pit telephone from time to time.

Iolo looked at his watch it was ten minutes to seven, he wrote the time down in his notebook and made the following entry.

'We are unable to get past the falls of ground caused by the explosions. There is no communication; pit telephone is out of action. Number of men is 4 including myself Iolo Pritchard district Overman. The men are Bernard Thomas district deputy; William Thomkins (Bill Pumpy) Philip Jones (pumps-man's assistant.)'

On the surface, power has been restored to the winding engines; mechanical and electrical engineers were making progress in the fan house. The rescue brigade had arrived at the pit surface and had established an incidence control room. Meanwhile a crowd of pit villagers had gathered at the colliery gates after hearing the pit hooter sounding long continuous blasts. They were anxious for news of the ill-fated miners.

Ethel stood among the worried women of the village. Management had posted men in strategic positions in order to act as a deterrent as they didn't want people invading the colliery surface, the press had not yet heard of the pit disaster.

In the fan-house engineers were working hard, Bob Blanchard chief unit electrical engineer had earlier made the decision to commission the standby fan as it had sustained minimal amount of damage to its switch gear. Mr Mainwaring the colliery general Manager flapped around issuing orders to the annoyance of the engineers. "Where's the ventilation officer?" he demanded, his waxed ginger moustache quivered.

"With respect, Mr Mainwaring, the ventilation officer is supervising the engineers in the fan drift they have to switch the doors over before the standby fan can be commissioned," answered Jack Williams, under-Manager.

"All right... go and tell him that in ten minutes time we will be ready to start the standby fan," ordered the general Manager.

The last of the men had been brought to the surface, by able bodied men. A mortuary had been prepared to receive the dead miners, fifteen in all. Four men were listed as missing; the majority of the men had miraculously escaped the blasts of the explosions, as they had arrived at the bottom of the downcast shaft before the explosions had occurred.

Meanwhile sat in the manhole on number 26s transfer point were the four very unfortunate miners trapped by massive falls of ground. Unable to escape their situation they had no alternative but to stay put, and hope and pray that they would be rescued before the gas got to them.

Iolo took his flame safety lamp out into the roadway just outside of the manhole. He studied the flame. "About five per cent," he shouted to Bernard Thomas. Bernard took a reading using the electronic CH_4 detector,

"Two and a half per cent, according to this," said Bernard looking very annoyed. "Let's have a look at the reading in the lamp," said Bernard, the men turned off their cap-lamps and again studied the gas-cap that burned around the wick in the flame of the flame safety lamp.

You're right! Five per cent it is, said the deputy, this CH_4 detector has had it." He hung the detector on a nail inside the manhole.

The men sat in the manhole looking very dejected there was no sign of the ventilation improving.

Iolo took out his note book and made the following entry. 'Friday 9 pm, Morale of my comrades is weakening, ventilation is five per cent CH_4 by flame safety lamp, D6 detector exhausted battery. Air is passing through fall areas but insufficient to dilute the gas in the gate road by which we hoped to escape from this hell hole.'

9:30 pm

Iolo looked out into the roadway; dust had started to fill the air he rushed out and stared downwind, grains of dust began to bombard his eyes, he shouted excitedly at his comrades. "The fan has started! The fan has started!" they came rushing out of the manhole and went to the fall area; they could hear the air passing through small gaps in the fallen ground. They listened intently for the sound of voices but none could be heard. Iolo examined the fallen ground by grabbing a handful stones the size of chippings. All they could do now was to sit and wait.

Meanwhile on top of the downcast shaft, First officer David Grimshaw inspected the rescue team members, he addressed his men. "Gentlemen of number one team there are four miners missing, management believe that these men are trapped beyond falls of ground, your mission is to find them, and you have your mine plan of the area where we believe these men are trapped." Number one team were coupled up to breathing apparatus and could not speak. "Ok number one team captain make your final inspection." Number one team captain inspected his team, each man made a thumbs up sign to signify that he was ok, the team captain examined every man one by one until he was satisfied that his complement of men was one hundred per cent safe. The tall banks-man watched intently as the mines rescue prepared to descend the shaft in order to establish a fresh air base from which to establish a safe place of operation. David Grimshaw spoke to the banks-man. "Ok banks-man you can make your signal. The banks-man pressed the signal button three times. The rescue team captain signalled five hoots of his hooter and the vice-captain signalled five hoots to acknowledge. The captain gave four hoots to signal his team to board the awaiting carriage. Eight brave men boarded the carriage. The banks-man lowered the gate of the carriage he signalled five to lower steady. The first officer watched as the men disappeared below the surface of pit top, they were now on their own facing unknown dangers.

Mike Thompson team captain studied the mine plan he pointed to the roadway that led to the number 26 district he marked a long arrow in white chalk on a wooden strut between arch girders, he then wrote the name of the team and the date and then signalled to his men to move forward

Fifteen minutes later the rescue team had reached the fall area and were taking mine air samples. The captain pointed to a broken red and black cable and began joining the cable, it was an intrinsically safe type of telephone cable used only on haulages and telephone signalling systems. The team retreated to the surface to report their findings and submit the samples of air that they had taken.

11: pm
Iolo sat in the manhole with his three comrades, young Philip Jones began to weep, Bill Pumpy tapped him on the knee with a broad hand to try and reassure him. Iolo pulled out his notebook and made an entry. '11: pm Morale is unchanged, Telephone is still out of action probably due to broken cable under fall area, ventilation is down to 4 ½ per cent CH4, unwilling to venture into the gate road until gas volume has been reduced further.'

Meanwhile on the surface Mr Mainwaring colliery Manager is addressing a group of people mostly women. "Ladies and gentlemen, I have dreaded this moment for most of my working life, I am finding it very difficult in finding the right words," he announced. Mr Mainwaring looked down at the floor and thought for a moment. "We have recovered the bodies of fifteen very brave men we have not yet located the four missing men. I am going to read out the names of the fifteen men who did not survive the incident," said Mr Mainwaring, his waxed ginger moustache quivered as he studied the list of names. Before he began reading he caught the eye of Ethel Probert he noticed her shaking uncontrollably and called to the medical attendant to stay close to her side. He then began reading the list of men who did not survive. "John Evans; lamp 1621; William Evans; lamp 1692,' he stopped reading as two women collapsed on discovering that a dear beloved one had perished. He went and spoke to the medical attendant, "I can't read anymore names, these people will have to go home to their houses and I'll have to speak to them there," he said, his hands shook violently, the document fluttered in his nervous hand. Ethel

Probert went up to Mr Mainwaring and asked to see the list of names, he held up the sheet of note paper with a shaking hand, she scanned the list for Iolo's name

"THANK GOD THERE'S A CHANCE," she screamed and fell to her knees and wept uncontrollably. She had somehow missed the announcement naming the four trapped men.

12: 00 midnight in the incidence control room

Fred Bishop colliery deputy Manager studied a plan of the Cwm Derw coalmine. He spoke to the colliery ventilation officer. "How's the barometer is there any improvement?" He asked.

"Seven hundred and fifty millimetres of mercury and rising fast, the storm has passed over us, we now have a chance," said the ventilation officer looking very pleased.

"Where do you think Iolo Pritchard and his men are?" asked the deputy Manager. Pete the vent as the miners called him rubbed his stubbly chin; his tired looking eyes peered at the mine plan.

"My guess is they are probably still in this area here," he answered pointing to a junction in 26s district. "In all probability from hearing the rescue report, the blast from the explosion knocked out the underpinnings two hundred yards out-bye of twenty-six' transfer point, not only but also the underpinning in-bye of the transfer point, must have been disturbed," he said pointing to the mine plan.

"Yes... I see but what about the afterdamp do you think they could have escaped it?" asked the deputy Manager.

"Difficult to tell, the area of the transfer point is a new repair job so the cubic area would be substantial; I've looked at the vent readings, the ones taken by the rescue men— air, is passing through the district but is very sluggish the gross make of methane may be diminishing due to the rise of the barometer. We must assume that the men are in the transfer point area. The distance from the transfer point to the up-cast shaft is almost two miles, that's travelling through twenty-six' face as well."

"So there's no way we can tell if they are alive or not?" said the deputy Manager, frowning.

"The afterdamp may have got them, but the readings I have seen show low levels of CO gas, so the fall of ground may have quenched the flame and the quantity of CO gas may have taken the shortest route leaving the area near the manhole relatively free except for some methane," reasoned the ventilation officer as he pointed a finger at the mine plan.

"Let's hope you are right."

"We have a serious decision to make," shouted David Grimshaw as he smartly strode into the incidence room, he strode up to the mine plan and pointed to 26s district. "It's a hell of a distance but can we get away with it?"

"You mean... send a team from this crosscut here, right away round the tail road down through the face and out to the transfer point here," said Pete the vent, pointing his finger at various places around the plan.

"Yes, it's a hell of a risk but bear in mind most of my men are volunteers, should we ask them to unnecessarily risk their lives, we don't know yet whether the four missing men are alive or not," said David Grimshaw. "No! We can't risk it… we would be hung drawn and quartered if it all went terribly wrong," he said, and had a worried look on his round tortured face.

"How is the work going on? How long will it be before they are able to get through any of the fall areas?" asked the deputy Manager.

"It's a hell of a place to work, we are filling sand bags with falling rubble the size of chippings we are operating a chain gang twenty yards long; the hole above is thirty feet or more. We desperately need to get the belt conveyor to work, volunteers are dragging a temporary conveyor return-end-unit up the roadway we hope to get the conveyor going in about two hours with some luck and a lot of hard work," said the rescue first officer.

Men were working everywhere, toiling on the intake side of the mine trying to get systems going in order to rescue their trapped comrades. Time was of the essence would Iolo and his men be alive when the rescuers got to them.

01: 00

Iolo studied his tired looking comrades he noticed that Bill Pumpy was breathing a little heavy he glanced at the flame in the flame safety lamp, the yellowy flame was beginning to emit smoke this indicated that the oxygen level was diminishing there was not enough air coming through the fall area, what air did get through was taking a short cut around a corner and into the main airway of the gate road. Iolo took out his pen and notebook and made an entry.

01: 00 'Flame in flame-safety lamp 'smoking' indicates low oxygen level. William Thomkins' breathing is becoming laboured. Philip Jones very quiet feeling sleepy, Bernard Thomas, asleep; must wake him.' Iolo carried the flame safety lamp into the centre of the roadway and observed the flame, he watched as the flame brightened and the smoke disappeared. "Bernard, look!" he gasped, "come here!" Bernard did not answer, Iolo went to the manhole and shook Bernard violently he failed to respond. "Bill, quick, lend me a hand, Bernard's unconscious!" shouted Iolo in gasping breaths. Bill Pumpy struggled to get off the makeshift seat inside the manhole; he grabbed Bernard by both legs. Young Philip made an effort and helped them move Bernard on to the conveyor near the corner of the junction. They lay him on his back on the belt. Iolo put an ear to the man's mouth and at the same time looked along the chest and listened for a breath. "He's not breathing," Iolo's hands shook nervously as he desperately tried to remember how to give artificial respiration. The other two looked on helplessly as Iolo pinched Bernard's nose and eased back his head in order to maintain an open airway. Iolo breathed into Bernard's open mouth he watched as the man's chest rose slightly, he painfully straddled the waist of the unconscious deputy, pushing hard on the tail end of the breast bone four times sharply. Bernard gave an almighty gasp and then automatically breathed in sharply. Iolo watched nervously laughing as Bernard began breathing on his own. Iolo rested his patient on his side and watched over him closely.

"We'll stay close to this side of the roadway from now on," said Iolo. He studied the faces of the other two they were looking healthier due to a little fresh air coming from the one side of the roadway.

Meanwhile on the colliery surface in the incidence control room, the final plan was being made. Fred Bishop deputy Manager spoke into the telephone. "I want twenty pair of manhole arches and I want them down the pit now." He listened patiently to the reply and then the colour of his skin turned a bright red. "To hell with the cost, get yourself and those cronies with you over to the place where you hide those supports that are going to hopefully, save the lives of four of our men and then I want you to carry them to the south shaft and there you will put them into trams and send them down the pit without any delay

71

and when you have done that I want you to do the same all over again; is that understood?" He then slammed down the telephone, turned to Pete the vent and grinned. "How many men do we have hanging around waiting for someone to ask them to do something," he asked.

"As many as you want," replied Pete the vent.

"Right, send them over to the stock yard I want all the timber supports, sandbags, fishplates and anything that will be useful to those men who are working on the fall area, I don't want them hanging about waiting for stuff, we must get to the other side as soon as possible" demanded Fred Bishop.

At the fall area men were dragging the temporary conveyor return-end-unit into place. Bill Parfit trouble maker and belt conveyor charge-hand was strangely doing his best even knowing that two bosses were trapped on the other side of the massive fall. He shouted orders and his commands were being carried out. Two men were drilling holes into the floor of the roadway in order to arrest the movement of the belt return-end.

David Grimshaw 1st officer came walking smartly up the roadway his spot lamp waved about like a miniature search light. "How are things looking?" he asked as he studied the temporary return end. "Nearly ready to join the up the belt," answered Bill Parfit.

On the other side of the fall the four trapped men were feeling better but they had drank the last of their water, food was not an issue as of yet. Bernard sat up on the belt, but Iolo still kept an eye on him. Bill Pumpy pulled out of his waistcoat pocket a shiny brass oval shaped box he opened it carefully and placed it on a knee he then took out of another pocket a penknife and carefully sliced off a thin sliver of chewing tobacco and put it in his mouth, Iolo and Bernard watched as they were always curious when some- one like Bill Pumpy had the time and patience to fiddle around with a long thin piece of 'bacca' and then chew it." Anybody like a chew?" offered Bill.

"No thanks, I'm trying to give it up," answered Iolo, Bernard, Grinned. Bill Pumpy went to a water column and filled his water jack the column held a little water as the water must have been turned off by the rescuers due to a broken pipe somewhere.

"I wouldn't drink from that pipe if I were you! I tried that trick many years ago it went straight to my legs they were like lead. I had a good old guzzle," grinned Iolo talking from experience.

"I only use it to wash my mouth out, before I put a new chew in," said Bill.

Iolo looked at the time and made an entry in his notebook. 02:30 'Men's spirit is good we have used all of our drinking water, William Thomkins using fire- range water to wash out his mouth.'

Mean-while on the other side of the fall area rescuers are moving forward now that the conveyor belt is operational. David Grimshaw rescue 1st officer has ordered his men to rest and change after shovelling for ten minutes; no man was to keep going until he fell exhausted. The ground above the rescuers fell time after time. Moving forward was proving to be very difficult. 3 am only five metres advance was made. The rescuers decreased the distance between manhole arches, and things picked up. Advances were being made. Survey department estimated fall area as twenty yards long, fifteen yards remain.

6: am only ten yards advance has been made in total, ten more to go. The ventilation readings are improving, and the rush of air is becoming louder as it is being forced by suction through the very small gaps in the rubble.

Iolo and his comrades had been aware of the presence of the rescuers as their voices could be heard and the sound of fast shovelling was a very pleasing sensation.

It was now more than twelve hours since the terrible blast that took the lives of fifteen miners and injured many more. Iolo watched as a small depression formed in the rubble caused by the removal of rubble below. Suddenly a hole appeared. Iolo could now see the sweat soaked face of one of his rescuers. The recue men pushed some steel supports through the hole, Iolo recognised them as manhole arches, a mining term for mini arch girders. The rescuers made safe the edge of the fall area. Iolo called to Bill Pumpy, he came almost running, the other two came following behind. Iolo and his comrades tagged on to the rescue man, Doctor Shaw was waiting at the fresh air base, ready to examine them. Bernard Thomas had recovered almost to the point of excellent health.

As the pit cage ascended the shaft there was an air of quietness, Iolo became aware of the cold and dampness as the air struggled to make headway down the shaft and into the mine workings. Iolo shuddered and pulled the warm coarse blanket tighter around him. Bernard Thomas, Bill Pumpy, and young Philip Jones were equally overcome by the sudden harsh reality of their escape from death. They remembered that other miners were involved in the mine explosion, they wondered about them, they were almost afraid to ask.

As the carriage slowed to a snail's pace they could see the daylight above them, and voices could be heard, the voices began to get louder as the cage ascended its final few feet to the Keps on which the carriage would finally rest and be relieved of its grateful burden.

The already bright morning lit by a pleasing sunshine suddenly exploded into a complex array of flash photography that lit up the darkness of the pit cage, Iolo and the others put up their hands to shield their eyes from the blinding flashes of the many cameras wielded by men in long black coats. Shouts of 'hooray' filled the air and miners held the people back by holding hands as the heroes little by little made their way to the medical centre refusing offers of help; they were miners and proud of it.

Ethel Probert sat by the telephone staring at it intently, her daughter, Bethan Morgan slept soundly on the sofa, and from time to time she would go and tuck the blue thick blanket under her daughter. Ethel stood over the phone almost willing it to ring. It was considered posh to own a phone in a pit village, but Iolo had to have a phone as he was a senior colliery official and was often contacted by management regarding the mine.

Ethel stared at the phone and shouted at it. "Why don't you bloody well ring, don't you know there's a crisis on," she shouted at it. Then suddenly the telephone burst into life, Ethel almost jumped out of her skin, meekly she picked up the handset. "Hello who is it what do you want?" she asked in a loud arrogant kind of voice.

"It's me," said a distant quiet voice.

"Stop playing around I'm waiting for an important phone call, put your phone down!" she said in that same voice.

"It's me Iolo!" replied the quiet irritated voice.

"O' my god you're alive!" blurted Ethel she called to her daughter Bethan. "Come here Bethan it's, Iolo… he's alive. You stay where you are, I'm coming now," she called into the phone.

One week later

"It's quiet in the village today hardly anyone about," informed Ethel as she returned from the shops. "Nice day out there, a clear blue sky makes a change from the weather we normally have round here," said Ethel quietly. Iolo sat in his favourite armchair thinking and listening to the radio.

"What times are the funerals? "Iolo asked quietly as he had not ventured out doors since the disaster only to assist in the investigation.

"Ten funerals today, some of the men as you know were from outside of the village, five burials are private so they are saying over the village," replied Ethel. She eyed Iolo with concerned eyes she could see that it would take some time to recover from the effects of the explosion.

Scarcely a street in Cwm Derw was unaffected by the disaster in one way or another.

Meanwhile at 37 Stanley Street Mrs Meredith wept openly, she sat sadly looking out of the small back kitchen window. She stared blankly at the black path that led to the garden gate, was she was waiting for someone? Mrs Meredith looked away from the window as Edith a daughter came to her.

"This damn custom of 'gentlemen only' funerals!" she said as she put an arm around her mother's shoulders. "We should move on. We're past the middle of the twentieth century and we women are almost barred from attending our loved ones funerals," she scowled. Other women dressed entirely in black hovered and whispered politely.

In the front room by the window, side by side were the open coffins containing Mervyn Meredith and his son Johnny, the room was dark and gloomy, little light filtered through the heavy curtains that adorned the wood framed window. The heavy smell of death lingered around the room. Dawn the elder of Mrs Meredith's two daughters looked down at her father's peaceful face and then at her young brother, she kissed two fingers of each hand and gently placed them on her dad and brother's face. Suddenly there came a gentle but firm rapping on the front door, Dawn jumped with fright as the room was previously still and quiet. "Mam, Edith, it's the undertakers," whispered Dawn through the adjoining door. Dawn went to the door and opened it.

A very tall grey haired gentleman dressed in a long black coat and trousers stood ominously at the door.

"Good afternoon, I'm Gordon Jenkins...undertaker," he said quietly. "I've come for Misters Meredith," he said in a voice that was deep and eerie.

"You had better come in then," Dawn beckoned with a hand.

Mrs Meredith came into the room and went to the open coffins, leant over each of them and kissed her husband and young son goodbye for the very last time. She stood back; her eyes reddened from weeping over many days watched the undertakers screw down the neat fitting coffin lids. Then the bearers came in almost all miners, heads bowed. The family wailed as the coffins were carried out of the house and into the waiting long black hearses adorned with wreaths and flowers.

Baptist church

Reverend Tomos Ahearn stood tall in the pulpit, he looked down at the two coffins that lined the aisle and then at the men who were sat in the pews, he raised his grey head and stared at the men who were standing at the back of the little Baptist church many more stood outside. Iolo Pritchard stood tall and ominous at the back.

Reverend Ahearn cleared his throat and began his short sermon as he had other sermons to administer that day. "We are gathered here today to celebrate the lives of Mervyn Meredith and his son Johnny, these two very brave men gave up their lives in order for us, and others, to enjoy a standard of life, not seen by our forefathers. One wonders if we could do without life giving coal. We use coal to light up our living rooms and power our hospitals, we use coal to make some of our medicines, for when we have a headache we will reach for a headache tablet made from coal. We clean our homes with chemicals that smell like pine, also made from coal. We fight a constant battle against Mother-Nature she never gives up her fight we have to win the coal from her. One day Mother Nature will win her battle against us, as scientists will find other ways to power our homes and industries relieving us of the burden of sudden death beneath this crusted earth of ours. Would you all now pick up your hymn books, and turn to page sixty-three, " *Rock of Ages, cleft for me, Let me hide myself in thee;*

Let the water and the blood, From thy wounded side which flowed, Be of sin the double cure; Save from wrath and make me pure".

Chapter VIII

May 1969 Plagued with water

Time had passed. Number 26s district has closed down due to the coalface reaching the boundary line. The colliery has recovered from the explosion caused by the lightning strikes, but the families of the dead miners will never recover from the loss of their loved ones, many others will need hospital treatment for the rest of their lives.

Iolo has taken on the responsibility of senior pit Overman on the afternoon shift. Ethel has become a grandmother for the first time, and busies herself helping with the grandchild.

Dayshift, twelve noon

Back at Cwm Derw colliery, Iolo's shift had begun, he was ready to sort the pit's problems as they arose, the day was warm and dry the telephone rang from time to time usually an official had something to report, as Iolo wanted to know about anything, no matter how small or inconsequential.

Deep in the bowels of the earth in a district called 27s, big Bob Stephens was screaming abuse at a journey of trams that had come of the rails:" What heathen built this road to hell? Damn him I say!" screamed big Bob, preacher to others. Jack Williams' under-Manager's lamp emerged, flashing out of the darkness,

"What's the problem Bob Stephens?" demanded the under-Manager, a slight grin appeared on his lined face. Big Bob picked up from the floor two wooden sprags and made the sign of the cross.

"This malevolent Iron snake has suddenly taken a dark dislike to me," said Bob in a scathing bitter voice.

"Can I give you a hand?" asked the under-Manager, grinning.

"Aye, if you would," replied big Bob. "Just push on the corner of this here tram and heave when I tell you... heave... come on... heave you evil eyed demon, heave this iron snake," cried big Bob the tram slipped onto the rails and Bob cried out loud "Praise the lord we have conquered this one eyed iniquitous snake." Jack Williams walked away laughing quietly to himself, he never knew quite what to say to big Bob.

Meanwhile inside at 27s coal face, it had succeeded number 26s. This new coal face had its problems, plagued with water from above. It rained from the roof in copious amounts, raining onto the men who struggled to work in cramped conditions; they wore heavy oilskins in a vain attempt to ward-off the often odious foul smelling water. Men were more affected by heavy perspiration than falling water. Ianto Pugh and his team worked 27s face, the men were experiencing problems with the coalface' armoured conveyor.

Ianto, team captain shouted orders over the face tannoy: "Put the tail motor in reverse, and give the motor a short burst of power," The operator pressed the speaker button and said over the tannoy system:

"Tail motor is in reverse, stand by and keep clear," The keep clear alarm sounded throughout the length of the coal-face and the heavy chain linked conveyor went backwards just a little. "Repeat the operation once more," ordered, Ianto. The conveyor operator repeated the warning and the chain crept backwards once more and stopped dead.

"Face electrician come to the speaker will you please?" ordered, Ianto Pugh.

"Face electrician here, what's your problem, Ianto?" he called over the tannoy.

"Isolate the face conveyor motors… the face chain has come out of the races, let the Overman know what has happened," shouted the team captain.

"Will do replied the electrician."

Jack Williams and the Overman Joe Watkins returned to the coal face just as the team members were jacking up one side of the face conveyor. "How long will it be before you get it going?" asked Jack Williams. He watched as Ianto supported the heavy steel conveyor by pushing long pieces of timber under the width of the heavy steel pan.

"With a bit of luck an hour should do it, this water running under our backs… it's blutty cold!" exclaimed Ianto. The under-Manager watched, feeling a little guilty as Ianto and a team member struggled with the heavy linked chain. Iced cold water mixed with coal dust ran up the sleeves of his oilskins as he lay on his side trying to line up the scraper bars that were connected across the chains.

Meanwhile in the lodge- office Iolo Pritchard was trying to gather information, he needed to know the position in 27s he would order the redirection of empty trams to other districts and they would be expected to take advantage of the situation.

Meanwhile in Cwm Derw village Ethel Probert stood outside a shop and studied the price of various vegetables that the owner had written in large letters onto the large glass window. The shop was owned by George Sweeny greengrocer to the villagers. George came out of his small shop and spoke to her. "I've got some nice taters inside, if you want some," he said.

"I could do with some chip taters," she said as she followed George into the shop.

Little George Sweeny opened a paper sack by pulling a piece of hemp string and the sack opened revealing large reds.

"Look at these beauties," he said as he dug down into the sack with short thick arms, he put some of them onto the weighing scales. "How much do you want Ethel?" asked George, he stared at her under thick bushy eyebrows and smiled.

"I'll have five pounds in weight please George," said Ethel.

"Iolo loves his chips then," said George, grinning.

"Aye he likes his chips all right," replied Ethel she grinned also.

A large redheaded lady came running into the greengrocer's shop shouting, "Help, help, the newsagent is on fire," Little George ran out of the shop closely followed by Ethel.

Smoke billowed out of the newsagent shop next door. Mrs Williams, owner, was busy throwing out bales of magazines onto the pavement outside, she coughed violently her complexion was a little red either from exertion or the effects of carbon monoxide.

"Ethel go and phone the fire brigade as quick as you can," ordered George Sweeny. He went into the shop and began pulling at Mrs Williams the shop owner.

"No, no, I must get my stock out," she cried and resumed coughing as she made vain attempts to re-enter the inferno.

"Leave the stock there Mrs Williams, your life is worth more than a few magazines," he shouted at her. George stared anxiously through the thick smoke, a dark figure was trying to open a back door.

"Where's your daughter Mrs Williams?" asked George, shouting at her.

"O my god, Myra! She's up stairs!" she cried.

"Is there anyone else in the building?" probed George.

"No just Myra— Myra!" she screamed as she darted into the fiery death trap, the heat intensified and the thick black smoke billowed out of the shop doorway and onto the street. George watched helpless as the smoke obscured figures hammered at the locked back door.

"I'll have to do something," shouted George. Ethel came running up the street clutching her large handbag.

"I've phoned the fire brigade they are on the way, where's Mrs Williams?" said Ethel, gasping for breath. George took a very deep breath and dashed into the newsagent shop in a vain attempt to rescue the stricken Myra and her mother. Ethel rushed in behind the brave George only to be beaten back by the intense heat of the fire. She shouted after him: "George, George, come back." George took no notice. Ethel heard the desperate screams of the women, the banging of George's fists and feet on the locked back door.

In the far distant the sound of the fire engine could be heard, the siren sounded as if it were approaching from every direction.

Outside the shop, crowds of onlookers strained their necks trying to see what was going on. Ethel used her reasoning, "Get back, we don't want any more heroes, George Sweeny is in there trying to get the Williams' out," she cried. The dreadful banging and screaming had finally stopped, the smoke was thicker and the heat was affecting the neighbouring shops.

The fire engine came up the side of the shops the wrong way. Firemen jumped smartly out of the appliance, they ran around the engine like the highly trained men that they were. Firemen ran out the fire hoses while other's tried to quell the flames that licked at the wooden framework of the shop doorway. Some of the firemen were using fire extinguishers. Others bravely went into the shop only to be beaten back by the intense heat of the raging inferno.

"It's no good, there's too much heat, I can't see them we'll have to retreat and cool the fire down," shouted the lead fireman.

Ethel and the other bystanders stood well back from the raging inferno while the gallant firemen fought with the blaze. Water gushed out of the shop and ran down the pavement like a small virulent river. The fire fighters aimed their hoses inside the shop. There was now no hope of the Williams' and of the greengrocer George Sweeny surviving the shop fire that was to cause so much grief throughout the small pit village.

Ambulances lined up near to the now smouldering newsagent shop. Bill Thorpe lead fireman and another fireman came out of the smouldering shop bearing a stretcher. The look on their sad faces said volumes about what they had seen. The corpse that occupied the all steel stretcher steamed as the blanket that covered it was wet from the water that ran hot from above the shop. "O' my god," screamed Ethel when she saw a thick arm hanging from the stretcher, it was that of George Sweeny, greengrocer to the village. The onlookers gasped in horror at what they were witnessing Myra Williams was being carried out of the building she too steamed with being soaked with hot water that ran from above the burnt out shop.

Meanwhile at the colliery Iolo Pritchard went about his business running the coalmine as he saw fit. Percy Higgins Powerhouse attendant picked up the phone and dialled the officials'-lodge office number. "Iolo Prichard", answered Iolo.

"Iolo I've heard that there's been a big fire up at the village, three people dead, so I've heard," recounted Percy Higgins.

"Is that right, Percy can you give me a line to my house please, butty," asked Iolo,

"Can do," replied Percy and within seconds the phone rang at Iolo's house.

"Hello what do you want?" said a voice that seemed to bellow from the earpiece. Iolo pulled the phone from his ear.

"Ethel it's only me, stop shouting," bellowed Iolo loudly.

"Oh, Iolo, it's been awful, George Sweeney and the Williams' burned alive I was there, and the police took a statement from me," she blurted.

"Ethel go to Bethan's house and stay there until the end of my shift just in case," ordered Iolo, he reasoned that the shock of witnessing the horrific events of the day could adversely affect her.

"Ok, I'll go there straight away," she answered.

"What's happening to the newsagent shop Ethel?" asked Iolo as he looked out of the back kitchen window.

"They say that the fish shop will be selling newspapers for the time being, anyone who wants a glossy magazine or something with have to go to Graig Ddu, well that's what they're saying over the village," said Ethel, she eyed Iolo as he was missing his morning paper.

All the villagers will remember the day that George Sweeny and the equally ill-fated Mrs Williams and her daughter Myra were burned to death.

The year was coming to an end and there was little sign that the newsagent shop would be up and running by the end of the year. Villagers were getting fed up with going without— for so long.

Iolo Pritchard took it upon himself to tackle the local council as he reasoned they had some responsibility in seeing that the newsagent was at least tidied up or a proper replacement was built near-by.

As it happened, Joe Parsons the village councillor walked into the bar at the Collier's Arms pub, and stood alongside Iolo Pritchard. "Just the man I want to see; about the newsagent shop, what do you know Joe, excuse the unintended pun; about the shop is there any news for us locals?" asked Iolo as he turned to face him.

"Iolo, if you went to council meetings you would know what was going on in the village, you asked me a question and I will try and answer it as truthfully as possible. You may not know; the owner of the newsagent and her daughter died intestate, we have had one hell of a job trying to find a relative. The council has to obey the letter and spirit of the law, so as soon as we have covered all the necessary steps and a new owner is established the shop will remain boarded up. Does that answer your question?" replied the irate councillor.

"It'll do for now… councillor, what are you drinking?" asked Iolo slightly pleased with the reply.

"I'll buy you a pint, it's safer," replied the councillor, he winked.

12 noon Christmas day at Iolo Pritchard's house.

Ethel, Iolo, Bethan and her husband David, little Guto bach in his highchair the newest member of the family were sitting around the dining table enjoying their Christmas dinner, suddenly the telephone rang loudly on the windowsill, everyone stared at it, who could it be as it was mainly used in connection with Iolo's work. Iolo got up from the dinner table and strode to the window. Slowly he picked up the phone and spoke into it. "Iolo Pritchard speaking who is it?" Iolo listened intently as the voice explained what had happened. Iolo slowly replaced the phone onto the receiver; he turned around and stared at the family, blankly. "Bill Pumpy's dead… he was killed this morning ten past ten," he mumbled.

"Bill who?" asked Ethel impassively.

"William Thomkins to his family," explained Iolo. "He failed to report to the surface by telephone. When they went to look for him they found him in a sump-hole overcome by blackdamp, silly man, all those years of experience, and he failed to examine the place for blackdamp, Bernard Thomas was the deputy, he should have been with him, god how did it happen?" Iolo shook his head in disbelief. "I killed him not the blackdamp!" exclaimed Iolo, he sat on a chair and put his head in his hands.

Chapter IX

June 1970 The inquest

It was just over two years since the explosion at Cwm Derw Colliery. Iolo Pritchard paced up and down the pavement outside the Coroner's court.

It was not often that he had much reason to visit Graig Ddu, which was the biggest town near to Cwm Derw. People were arriving by public transport. Bernard Thomas stepped off the red double decked bus and walked smartly to where Iolo was pacing back and forth.

"How're you Iolo? It's a nice morning to hold an inquest, plenty of interest. I see the press are on the boil, it's been a long time since the pit went up," said Bernard nervously straightening his black necktie.

"Aye, it's been a long time. I've been pacing up and down this bit of the pavement trying to remember the events of that… bloody afternoon," said Iolo nervously, it showed in his voice as he spoke.

"Where's your missus I can't see her around here," queried Bernard.

"She's around here somewhere talking to someone I shouldn't doubt," answered Iolo. "Where's *your* missus then Bern?" asked Iolo, smiling.

"She wouldn't come, her brother was one of those killed in the explosion," replied Bernard.

"Of course! Simon Watts, he was a decent bloke," remarked Iolo he stared blankly for a moment as he remembered.

The door of the stone built building opened, a man wearing a black gown stepped out and surveyed the amassing crowd. Iolo glanced at his wristwatch it was ten minutes to ten almost time to go into the Coroner's court.

"Would all witnesses and anyone who has an interest in this morning's inquest please report to me immediately," called the

Coroner's official, he was a tall man who looked as though he may be a doctor or maybe a lawyer.

One by one the witnesses had their names recorded as being present and a court official showed them to a room where they were to wait until they were called to give evidence.

In the courtroom all those who did not have a direct interest sat at the back of the court, the press were sat at the place appointed for them. Ethel sat next to a woman who had lost a brother in the Cwm Derw colliery disaster, they chatted nervously.

"All rise," called the court official as the Coroner Mr James Connick came through double wooden doors. Everyone rose off their seats and bowed towards the Coroner as he sat, the intended respect was for Her Majesty's coat of arms which was prominently displayed above the Coroner's chair. The Coroner nodded acknowledging the act of respect. He sat his large frame onto the throne like chair and waited patiently for the spectators to settle. A loud single tap of the gavel signalled the start of proceedings.

"Ladies and gentlemen of the gallery we are not here today to pass judgement, we are here to find out what happened on that fateful day, May third, nineteen sixty-eight, I want you to listen carefully to the evidence, some of it will be very disturbing. If any of you suddenly feel unwell at any time, would you please raise your hand, a court official will come to your aid," he explained as he peered intently over his half round spectacles. "As you can see no jury has been appointed, the obvious reasons will be evident as the proceedings gather momentum as it were," he explained. "I will oversee this inquest and I have appointed the mines inspector Mr HG Darlington to give an overview of the Cwm Derw colliery."

Mr Darlington went to the witness stand to deliver his very detailed overview of Cwm Derw colliery. "Ladies and gentlemen of the court, I have been her majesty's inspector for Cwm Derw mine for about ten years, Cwm Derw mine is generally a safe mine, it has had its problems." The inspector droned on giving more detail than the audience anticipated. "It has suffered from inrushes of water, nothing that I would call life threatening." Ethel listened patiently as he went on and on. The inspector stopped and briefly studied his notes, he brushed back his thick brown hair with long fingers and glanced at the Coroner to signify that he was about to continue with the overview.

"Cwm Derw employs at present one thousand and seventy two men below ground and produces about seven hundred and fifty thousand tons of prime coking coal for power stations and industries annually." The inspector gave great detail concerning the ventilation system and then the statistics. "The accident rate was fourteen point one, per one hundred thousand man-shifts, that is January, nineteen hundred and sixty seven, to January nineteen hundred and sixty eight, these are the figures prior to the nineteen sixty eight explosion at Cwm Derw mine." He stopped reading and studied the faces of his audience. Most seemed unconcerned at the statistics. The Coroner nodded to the mines inspector to signal that he was to give the result of his findings regarding the Cwm Derw explosion.

"Ladies and gentlemen of the court, at approximately three fifty five pm on the third of May, nineteen hundred and sixty eight, an explosion occurred in the main intake airway some one thousand one hundred yards in-bye of the downcast shaft. From my examination of the workings it was apparent that there was a flash that emanated from a three thousand three hundred volt armoured fixed electric cable, this was evident by the scorch mark around the intrinsically safe heavy duty cable joint near to the edge of underpinning that extended some twenty yards in- bye of the edge of the repair lip, at site. A heavy fall of ground destroyed the safe integrity of the cable so joined to the cable joint. We must bear in mind that the barometric pressure was falling sharply and was reported earlier in the day. The ground above the underpinning area was of a friable nature due to water saturation from old workings above, again we must remember that because of the nature of intake airways methane gas was very rarely found. Captured methane gas flowed from the friable ground as it cascaded from above the underpinning, at the very same time the inclement weather on the surface produced an electric storm that firstly destroyed the lightning conductor that protected the fan-house, a second lightning strike hit the fan-house destroying the electrical switchgear previously protected by the lightning conductor fastened to the building namely the main fan-house. This caused an electrical power surge, the electrical surge would take any short path to earth, unfortunately the only weakness in the electric circuit was at the lip of the repairs at the edge of underpinnings it was this electrical discharge that ignited a small amount of methane gas, which in turn threw up a fine cloud of flammable coal dust which exploded with such violence that it took the lives of fifteen miners and severely injured others."

The inspector of mines looked at the Coroner and noted that he seemed to understand what had been described to the court.

"Would you call the first witness please," asked the Coroner. The official called out Iolo Pritchard's name, he came walking smartly into the courtroom and gave a short bow as instructed by the court official and stood at the witness stand.

"I swear by almighty god that the evidence I shall give is the truth, the whole truth and nothing but the truth."

"Are you Iolo Pritchard of number three Herbert Road Cwm Derw, were you employed at Cwm Derw colliery as a colliery Overman on the third of May nineteen sixty eight?" he asked. He stared over the top his half round spectacles at Iolo and waited for him to reply.

"Yes sir," replied Iolo. His legs began to shake as he wondered how long it would be before he could escape to the gallery and sit beside Ethel.

"Can you describe the events that led to the explosion? Begin your account from the time you arrived on the premises," he asked.

"Yes... I arrived at the colliery at about half past one on the afternoon of the third, the weather was very windy which made me think of the barometer," said Iolo.

"Can you explain to the court the significance of the 'barometer'?" asked the Coroner.

"The barometer is an indicator of the potential for bad or good weather," answered Iolo. At the same time the Coroner studied the faces of the people who were sat in the gallery.

"What bearing would the weather have to the underground workings of the mine?" He asked again.

"Low atmospheric pressure would be indicated on the barometer, this would tell the officials that they would have to be extra alert when making examinations for gas," said Iolo.

"Yes... I think the court understands the principle, but I can see them asking how does it affect the mine workings?" he asked.

Mr HG Darlington inspector of mines stared at the Coroner, he glanced at the inspector.

Iolo stopped he was clearly trembling. He composed himself and began to explain to the court how atmospheric pressure affected mine workings.

"Boyles law says that at a constant temperature the volume of a fixed mass of gas is inversely proportionate to the pressure, this means that if there is a decrease in atmospheric pressure the volume of gasses in the waste and in cavities and cracks in the roof of the mine increases and vice versa," said Iolo remembering his school of mines training.

Mr James Connick sat with a hand under his chin listening intently at Iolo's attempts in recalling mining science.

"Ok, that was very enlightening," he remarked." What happened when you reported to your superior?" asked the Coroner.

"My superior is Mr Jack Williams he was still down the pit when I reported to the official's lodge," answered Iolo.

"This barometer you were talking about... where on the surface of the mine is it situated?" he studied his notes.

"On the wall in the lodge- office," answered Iolo, he began feeling a little confident.

"What was it reading when you signed on?" queried the Coroner.

"Six hundred and ninety millimetres of murcury," answered Iolo.

"Is six hundred and ninety millimetres of mercury particularly low?" he enquired, a thoughtful gaze appeared on his broad features.

"Not really, but the register showed that it had been falling steadily since early in the morning," answered Iolo, confidently.

"By how much?" he asked. He peered at Iolo through his spectacles and not over them as he usually did.

"Two or three mill, "answered Iolo trying to answer with confidence.

"That's millimetres, I take it?" queried the Coroner.

"Yes sir," confirmed Iolo.

"What happened when you eventually went down the mine, did you notice anything unusual?" he asked.

"Not immediately," said Iolo, after he thought for a moment.

"When you proceeded to your designated place of work what route did you take?"

"I travelled via the main intake roadway," answered Iolo.

"How did you cross from return airway to intake airway?" asked the Coroner as he turned over a page of his notes.

"I used the cross cut," answered Iolo.

"Can you explain to the court what a cross cut is?" he shuffled uneasily on his chair.

"A cross cut is a short roadway that connects the intake and return airways separated by sets of ventilation doors, about fifty yards in length or so, but it is usually designed to suit the maximum number of trams allowed to travel that section of roadway. No trams travel the bottom crosscut. So we can say it's no more than say fifty yards in length," answered Iolo, thoughtfully.

"So you travelled via the main intake airway, is this the same airway that transports coal from the coal faces?" enquired the Coroner again he studied his notes.

"Yes sir it is," answered Iolo.

"Mr Barrington would you please set out the west plan of Cwm Derw mine," ordered the Coroner. The court official went to the easel that held rolled up plans and other information for the benefit of the court. He pulled down a ventilation plan of the west side of Cwm Derw mine and then returned to minding the door.

"Mr Pritchard, can you see on the mine plan the route that you took on the third of May?" asked the Coroner.

"I can Just about see it from here," said Iolo squinting at the plan.

"You'll find a baton at the foot of the easel, can you point out the route you took to your designated place of work?" asked the Coroner indicating that he could leave the witness stand and begin demonstrating.

Iolo left the witness stand and stood in front of the easel that displayed the mine plan. He pointed the baton at the cross cut and demonstrated the route explaining what he saw on his journey towards 26s district. Mr HG Darlington inspector of mines reached to the floor and retrieved a small replica of the same plan.

Mr James Connick, Coroner watched with great interest as Iolo pointed his way around the mine plan.

"Can I stop you at the point on the plan marked with a cross?" he asked . Iolo stopped and began to wonder what was about to happen.

"According to my notes this is the place where the inspector for mines found that the explosion had occurred," he said. His brow furrowed and he began to stare at the people in the gallery.

Mr HG Darlington nodded to indicate that he agreed that that was the place on the mine plan.

"Can you, Mr Pritchard, describe to the court what you saw and reported over the telephone?" he asked.

"On approaching the repair holt I observed coal dust was being raised from the conveyor belt because the roadway beyond was low and lacking cross sectional square area causing a higher velocity of air current passing over the conveyor belt causing litter and dust to be raised into the air" explained Iolo, the people in the gallery began to sit up and take notice as Iolo described what he reported prior to the explosion.

"It was useless watering down the dust as it would quickly dry out owing to the brisk ventilation," explained Iolo. "The only solution was to enlarge the roadway; this enlargement was suspended due to skilled men leaving the industry because of low wages," explained Iolo.

"Mr Pritchard we are not here to explore the manpower problems concerning the Cwm Derw mine," he raised his voice as he said it.

"Sorry sir, I'll try and remember that," said Iolo. The Coroner looked at the mines inspector and sort of winked very quickly.

"Mr Pritchard what happened when you reached the coalface what did you encounter?"

"As I approached the face I spoke to the boys whose job was to supply the face with timber supports and most other things, then I had a short conversation with the leader of the ripping lip team," answered Iolo, he wondered where this was leading.

"Can you tell the court what the leading hand told you?" he asked. Iolo struggled to remember what happened next.

"I think he told me, he could smell gas, I said, methane was colourless and odourless; there was no scientific evidence that gas could be detected by smell. Never the less he insisted he could smell gas," said Iolo. Mr Darlington looked at the Coroner and raised his hand.

"Can you enlighten the court as to whether methane gas could be detected by smell Mr Darlington?" asked the Coroner, he frowned at Iolo, and quickly made notes.

Mr Darlington rose to his feet and began giving an explanation as to whether methane could be detected by smell.

"Many miners will tell you that they can smell gas but what they are detecting is not methane but impurities mixed in with the gas giving the illusion that it has an odour," explained the inspector. "An example of the impurities in firedamp as we call it would be, ethane, propane, ethylene, hydrogen sulphide and other trace gases depending on the geology," explained the inspector.

"I see, so it's other gases that this man could smell," said the Coroner brushing back the sparse hair on his balding head." You may be seated Mr Darlington.

"Mr Pritchard," he continued, what did you do when the leading hand said he could smell gas?"

"Nothing immediately," answered Iolo.

"Why was that?"

"Because at that time the district deputy came out of the face and approached me," answered Iolo.

"Did he have anything of importance to say to you?" asked the Coroner as he peered over the top of his half round spectacles. He immediately consulted his notes.

"Yes sir," answered Iolo.

"Did it concern the state of the ventilation of the mine?"

"Yes sir, he said he had received a message by telephone from the met office giving a warning that the barometer was falling sharply he said the reading was six hundred and ninety millimetres of mercury at two o'clock that afternoon; it had dropped to six hundred and seventy as we spoke; the lowest he said he had ever seen," recalled Iolo, he looked at the clock on the wall in a far corner, almost eleven o'clock. Perspiration began to run down his square features a bead of perspiration hung from his nose and it irritated him.

"Can you explain to the court the reason why the Met office would want to phone a pit deputy?" he stared at Iolo.

"The met office has been informing collieries about falls in the barometer for over eighty years," answered Iolo. "I believe It's because the met office gathers barometer readings from all over the country, and can give a more accurate explanation of moving trends, there are no barometers below ground," explained Iolo.

"Very well, I'll accept that explanation," he said, grinning.

"What happened then?" enquired the Coroner.

"I told him of the state of the trunk conveyor road way, he agreed and said he and the deputy responsible for the airway had reported it in the M and Q book" recalled Iolo, confidently.

"This book of forms… is it this one, form, two- three- five? The Mines and Quarries book you refer to?" he made a note.

"Yes sir, it is," answered Iolo.

"What happened after that?" he asked, he had an eager looking glint in his eye.

"We made thorough examinations of the waste and roof and sides, the deputy had already erected hurdle sheets from the face- ripping lip to about two hundred yards out-bye, the general body of air as we call it…it was already established as nought point eight per cent of CH4 by the deputy, earlier," recalled Iolo. Perspiration continued to bother him.

"How did you know that the general body of air contained nought point eight of methane?" asked the Coroner, he rested his large frame against the back of the throne like chair and waited for Iolo to answer.

"The deputy told me he had found that percentage," We later took further readings from a D –six, methane detector," answered Iolo.

"You mean you put all your trust in a machine, why didn't you use your flame safety lamp, Mr Pritchard?"

"We could not confirm the reading by lamp as the lowest reading possible is one and a quarter per cent by volume, we never put all our faith in machines because experience has taught us that if a machine can go wrong you can bet it *will* at some time or another," explained Iolo.

"You're saying that the flame safety lamp of the kind you use is infallible?" asked the Coroner, he glanced at the mines inspector and he nodded.

"To a point, human error can play a part in wrong or too low a reading," explained Iolo. The mines inspector again nodded in agreement.

"What did you do about the gas considering what you saw in your lamp?" he probed anxiously.

"We took another reading by lamp and found one and a quarter per cent CH4 in the general body of the roadway air," said Iolo. He was now struggling to remember fact and figures. "I then sent the deputy to the gate road to take some readings there just in case," answered Iolo. "I then continued to monitor the general body for an increase in the percentage of gas," explained Iolo.

"Did the gas content increase?" he probed.

"Yes sir, the deputy made his examination of the gate road and contacted me by telephone," explained Iolo.

"So what did the deputy of the district say over the telephone? What decisions did he make concerning the ventilation?" the Coroner was exploring every avenue looking for weaknesses in Iolo's methodology.

"The deputy instructed the district electrician to isolate the electrical power to the tail road because the law says electrical power must be isolated when the percentage of methane is found to be one and a quarter per cent or lower in some cases." explained Iolo.

"Was the power turned off by the electrician?"

"Yes sir, it was," answered Iolo.

"Mr Pritchard you said in 'some cases'— explain to the court what you meant by *some cases*," he instructed.

"There are parts of a mine where certain kinds of explosives are used, the inspectorate will only allow the firing of shots where the percentage of methane does not exceed nought point eight per cent," explained Iolo.

"This is where exemptions are in force I take it?" he asked, then glanced at the mines inspector; the inspector looked away as if to say the explanation was not entirely correct.

"We can safely say all electrical power to the tail road is turned off and no explosion or fire could occur."

"No, we can't say that because the air in 26s moved at about thirty feet per second, carrying the gas with it which means the out-bye places and districts would be polluted," explained Iolo, patiently.

"Bearing in mind what you have explained to the court, what, did you do next?" asked the Coroner he glanced at his wrist watch.

"I went to the crosscut and isolated the power there. But before that, I telephoned all districts out-bye and informed them of the position regarding the gassy ventilation, and then I retreated in-bye. I scrambled up the face conveyor it was quicker, and joined Bernard Thomas deputy, we made readings of the ventilation as we went, they started to get higher," said Iolo.

"Can I stop you there?" he said, then quickly flicked through his notes. "What readings did you get when you were making your way out of your district?" he asked.

"We were getting five and a half per cent CH4," replied Iolo.

"Ok, you were near to the 26s intake junction, explain to the court what happened there."

"I heard a noise like a puff of wind and a sound like doors opening and closing then I fell over and a hot wind passed over me. Bernard and me then got up and made for the manhole which was only a few yards away, the dust and heat was terrific how we managed to find our way to the manhole is a miracle in its self," remembered Iolo.

"You may now stand down Mr Pritchard. The court is now adjourned until ten o'clock tomorrow morning," announced the Coroner.

"All rise," announced the court official loudly. The court room suddenly filled with chatter as the Coroner strode smartly out of the court room.

Chapter X

Day Two

Iolo sat on an iron bench outside of the Coroner's court talking to Ethel.

"You shouldn't be giving evidence for much longer should you?" queried Ethel. "I mean, how much more to your story is there," asked Ethel she turned her head as the court official touched her on the shoulder.

"Excuse me Mr Pritchard but the Coroner will be resuming proceedings shortly," said the official in a loud posh voice. Iolo and Ethel got off the iron bench and made their way into the building. Ethel went to her seat and sat next to the woman who had lost her brother in the explosion. Meanwhile, Iolo waited to be called to give more evidence.

"All rise," called the court official loudly. The Coroner walked briskly through the double wooden doors and went to the chair that resembled a modest throne he sat his large frame on it and made himself comfortable.

The Coroner reminded the audience of the previous hearing to make sure that there was some degree of continuity.

"Call Iolo Pritchard," said Mr James Connick. The court official called Iolo's name and Iolo duly entered the courtroom.

"Are you Iolo Pritchard of number three Herbert Road Cwm Derw, were you employed at Cwm Derw colliery as a colliery Overman on the third of May nineteen sixty eight?" he asked formally.

"Yes sir," answered Iolo. The Coroner thumbed through his notes and studied them briefly.

"Mr Pritchard, We heard previously that you and the deputy Bernard Thomas fell over just as the explosion occurred, you say that you heard a noise like 'a puff of wind' and further noises that sounded like ventilation doors opening and closing," he stared at the spectators intently over half round spectacles. "You then made for the nearest manhole a manhole used by the transfer point attendant, where you were overcome by dust and extreme heat. Is that correct Mr Pritchard?"

"Yes sir, that is correct," answered Iolo, loudly.

"Mr Pritchard, what did you do next?" asked the Coroner. Iolo thought for a moment and began to answer.

"We waited for the heat and dust to subside," replied Iolo, remembering.

"When the heat and dust eventually subsided, what did you do to ensure the survival of your comrades? Did you go and see the site of the explosion?"

"We were informed of the fall of ground by Bill Pumpy and his assistant, they escaped the blast owing to them working in a snicket place," said Iolo, remembering.

"You say a snicket place, is that a mining term?" asked the Coroner.

"A snicket road is generally a short roadway that is mainly used to store stuff or it can act as a standage for water," explained Iolo.

"How would this snicket road be ventilated, wouldn't it have been affected by the afterdamp?" he asked, then stared at Iolo, intently.

"Under normal circumstances the air mover that was ventilating the snicket would have polluted the snicket with afterdamp but the blast had knocked the air mover down so that the air was directed away from the snicket," explained Iolo.

"I see, so providence was on their side then!"

"They were very lucky," Iolo commentated.

"You may stand down Mr Pritchard," said the Coroner. Iolo walked smartly away from the witness stand and sat down beside Ethel, she patted him on the knee fondly as if to say well done.

"Can we have Bernard Thomas please," called the Coroner.

"Bernard Thomas," said the court official, loudly. Bernard walked smartly into the courtroom and briefly glanced at the audience in the gallery. He grabbed the edge of the stand firmly his hands trembled but not enough for anyone to notice. Bernard said his oath of truthfulness while the Coroner eyed him.

"Are you Bernard Charles Thomas of 14 Rectory Road Cwm Derw, and were you a deputy employed at Cwm Derw colliery on the third of May nineteen sixty eight?" asked the Coroner.

"Yes sir," replied Bernard.

"Mr Thomas, can you describe the events that led up to the explosion? Begin your account from the time you arrived on the premises," asked the Coroner.

"I remember it was a windy old day as I walked down the pit drive, I spoke to an official who had been working in a district on the other side of the pit. He told me that the barometer had been falling slowly all day. The reading was six hundred and ninety millimetres of mercury at two o'clock when I signed on. The day shift deputy told me he had problems with layering in the return road," remembered Bernard.

The deputy gave his account of the lead-up to that fateful explosion just as Iolo had done earlier.

"Thank you Mr Thomas you have been most helpful, you may retire to the gallery." Bernard wasted no time in making his way to the gallery.

The Coroner beckoned to the mines inspector he went to him and had a brief conversation. Iolo watched from the gallery and wondered what would happen next. The mines inspector returned to his seat.

"Call Brian Powell," said the Coroner, the court official called out 'Brian Powell.'

Brian Powell a tall lean man came through the double doors of the courtroom he stopped briefly to readjust a pair of old wooden crutches, he cursed under his breath as he fumbled with the contraption. The court official came to his aid and guided him to the witness stand. Brian Powell swore the oath of truthfulness.

The Coroner studied him briefly and consulted his notes. "Are you Brian Powell of seventeen Colliery Terrace, Cwm Derw and you were employed below ground as a face worker at Cwm Derw colliery on the third of May nineteen sixty-eight."

Brian Powell paused before answering, he glanced around the courtroom, piercing blue eyes stared out from behind a heavily scarred face, staring at the Coroner he answered, "Yes," his equally scarred hands grasped the hand rail of the witness stand firmly.

"Mr Powell can you tell the court what happened on the third of May nineteen sixty-eight, can you begin your account from the time you arrived on the colliery premises?"

"I'll do my best to remember, my memory is not that good now days," he said in a slow and awkward way. "I was late for work that day, one of the kids had an accident in the school playground and I had to take her to the local hospital for treatment. By the time I had got to the pit I was nearly half an hour late and I had to ask the afternoon under-Manager for permission to go down the pit, he said it was alright as he had heard from one of my work butties that I would be late," he remembered.

"Is your child ok now?" asked the Coroner politely.

"Yes sir, she's fine," answered Brian.

"When you eventually got down the pit as you put it, did you notice anything unusual?" He stared at the scarring on Brian's face and hands.

"I remember the pit bottom fireman taking readings with a methanometer and writing in his notebook, I guessed that there was gas about," said Brian, remembering.

"Mr Powell can you explain to the court what a fireman is, my recollection of a fireman is of a man that puts out fires," said the Coroner, grinning.

Brian waited until he had stopped grinning. "The proper name is deputy but we down the pit call him a fireman because it goes way back when they set fire to pockets of gas in the roof," explained Brian.

"Ah yes, I remember now, you are quite correct Mr Powell," remembered the Coroner. "What happened next, what did you see other people doing?" he asked.

"Nothing much I had my head down and was walking up the main return road pretty quick as I was already late and would be cropped wages," explained Brian.

"So nothing much happened. Did you see any more officials making readings of gas as you put it?"

"Not until I got in the gate road," said Brian, struggling to remember exactly.

"You say, not until you got in the gate road, who did you see making readings Mr Powell?"

"The fireman, I mean, deputy was making readings," said Brian,

"Can you see the deputy in the courtroom if so could you point him out?" asked the Coroner as he peered over the top of his spectacles.

"Bernard Thomas, he's sat in the back," said Brian Pointing towards the back of the courtroom.

"Did you discover the extent of the make of gas? You said 'he' the deputy was taking readings, did you ask him about the situation?"

"No sir," replied Brian.

"So when did you suspect that the ventilation was playing up, Mr Powell?"

"Jack James the man working in the rib side of the stable hole said that his lamp was showing gas,"

"How did this Jack James know the lamp as you put it was showing gas?"

"I just took him at his word, anyway he was supposed to make an examination for gas," said Brian.

"So we can safely say that most of the workforce knew that there was a ventilation problem then?" said the Coroner he then studied his notes and briefly glanced at the gallery.

"How long was it before you were told to leave the district and how did the men take the order to abandon ship as it were, Mr Powell?"

"It wasn't long! I just got the tools off the bar and then I put them back on again, most of the men didn't hang around, they were gone like a shot out of a barrel, others wanted to know how much gas was about. They were saying that they shouldn't have been allowed in the district if there was gas about," remarked Brian Powell he stopped and thought for a moment his scarred lips quivered.

"You say that some of the men were saying that 'they should not have been allowed in the district if there was gas about, Mr Powell," he had a quizzical look about him and sought the advice of the mines inspector. The inspector went over to the Coroner and explained in a quiet voice what mining law said about the removal of workmen from a district affected by concentrations of methane gas.

"Mr Powell do you know what mining law says about the removal of men from a district affected by gas?" asked the Coroner looking at the people in the gallery and then at Powell

"Not word for word, but men must be withdrawn when a certain percentage is in the main body of air," answered Powell.

"A percentage of what, is it gas, coal dust, Mr Powell?" the Coroner asked sarcastically.

"It is gas," replied Powell.

"How much gas did the men think should have been in the main body of air in order for them to believe that they should not have been allowed in the district in the first place?" asked the Coroner who was by now realising that he was to have a hard time interrogating miners who didn't know the letter of the law and were being led by trouble makers.

"I think they were saying two per cent," answered Powell.

"Mr Powell, you stated earlier that you 'went down the pit' as you put it a clear half an hour after the main workforce. Who told them that the district was being affected by 'gas' and by how much?" asked the Coroner in a slightly raised voice. "According to the deputy's report on the preceding shift the general body was reported as being nought point six per cent, how did they know it was two per cent methane?" asked the Coroner.

"I've no idea, they must have made it up, just guessed it, I expect," said Powell his hands were beginning to tremble.

"Mr Powell, in your honest opinion and remembering that you are on oath, were there trouble makers working on your coalface?" Brian Powell thought hard as he painfully turned and studied the people in the gallery. Composing himself he faced the Coroner his scarred lips quivered as he began to answer the Coroner's question.

"Twenty six' district was considered a good a district, there were one or two stirrers working there," answered Powell who was by now wondering where all this was leading to.

"Mr Powell you say that there were one or two stirrers working on twenty six's coalface. Do you see any of them in this courtroom?" asked the Coroner loudly he peered over the top of his half round spectacles; he looked at the faces in the gallery studying them one by one. Powell answered quickly.

"No sir they're not here today," his piecing blue eyes stared out from behind a mutilated face scarred by the intense heat of the flame that emanated from the explosion at Cwm Derw colliery.

"Would you write down the name of the main 'stirrer' as you eloquently put it Mr Powell?" asked the Coroner.

"I'll need some paper and a pen, then," said Powell, slowly. The Coroner called to the court official the tall figure of a man walked smartly to where the Coroner was sitting and picked up a pen and a large piece of paper, he quickly went over to where Powell was waiting in the witness stand. Powell stood silently and paused, he held the pen in a left and scarred hand, he dropped the pen audibly onto the wooden floor and apologised.

"Oh, I am sorry Mr Powell, how silly and insensitive of me, I didn't realise that you were not able to hold a pen and paper, can you whisper to the court official the name of the main trouble maker?" he asked apologetically .

Powell whispered the name of the 'stirrer' into the official's ear the official wrote it down and then passed it to the Coroner who immediately read the note. The Coroner whispered to the official and he nodded and went to the door where he passed on the message.

"Mr Powell, thank you for that, we will see the person in question here in court tomorrow morning. We will now carry on from where we left off. Can you take us through the journey from the coalface to the point where you were unfortunately and seriously injured?" asked the Coroner, he shuffled uneasily on his substantial chair and waited for Powell to compose himself.

"I had just got the tools off the toolbar when the fireman, er... I mean deputy said that the ventilation was gassy and was touching two per cent, and he said that we had to get to the pit bottom area," said Powell slowly.

"How did the deputy sound did he sound panicky or just mentioned it as a matter of fact?" asked the Coroner in a quiet sort of voice. Powell thought long and hard before he answered.

"He sounded normal to my way of thinking, Bernard Thomas isn't the sort of man that would lose his head in a crisis," answered Powell, sounding positive.

"I take it that your colleagues just got up and went, that is when they were told to do so!" suggested the Coroner.

"They made sure that their tools were locked up first," answered Powell painfully grinning.

"So we can safely say that all the men left the twenty six district all at once then," he consulted his notes and stared at the gallery.

"What happened when you all reached the bottom of the downcast shaft, were there many men there before you?" asked the Coroner his voice picked up as he spoke.

"About two hundred and fifty men I should think...some of the pit had already got to the surface... we were some of the last to get there considering that we were the only district who were told to leave," said Powell, hesitantly.

"Hmm, sounds like all hell broke loose when they heard that a district on the other side of the mine had been given permission to leave their place of work," suggested the Coroner, disgust showed on his broad features.

"What happened then?

"Everybody was shouting at the hitcher... the pit bottom deputy tried to hold the crowd back... we at the back could see that he wasn't getting anywhere, the hitcher eventually managed to get all but about fifty men onto the cage... some of the men from twenty six' got on the last run... the cage must have reached pit top when the air suddenly went backwards, I was at the very back of the crowd and was knocked to the ground... I then felt a searing heat, next thing I was in hospital and my family was standing around my bed." Remembered Powell as the memory came rushing back.

"You had a lucky escape, so to speak," said the Coroner, quietly.

"You could say that, my family has still got me, can't say that for the others who didn't make it," said Powell. Mr James Connick studied his notes and began to rise from his chair.

"Court is adjourned, and will resume tomorrow morning at ten o'clock," said the Coroner as he left the chair.

Out- side the court Iolo and Bernard was wondering which of the stirrers would be subjected to a subpoena.

Chapter XI

Day Three

This was the third day of the hearing at the Coroner's court in the town of Graig Ddu. A red double deck omnibus pulled up outside of the Coroner's court.

Iolo and Bernard Thomas watched as the passengers stepped off the bus and made their way to their respective destinations, most people were eagerly making their way to the Coroner's court.

Just as Iolo and Bernard thought that all of the passengers had got off the bus a lone man stepped down onto the pavement. "Dagnabit, I bloody well knew it! Billy Parfit was the one Brian Powell said caused the trouble on Pit bottom," squealed Iolo, he looked pleased as he and Bernard eyed the colliery trouble maker.

"Morning Billy Parfit, bit of a stink round here, come to sort it out have you?" called out Bernard Thomas. Parfit eyed the pair of officials with one contemptuous look. Parfit walked towards the Coroner's court slow and awkward as others suddenly realised he was the one who had been subpoenaed by the Coroner. The tall elegant official stood on the steps of the court, taking names, Billy Parfit tried to brush past him but the official stopped him in his tracks.

"Name please," asked the court official, he barred the way; Parfit had no option but to give his name, and address.

Billy Parfit sat on an uncomfortable wooden chair crossing and uncrossing his spindly legs as he waited to be called to give evidence.

"William George Parfit," called out a loud voice, the door opened; the court official went to Parfit and asked his name." Are you William George Parfit?" asked the official in a loud clear voice.

"Yes, I am William George Parfit!" he answered disdainfully. The official explained what was to happen and he had to do as he was told.

In the court room the people in the gallery waited with baited breath for the appearance of Billy Parfit. The room filled with chatter as the gallery discussed the nature of Parfit's appearance at court.

Parfit walked towards the witness stand, he eyed the few pit officials who watched with gleams in their eyes. They guessed that Parfit would be given a hard time as he was considered a trouble maker by most of the colliery officials.

"I swear by almighty god that the evidence I shall give is the truth, the whole truth and nothing but the truth," said Parfit looking very uneasy.

"Are you William George Parfit of thirty-two riverside cottages Cwm Derw, and you were employed as a conveyor belt repairer at Cwm Derw colliery on the third of May nineteen sixty eight?" asked the Coroner, he eyed him cautiously for a moment and then studied the faces of the people sat in the gallery.

"Yes sir."

"Mr Parfit describe as best you can the events that led up to the incident at Cwm Derw colliery on the third of May. Begin your account from the time you arrived on the premises," ordered the Coroner.

"I don't remember much about it, really, only it was a bit windy that afternoon as I walked down the pit drive," answered Parfit trying to act dumb.

"Don't worry too much about your poor memory, Mr Parfit, I will try my best to help you remember," said the Coroner, smiling as he had already got his measure. "Do you recall going into the colliery canteen and sitting amongst the other men on the afternoon shift?" Parfit thought long and hard before he answered.

"I'm in the canteen most days of the week, they all seem the same to me, one day is just like another," answered Parfit trying to outwit the Coroner.

"Let me put it another way, on the day in question did some of the men discuss with 'you' the state of the ventilation in number twenty six district?" he asked staring at Parfit over half round spectacles, he briefly studied his notes.

"The ventilation may have been discussed but that was more than a year ago, how can I be expected to remember all that time ago!" answered Parfit showing signs of being ruffled.

"Then I'll put it to you another way Mr Parfit!" he was annoyed at Parfit trying to stall proceedings. "A witness has said on oath that 'you' stated that 'you' was looking for any excuse to go home early from your shift is that correct Mr Parfit?" asked the Coroner raising his voice. Parfit looked around the courtroom studying the faces of the people in the gallery.

"I may have said that I was looking for an early note, I remember having business to attend to in the evening," said Parfit clearly looking ruffled.

"So your memory is finally returning, at last; we may get somewhere now!" remarked the Coroner, looking pleased. "What happened when you collected your lamp did you go down the mine straight away?"

"I think I called into the under-Manager's office in the officials' lodge," answered Parfit.

"What for," he asked curtly.

"I wanted to go home early, as I had business to attend to," answered Parfit, coyly.

"Did the under-Manager give you permission to go home early, then?" asked the Coroner.

"No," he answered.

"Why not?"

"He doesn't like me." Answered Parfit, frowning.

"Why do you think that the colliery under-Manager has a dislike towards you?" he asked, smiling to him-self.

"I've been accused of being a trouble maker," answered Parfit, the gallery burst into loud laughter.

"Order, order, shouted the Coroner," he slammed his gavel on to his desk the court came to an abrupt hush.

"So you have been accused of being a trouble maker Mr Parfit?" remarked the Coroner he eyed the gallery before continuing with his questions. "When you finally went down the mine did you notice anything unusual?" he asked, peering over his spectacles.

"Things looked ok to me; I overheard officials talking about gas in the twenty six district," recalled Parfit.

"Did these officials mention certain amounts of gas during their conversations?" asked the Coroner studying Parfit over his spectacles.

"They were talking about the barometer, dropping throughout the dayshift and that point six was in the general body," said Parfit. The Coroner eyed him cautiously before asking any further questions.

"Mr Parfit! I want you to think very hard before you answer my next question," said the Coroner in a quiet voice. There was a deathly hush as he slowly thumbed through his notes. Parfit was visibly trembling he guessed what the next questions would be.

The Coroner eyed Parfit's white knuckles as he tightly gripped the sides of the witness stand.

He coughed into his fist and then fired the next question. "Mr Parfit, when you finally got into the twenty six' district, what did... you...do?" asked the Coroner hesitantly.

"I examined the conveyor drive and then I watched as the belt went around I was looking for bad joints and that," answered Parfit.

"Mr Parfit, we'll assume that the conveying system is one hundred per cent safe and you finally arrived at the backend of the conveyor and inspected it. What was happening around you?" asked the Coroner with a gleam in his eye.

"The deputy was making… readings with a methanometer," answered Parfit, slowly.

"So the deputy was making readings as you put it, did he speak to you directly regarding the ventilation?" asked the Coroner.

"No... Sir," answered Parfit again in a slow fashion.

"Mr Parfit, what did you do next?" asked the Coroner, he glanced quickly at the people in the gallery.

"I went down the face to talk to the boys," replied Parfit.

"What about?" asked the Coroner; quickly.

"Just for a chat about things," answered Parfit.

"What did you discuss with the *boys down the face* as you put it?" asked the Coroner.

"We were saying about the gas and the deputy didn't seem bothered about telling us about it," said Parfit.

"Why did you think that the deputy would want to discuss the state of the ventilation with a conveyor belt mender?" asked the Coroner, smiling.

"I just like to know what's going on. After all I have to breathe the stuff and we all had a right to know what was going on," answered Parfit, ignorantly. The Coroner peered intently at Parfit over the top of his spectacles.

"Can you explain to the court what you meant by *"breathe the stuff"* Mr Parfit?' asked the Coroner with a serious look about him.

"Well, I mean, they don't tell you the whole truth about it do they?" answered Parfit and the gallery laughed out loudly.

"The whole truth?" questioned the Coroner, smiling.

"Yes, I mean… they don't tell you whether gas affects the brain cells or not," said Parfit. And the gallery laughed again. The Coroner could see that Parfit was clutching at straws and was beginning to lose the argument.

"I put it to you Mr Parfit that you purposely went '*down the face*' as you put it; in order to coerce the workforce into walking out of the district to further your own end, that is to say you failed in your attempt in obtaining proper permission from the colliery under-Manager so you sought other means to get your own way," stated the Coroner in a quick fire rattle of words.

The Coroner thumbed through his notes and studied the people in the gallery.

"Mr Parfit, so you had a bit of a chinwag with the boys, and then what happened?" asked the Coroner.

"Bernard Thomas the district deputy came down the face and told us to assemble in the gate road as the gas content was nearing two per cent in the general body of air," remembered Parfit.

"So you were getting nearer your wish but a bit sooner than you expected," said the Coroner, sarcastically.

"What do you mean by that?" Retorted Parfit, angrily.

"I'll ask the questions here Mr Parfit," said the Coroner, quickly. "When you crawled back up the face to the gate road, what went on, then?" asked the Coroner, he had a quizzical look on his face.

"We waited for the deputy to get back to the gate road but he was taking a long time," answered Parfit he gazed at the Coroner suspiciously.

"Mr Parfit how long was it before the deputy returned to the gate road?"

"About twenty minutes I should imagine," answered Parfit.

"What happened then, did the deputy make more readings?" asked the Coroner.

"Yes he spent a long time taking readings, I was getting worried that the gas was getting worse and we would be caught up in an explosion or something," said Parfit, he stared at the floor briefly and then at the Coroner.

"Mr Parfit, under oath the deputy put himself across as a very competent man, I should think with his training he would know more than '*you*' about the law in regards to mine ventilation," retorted the Coroner angrily. "We will leave the district in competent hands and move on to the area around the bottom of the downcast shaft. What was the position when you eventually reached the bottom of the shaft?" asked the Coroner.

"Men from other districts were queuing up, we didn't like it as their districts weren't affected by as much gas as ours," explained Parfit with an air of indignity.

"You mean the men revolted because some-one else was having something that they were not having?" suggested the Coroner.

"Yes, something like that!" answered Parfit.

"Mr Parfit, how many men were behind you in the queue at pit bottom?" asked the Coroner, quietly.

"About twenty men or so," answered Parfit, suspiciously.

"And how many men were ahead of *you* waiting in the queue?" asked the Coroner again in a quiet sort of voice.

"Somewhere around fifty men or so," answered Parfit again with a hint of suspicion.

"So there were around fifty men ahead of you waiting to ascend the shaft, hmmm, what happened to the other fifty or so men on the afternoon shift?" asked the Coroner.

"I've no idea," came the reply.

"Mr Parfit, could you tell the court of the mood of the men while they waited for someone to give the order for the pit to begin winding men up the shaft?" asked the Coroner.

Parfit thought long and hard before he answered.

"Most of them were saying… what if the pit went up? And were screaming at the pit bottom deputy to wind men, but the deputy wasn't having any of it. He was waiting for orders from the under-Manager. I took it upon my-self to go and talk to the deputy about the situation, the men were screaming blue murder and rushed the pit," answered Parfit confidently.

"Mr Parfit, can you explain to the court what *'rushing the pit'* means, you may take your time," said the Coroner, smiling.

"Rushing the pit means the crowd breaking the order of the queue all trying for first place," replied Parfit.

"Very well put Mr Parfit," remarked the Coroner. "So why do you think that the under-Manager was slow in giving the pit bottom official; orders in regards to winding men?" asked the Coroner, he looked at the gallery and then thumbed his notes.

"He didn't want to give the men anything I expect," answered Parfit.

"What if the district deputies reported that the gas content of the districts was receding, what would happen then?" asked the Coroner peering over the top of his half round spectacles.

"We would have had to go back to work I expect," answered Parfit.

"So the under-Manager had got word that the general body of gas in twenty six' district was not going to recede in the very near future, and he was also informed of the conduct of the men *baying* to be let up the pit, as it were. What happened when the pit bottom deputy gave the order to the pit bottom hitcher to begin winding men," asked the Coroner.

"The men...were shouting to me to get back in the queue where I had come from, but me being pig headed refused, they were pushing and shoving, so the hitcher went back into his manhole because he said it wasn't safe to stand in front of animals," said Parfit, by now guilt was showing on his furrowed brow.

"How long in minutes, was lost, in waiting for the crowd of men waiting to ascend the shaft in order to settle down?" asked the Coroner loudly.

"About five minutes I should think," answered Parfit slowly.

"Would that be long enough to do one winding of the shaft do you think?" asked the Coroner.

"Yes... sir I think so," answered Parfit.

"Mr Parfit, describe to the court how the men reacted when the order to begin winding men up the shaft was given," asked the Coroner as he reached for a pen. Parfit eyed the stenographer as he posed with fingers at the ready.

"The hitcher shouted at the men to get back or he would get back in the manhole, some of the men obeyed others were shoving the queue forward. The hitcher would not be panicked into giving the signal and lifting the gate of the cage. The men quietened down a bit until the gate was lifted and then all hell broke loose, the first men in the queue were shoved onto the cage some fell on to the floor of the cage and were trampled on... I was one of the last to get on the cage; the cage must have held about thirty men on each deck at that point," recalled Parfit. A horrified look appeared on the Coroner's face as he realised the mayhem that ensued as the miners' panicked thinking that the mine would blow up at any moment.

"Carry on, Mr Parfit, explain the situation as the cage ascended the downcast shaft," said the Coroner; he appeared very concerned as the story was being unfolded before him.

"As the cage was getting nearer pit top, someone said that they thought they had heard a sort of bang… and I felt a puff of wind; men started screaming and shouting, there was nothing anyone could do…when the cage finally rested on the keps and the gate was lifted the men went mental, no one seemed to know what to do, men ran around looking for telephones they wanted to know what had happened, did the pit blow up? Or was it something else?" recalled Parfit, the Coroner noted a tear in the eye of the man who had been bombarded with questions for more than an hour. He was determined to find out the truth, why did fifteen miners lose their lives on the third of May nineteen sixty eight?

"Thank you Mr Parfit, you may now step down. The court will adjourn until ten o'clock tomorrow morning when I will deliver my verdict regarding the deaths of the fifteen miners at Cwm Derw colliery. You may now all rise and thank you for your patience."

Chapter XII

Off to the Races

Iolo and Bernard Thomas stood at the bar in the Collier's Arms pub; they were busy discussing the Coroner's verdict. "That Coroner did a good job, considering the facts, I mean the lightning played a big part in the deaths of the men, poor sods, we were very lucky... god must have been on our side," said Bernard as he stared into a half empty glass of beer.

"Aye, you can say that again, a misadventure he called it, god was not on the side of those poor men who didn't make it to the surface, alive, and they say lightning doesn't strike twice in the same place, except for the third of May," remarked Iolo, he sank the remainder of his drink and bid the others in the pub farewell.

Iolo strolled towards the houses thinking about the past inquest, it seemed a long three days. The afternoon was dry and bright as Iolo walked down the garden path to the front door but as he fumbled for his front door key the door opened. Ethel stood and eyed him; he seemed steady on his feet she thought, considering that he had been drinking with Bernard Thomas who was known to sup a pint or two. "You have a visitor," she said and Iolo detected that there was something afoot, Suddenly Iolo was filled with dread as he wiped his feet on the brown coconut matting just inside the front door of the immaculately kept Coal Board house. Iolo was expecting the worst as he peered round the door of the lounge.

"Hello brother, long time no see," said Caradog Pritchard who happened to be sitting in— Iolo's favourite armchair.

"Er, hello to you too Caradog, what brings you here?" asked Iolo cautiously.

"Me and the missus were wondering about you, what happened at the inquest? I would have attended but my hip was playing up," complained Caradog as he painfully tried to get out of Iolo's armchair.

"Don't get up, I'll sit on Ethel's chair," said Iolo as Ethel came in with a tray of tea and sandwiches.

Iolo described what went on at great lengths, about the inquest, Caradog listened in awe as Iolo described the final moments told by Billy Parfit.

"Parfit was always a trouble maker," confirmed Caradog, shaking his head. He was the same when he worked with me as a youngster, always trying to get men going, trying to pit one man against another," he added and chuckled at the thought of it. "So Parfit wasn't entirely to blame then, it must have been a terrifying few minutes before the pit went up so to speak," said Caradog quietly staring into his cup of tea.

"There was something else that I wanted to ask you?" said Caradog he looked to where Iolo was sitting.

"Well brother, I've only a few quid on me until payday, how much do you want then," said Iolo reaching for his wallet.

"Put it away Iolo," said Caradog eyeing the fat wallet in his brother's big hand. "I was going to say, there's a place on a trip to the Epsom races from the workmen's club, and I want you to come, it'll only cost you two quid, you don't go anywhere do you?" said Caradog with a pleading look in his eyes. Iolo looked at Ethel, she glared at Caradog, her eyes narrowing.

"You won't get him drunk will you? And I hope that… Bernard Thomas isn't going, the pair together drinking, I dread to think," said Ethel with a worried look about her.

"Don't worry Ethel, girl, it's only a trip to the races," said Caradog trying to reassure her.

"I've heard the women talking over the shops about the state that their husbands got into on so called trips to the races," said Ethel as she disappeared into the kitchen.

Caradog winked at Iolo and whispered "I'll sort it at the club then," he got up from where he was sitting and shouted to Ethel. "All fixed then, Eth' I'll see my- self out."

Ethel stood at the kitchen sink washing a few cups; shaking her head as the front door slammed shut.

As the days went by Ethel had given Iolo a few digs about the impending trip to the races. Iolo thought more and more about his wife Anwen and her lover Maldwyn Evans. He wondered about ghostly stories that some of the miners were talking about, some said they had seen unexplained men near to pit bottom where the fifteen miners were burned to death in nineteen sixty eight. Others said they had heard strange noises near to twenty six' return road and had experienced strange rotting like smells. Iolo wondered more and more, would he go mad like they do in films and such.

Talk was going round the colliery, the trip to the races would be the best for years, men were speculating on what horse would win the big race and a sweepstake had already began for those who were unable to go on the infamous excursion of the year.

Saturday Morning June 6th

Iolo and Caradog were sitting on the coach as other colliery workers and a few men from other industries boarded; noisily exchanging good natured banter. As they were settling down for the journey, Big Ray Chapman club chairman boarded the coach, holding a large piece of paper he began calling out names, and made a tick when anyone answered 'here' or any other word resembling an affirmative.

Iolo and Caradog exchanged gossip and talked about old times remembering old characters from the past.

"Remember Dai twp? Walking half a mile to look for a brick to put under a tram that had come off the track," remembered Caradog.

"Aye, I remember, one of the trams was full of bricks, but he didn't want to spoil one so he said," remembered Iolo, chuckling.

The Epsom racecourse was more than three hours away from home but the men were taking it all in their stride. They passed away the time reading newspapers and studying form in readiness for taking on the race-course bookmakers. Other men in the party would stop off in town spending the day in a local public house or workmen's club but never too far away from the bookmakers', darting to and fro, gambling their hard earned cash in modest amounts, winning and losing with equal aplomb.

At the race course the Cwm Derw punters gathered round as club chairman and organiser of the outing spelled out what they had to do in an emergency. "Well, boys, enjoy your selves and don't forget the coach will leave this venue at precisely five o'clock sharp," explained Ray Chapman. "Don't forget to watch out for pick pockets, some of you will remember Peter Burns had all his money in his wallet, so I suggest counteracting any thief taking all of your money by spreading it about your person. One more thing… try and stick together keep a good eye on each other. And if you spot anyone going after your hard earned money give em a hard time," he lectured.

Iolo remembered the advice given by the club chairman he held on tightly to his wallet and often reminded Caradog about keeping an eye out for pickpockets and painted ladies. Caradog was well versed in the misadventures of visiting Welshmen as he had his wallet pinched several years ago.

Iolo looked around and was amazed at the money being thrown at the course bookmakers', some men seemed to be begging the bookies to take their money off of them, as they waved fists full of notes at the eager men wearing Trilby hats. He studied the prices chalked onto long blackboards and seemed baffled as to how the bookies arrived at the figures quoted on the boards. Tic-tac men waved their arms signalling to no one in particular stopping briefly to scrawl coded numbers onto dirty white smudges of the bookmaker's blackboard.

Caradog nudged Iolo painfully in the ribs as the price of his fancied nag seemed to improve in his favour. "Iolo what do you fancy in the big race? Maybe beginner's luck, why don't you put a little fiver on it?" suggested Caradog.

From time to time Iolo's mind wandered, his head filled with thoughts of Anwen and her lover resting half a mile in the bowels below Cwm Derw and wondered whether he would be found out and suffer the terrible consequences of his dastardly deeds.

Iolo had given the big race some thought whilst studying the racing pages, he had plenty of time for study as the coach rumbled towards its destination. 'Lupe' he mumbled quietly.

"Er, what was that Iolo, did you say— Lupe?" questioned Caradog as he searched for the jockey's name. "Sandy Barclay, are you sure brother, he's not one of my favourite jockeys," said Caradog, he eyed Iolo with disdain as he was sure that his fancied nag would win the big one and not *Lupe*.

Back in Cwm Derw, the villagers were getting on with their lives and those who could not go on the legendary racing trip of the year were filling the workmen's club and Collier's Arms public house. Howell Davies landlord of the Collier's Arms adjusted the television from a rickety old chair. Men stood at the bar gazing at the monochrome telly and from time to time one of them would disappear leaving a half drunk pint glass standing idly on a soaking wet bar towel, safe in the knowledge that no one would even think of supping it, lest they get a taste of something horrible floating on top of the brown sudsy looking tipple.

Fred Morgan club vice chairman and butty to Caradog Pritchard was on duty for the weekend. Fred eyed the members as they came through the door each of them scrabbling for their usual seats. Lil the stewardess leaned on the bar eyeing the members as the air filled with friendly banter and mild cursing. Fred Morgan leaned on the bar and took a sip from his frothy tipple raised his glass high and calmly said, "to absent friends, and may they all have winners," the membership raised their glasses and mumbled loudly in unison, 'here, here.'

The membership at Cwm Derw workmen's were getting exited the air was electric as the big race drew near.

At the Collier's Arms pub, the punters all of them experts were exchanging their views on what horse would win.

"DAGNABIT; my bloody wallet some sneak thief has pinched my wallet!" wailed Iolo, pitifully; desperately searching his pockets in vain.

"There he is! I thought he was too sociable, all hands and a big nose," shouted Caradog, pointing in the direction of a fleeing figure. Far in the crowd a long arm with a wide bony hand reached out grabbing him firmly by a thin sticklike arm.

"He who steals my wallet steals trash," bellowed big Bob, He held the struggling big nosed thief in long strong arms until someone came to arrest the thief.

"Well done big Bob, don't let him go, the police are coming, hold onto him tight," shouted Caradog, grinning.

"All right, all right, let the dog see the rabbit," said a tall police constable, "beaky Thompson is it?" he said staring at the thief. "What has he done? Turn out your pockets, Beaky lad?" said the constable. The beaky nosed lad stood upright and straightened his ruffled clothes, his long thin features were a fresh colour and dark blue staring eyes studied big Bob momentarily. As the young lad slowly emptied his pockets it became obvious that he was not in possession of Iolo Pritchard's hard earned cash. "How much of your valuables are missing sir," asked the bemused police constable.

"About a fiver, I expect," answered Iolo, grinning widely. He pulled up a trouser leg to expose a thick stocking leg. Caradog grinned and the policeman grinned likewise. This here lad passes on the stolen items to an accomplice, I'll have to let him go, but I can escort him off the grounds," said the policeman. The young errant race goer looked frightened as crowds of onlookers shouted loud abuse at him.

Meanwhile at Cwm Derw things weren't quite so lively, the punters gathered around monochrome tellies' hoping to win a few shillings or so. The Collier's Arms pub was no different to any other pub in the country. All around the land people were waiting for the 'off' and our miners at the course were no exception.

The miners of Cwm Derw strained their necks as the course commentator shouted 'THEY'RE OFF.' the crowd roared their approval the horses hooves thundered as the jockeys crouched over their mounts, whipping, modestly shouting at the runners. The cry of 'come on Lupe you can do it' reached Iolo's ears he was not the only one who had backed the horse that brother Caradog hadn't fancied. The atmosphere was electrifying as the galloping horses thundered by, racing for the finish.

At Cwm Derw workmen's club the air was equally electrifying, members shouted mild obscenities, Fred Morgan tried to keep order he wondered about his butty Caradog Pritchard and brother Iolo. Chairs rattled across the floor as members rode imaginary horses whipping them frantically, urging their fancied nags, hoping for a winner but most of all they were enjoying the atmosphere of the big race right on their doorsteps.

Iolo and Caradog screamed at the leading horse, Iolo momentarily glanced at brother Caradog he hadn't bet on Lupe winning the race… or had he? The galloping, roaring sound of hooves thundered by, the crowd screamed and the commentator shouted over the loudspeaker 'LUPE IS THE WINNER.' Caradog patted Iolo on the shoulder saying, "well done brother." There were long faces and grinning faces as the punters collected their winnings, some punters seemed to be wiping away a tear or two.

Back at Cwm Derw workmen's club Fred Morgan grinned at the membership as they bemoaned their choices of nags. Lil, club stewardess began clearing up as the membership being lighter in the pocket filed out of the club and breathed fresh air for the first time in a while.

The Collier's Arms pub was quieter now as most of the drinkers and punters had left for the bookies or faced the womenfolk, being the worse for wear.

Ethel Probert sat in her fireside chair watching the small television screen, scrutinising the crowds at the Epsom racecourse hoping for a glimpse of Iolo Pritchard her live-in lover.

Back at the racecourse the Cwm Derw punters were making their way to the coach park. Caradog and Iolo were among the first to board the coach they sat staring out of the window, gazing at the hordes of punters making their way to coaches that were bound for destinations around the country. However, the Cwm Derw punters had a workmen's club booked for them by the Cwm Derw club committee, the host club was situated somewhere along the route home. Ray Chapman and the coach driver were the only ones who knew of the destination and were keeping the secret close to their chests.

Iolo was amused to see big Bob…ambling towards the coach clutching a bag of fried chips and from time to time he would offer the packet to passing punters, they turned away in horror as he reached out offering to share his meal of the day.

Ray Chapman walked slowly up the aisle of the coach counting the heads of Cwm Derw punters. "Ok driver all present and correct."

Most of the members dozed as the coach made its way to the secret destination. Caradog and brother Iolo snoozed, heads swung to and fro as the coach swayed and lurched on its tiresome journey to the unknown destination.

As the coach came to an abrupt stop in a makeshift car park Iolo raised his head and nudged brother Caradog. "Looks like we're here then!" said Iolo, sleepily.

"Come on you dozy lot, the bar's open," called Ray Chapman, club chairman. Big Bob, was first to get out of his seat.

"And the lord spake unto Aaron saying do not drink wine nor strong drink, nor thy sons with thee," spoke Bob loudly.

"Shut up big Bob, go and get the beer in," called little Mervyn Coles, excitedly, he didn't give a damn.

Iolo stepped off the coach and shook out the tiredness from his stiff limbs, he stared at the ramshackle building; a large sign above called out Bodsworth Workmen's Club in big red letters. "Hey, Caradog no wonder big Ray Chapman kept the name of this place quiet," said Iolo in a critical sort of voice.

Caradog stared at the foreboding building, his eyes were wide open, he grinned toothlessly saying "Aye, I remember a place like this during the war, all baggy arsed men and no beer," he chuckled. Iolo grinned and began the short walk to the two corrugated Nissen Huts built side by side and joined together in the middle. As the coach party neared the premises the door unceremoniously opened and a large man stepped into the opening hands on hips, he eyed Iolo and then Caradog.

"You are the Cwm... Cwm what's its name from Wales?" he asked.

"Aye that's us, where do we go?" asked big Ray Chapman. He stared at the bushy faced man who stood in the doorway.

"Yes, er, the bar has just opened, please be free and relax after your long journey, would the leader of your party please sign the visitors book," he asked, smiling broadly.

"That's me," said Ray Chapman I booked you over the phone," he confirmed.

"Iolo and some of the others hurriedly made their way to the Bar while the rest went to visit the toilets and to reserve some seats.

Caradog looked at the clock that hung above the bar it was showing 8 o'clock, the local headcount was disappointing. The people who bothered to welcome the Welshmen were few but friendly and were calling to them "give us a song Taff." Big Bob got off his seat and ambled to the stage. "Where's the pianist then, he grumbled as he climbed the two steps to the stage. The man who had sort of welcomed the men of Cwm Derw into his club stood on the stage and introduced himself. "Good evening ladies and gentlemen, my name is Sylvester Stanwick and I am the club's chairman. We will begin our night of entertainment with a concert given by our good friends from over the Bristol Channel, the Cwm... Cwm Der-oo male-voice Orpheus, and my first virtuoso is?" he stared at Bob, "er what's your name sir?" asked the chairman.

"Bob," he answered politely.

"What are you going to sing— Bob?" asked the chairman he grinned cheekily.

"Why, why Delilah?" answered big Bob. The men of Cwm Derw began to sing along with big Bob and the few locals were enjoying the atmosphere. Iolo had noticed some people were leaving in a hurry, he wondered why, his anxiousness was soon relieved as people were coming into the club, word had got round that there was a good night to be had at the workmen's club. Big Bob was leading the sing-along from the stage, no music was being played, but it didn't seem to matter. More and more people were crowding into the small Nissen Huts and enjoying the atmosphere.

Iolo had noticed an older woman playing the fruit-machine and eying Caradog from time to time. She seemed the same age as brother Caradog, but he as yet hadn't noticed.

The night was awash with beer and good singing and Caradog still hadn't noticed the woman playing on the fruit-machine staring at him with inquisitive eyes. He was enjoying the beer and sung loudly at the top of his voice when he felt someone tapping him softly on the shoulder. "Excuse me but is your name Cardog?" Asked a woman; mispronouncing his name.

"Caradog is the name," he answered as he turned to face his inquisitor. He squinted at the woman through beer affected eyesight. "Do I know you missus?" asked Caradog, hesitantly.

"I thought I recognised you, you were here during the war, you look a lot older now," she blurted, unsmiling.

"Was I?" exclaimed Caradog, drunkenly.

"Yes, it's you all right, you liked the beer even then," she remembered. "Is there somewhere where we can talk?" she asked, and then nodded in the direction of a corner of the building. Caradog got to his feet and followed the slim silver haired woman. The nicely dressed woman and the drunken Caradog began being re-acquainting themselves.

Iolo hadn't noticed Caradog going off with the silver haired woman who had been watching him all night. The Cwm Derw choristers drank and sang, the more they drank the better they sang. Caradog returned to his seat and sat on it with a heavy thud, Iolo noticed that brother

Caradog looked a little soberer and seemed to be in another world gazing inexplicitly to the bar.

"Are you alright brother?" asked Iolo, showing concern. Caradog was surely affected by the conversation he had with the silver haired woman.

"Aye, a little soberer but I'll tell you all about it on the way home," answered Caradog. Iolo looked a little puzzled as he hadn't noticed brother Caradog going off with the mysterious silver haired woman.

Meanwhile in Cwm Derw, Ethel was preparing for bed she gazed at her nakedness in a long oval mirror as erotic thoughts of Iolo were with her, she studied her hands cupping her still firm, white breasts; she gently caressed them and she was now aroused. Ethel lay naked on her bed and in the mirror on the wall she watched her long sensual fingers touching, probing, squeezing, and within a minute she purred and fell asleep, naked. But her dreams began to torture her tired mind, manifestations of the violent, cruel death of her husband and the night she witnessed Iolo carrying his murdered wife's corpse to the waiting car outside.

A tortuous hour had passed and the sleepy Ethel awoke, a kind of fear gripped her as she tried to shake off the nightmare that had tortured her as she slept naked alone on her bed. She gazed bleary eyed at the tin plate alarm-clock ticking loudly at the bedside. "Eleven o'clock, I wonder what he's doing now?" she mumbled quietly. "Sunday tomorrow, I hope it's nice, we could spend some time in the front garden," she mumbled again.

Ethel got between the cool freshly laundered sheets, she thumped her pillow hard before her tired head rested neatly on the crisp white pillow, her thoughts turned to the future, she and Iolo had discussed marriage and had dared to think of the consequences of the demise of Anwen and Maldwyn, would Iolo ever get found out? She must have wondered every night since that dreadful night in December 1967.

The Cwm Derw miners noisily boarded the coach, home was two hours away, and the happy locals' were thanking the boys and wishing them a safe and pleasant journey. Everyone safely aboard; the coach slowly pulled away from Bodsworth Workmen's Club. Caradog looked away sheepishly as the lonely silver haired woman stared at the coach scanning for Caradog. The coach rocked gently the engine hummed and went silent as the intoxicated Miners of Cwm Derw gently nodded off to sleep in a drunken haze. Iolo and Caradog however, had things to discuss.

"You were saying brother, you had something to tell me," said Iolo he stared at his brother with tired drunken eyes.

"Aye, that woman… that… that came up to me in the club, she remembered me from when I was stationed near there during the war," said Caradog his tired worried eyes stared into Iolo's eyes searching for something.

"So, why should she worry you, that was a long time ago during the war?" said Iolo beginning to wonder if his brother had got up to mischief all those years ago.

"She reckons I gave her a kid, and then I supposed to have run off leaving her to it," replied Caradog still staring into Iolo's tired looking eyes.

"So you didn't leave your name and address then," said Iolo with a slight smile that said —while I'll never—.

"It was in the war, I was all over the place, here one day gone the next, we were told to never give away information that might be useful to the enemy," said Caradog, his eyes turned to the sleeping men on the adjacent seats.

"Did the woman give her name, what was the name of the kid that you supposed to have fathered?" asked Iolo unable to take in that he may be an uncle to an Englishman.

"Her name is Ethel, same name as your missus, and the kid's name is James, he's twenty five and in the Royal Air Force," said Caradog with a sort of pride in his voice.

"Are you going to keep in touch with her and the *kid?*" questioned Iolo staring dead ahead.

"What will my missus say she'll go spare if she finds out?" replied Caradog, looking very worried.

"Rowena is a fair minded woman, anyway all this happened during the war when you wasn't even engaged to her," said Iolo raising his voice.

"Quiet mun, if this gets out I'll be the talk of the village," exclaimed Caradog, looking annoyed.

Unknown to Iolo and Caradog, Bill Parfit was sitting behind them fully awake and taking in every detail of the conversation.

Early Sunday morning

Iolo was becoming aware that the coach was stopping to let off its passengers he raised his head and stared bleary eyed as men were being dropped off at various places around the village. Bill Parfit brushed by the seats that Iolo and Caradog were sitting on. Caradog raised his weary head and stared into the eyes of Bill Parfit he stared back with a look that said 'I know what you were talking about'.

Iolo was the last person to be dropped off, the coach moved off depositing a droning hum in Iolo's ears. He stood motionless waiting for the hum to dissipate. When the hum finally subsided Iolo walked slowly towards home his thoughts turned to his brother.

Iolo momentarily stopped in his tracks the quietness of the village now evident, he could almost hear the loud ticking of the many tin-clocks on low bed-side tables, some men would open one eye like a sleeping dog keeping an eye on the early silent morning save for the odd gasping, snoring, spouse, noisily disturbing the peacefulness that would soon be broken by the loud tin-clocks drumming loudly on the low wooden tables. Others snoozed on, oblivious of men rising early for their Sunday morning shift at the silent Cwm Derw colliery.

At the house of Iolo Pritchard, things were quiet as the key was pushed into the old and worn brass lock, Judy, Iolo's faithful cocker spaniel came silently to greet him, licking his hand and then retreating to the warmth and cosiness of her basket near the glow of the open coal fire. Ethel could be heard sighing and wheezing in whistled breaths in the bed above the kitchen. Iolo touched the oven door with the back of his hand, it felt warm and a faint odour of a casserole reached his sniffing nostrils. The heavy door opened to reveal its contents. "Liver and bacon" said Iolo. Quietly, he carried the casserole to the kitchen table eating it luke-warm straight out of the pot. Judy watched, her tail thumped loudly on the oilcloth in anticipation.

Late Sunday morning

"Well, you stank of drink when you came to bed this morning, I hope your brother looked after you," said Ethel, she stared over a steaming hot cup of tea at the bleary eyed Iolo.

"We had a good day out, I backed a winner," said Iolo staring vacantly up at the kitchen window, he remembered the incident with the silver haired woman at the workmen's club. Ethel could see there was something going on behind the bloodshot groggy eyes of her partner.

"Something happened yesterday, didn't it?" she questioned, her eyes narrowed and she wondered. "Iolo Pritchard, what happened yesterday? You know you're a poor liar, you know you'll let it all out eventually," she teased him.

"It's Caradog," uttered Iolo, quietly.

"He's alright is he?" questioned Ethel, her eyes opened wide and stared at Iolo, waiting for bad news.

"Aye, he's alright, but he had a bit of a problem," revealed Iolo. Cautiously he began to tell her the story of the slim, silver haired woman at the workmen's club. Ethel's eyes lit up taking in every detail of what she heard.

"I always thought your brother was a bit of a ladies man, my mother warned my sister about him, it's a good thing she listened, my mother was right," said Ethel. She grinned and vowed to keep the secret to herself.

Monday afternoon

The afternoon shift started off on a good footing, except for Bill Parfit sitting on a low wall outside the fitting shop, men gathered around the trouble making rogue listening to what he had to say and from time to time he would look in the direction of the officials' lodge. Men laughed loudly and continuously. Iolo was busily talking to the Manager on the telephone,

"Iolo get those men down the pit they look as though they have lost all track of time, and tell Bill Parfit I want to see him here in my office before he goes down the pit!" bellowed Mr Mainwaring, colliery Manager, he watched them with annoyed eyes from his office window. "Yes Mr Mainwaring, I'll go out there and send them down the pit, anyhow the pit hooter is about to go off," answered Iolo he put the phone down and promptly marched out of the office and onto the colliery yard to confront the jovial laughing miners.

Bill Parfit stood outside the colliery Manager's office wondering why he was wanted. The door of the office opened sharply, Mr Mainwaring shouted, "Come in Bill," the troublesome miner cautiously walked into a spacious office bedecked in wide strips of polished conveyor belting. Parfit momentarily stared at the photos of past colliery Managers that were dotted around the office wall, each man seemed to eye him as he strode by them to the waiting colliery Manager sat at his desk.

Mr Mainwaring sat tapping the bulbous end of a pencil on a large pad of blotting paper. "Sit down Bill," commanded Mr Mainwaring. "I'm concerned about your conduct, I've had several reports about you, disturbing reports; you seem to have the ability to stir up the imagination of the colliery workforce. Whenever there has been a flash dispute, you always seemed to be in the middle of the dispute urging other men to withdraw their labour. What do you say in your defence?

"I want representation by my union before I say anything," replied Parfit looking red in the face.

"Fair enough, Bill, but what would you say if I asked you to attend a potential pit deputy's course? I would rather have you on our side than have you constantly interrupting production at this colliery," said the Manager uncharacteristically smiling in this sort of circumstance. Parfit stood motionless, stunned by the sudden offer of going over to the other side.

"I'll need time to consider your offer Mr Mainwaring, I'll have to discuss this with my family," answered Parfit, his face took on the look of a bewildered and suddenly anxious man.

"I've taken the liberty in getting an application form… from the training office," said the Manager pushing the form in Parfit's direction. Parfit cautiously picked up the application form stared at it for a brief moment before asking for something to put it in, as he was about to go down the pit and do his shift.

Polling day June 18 1970

Thursday was docket day, and today the country went to the polls. Iolo Pritchard strolled up to the pay clerks open office window. "Robert Holder, pay clerk, reached out to Iolo, holding a payslip, the pay clerks seldom had to ask a miner for his pay number, every man's number seemed to be etched in the clerk's head. "Have you voted,

Iolo?" asked the pay clerk smiling as Iolo took the green printed slip out of Robert's long thin fingers.

"Yes, I've voted, but it'll make no difference to the end result, they can put a donkey up for parliament and you can be sure a miner will vote for it if it's got a labour rosette pinned to it," answered Iolo, grinning, cheekily.

"That's one of my grandfather's sayings, he always said it; Iolo, things never change," shouted the pay clerk to him as he walked towards the pithead baths.

Every Thursday Iolo made a visit to the 27s district this he had done since he took on the senior Overman's job just after starting back to work after the terrible explosion that tore apart the lives of the many men who lived through it.

"Voted have you, Iolo?" said Charlie Dicks as he raised the gate of the pit cage.

"Aye, I voted, I put my cross in the same spot as always, same old donkey," answered Iolo as he ducked under the gate.

"Harold, will get back in, you watch," shouted Charlie Dicks, grinning as always. Iolo walked smartly away from pit bottom, hands clasped behind his back as usual and habitually inspecting the roadways as he went. Return airways always stank of something whether it was from explosives after shot firing or just a plain damp smell, but Iolo always sniffed as he approached the mouth of the old 26s district, men had often complained of a foul smell and some had even reported hearing strange noises like people whispering. Iolo stopped, sniffed and listened where the old 26s was stopped off, his imagination started to get the better of him, he thought for a moment that he heard a strange whispering sound, then suddenly the rope haulage moved, Iolo jumped with fright, he wasn't expecting the haulage rope to move. Quickly Iolo moved; hands clasped behind his back racing away from what may have been the ghosts of his wife Anwen and her lover Maldwyn Evans.

At the mouth of 27s district lights busily flashed as men coupled up trams in preparation for taking the journey in-bye of the district. Iolo stopped and watched them from a just a few yards away; men shouted orders, trams slammed against each other noisily. "Ye gods, hallelujah," shouted a voice. "Praise the lord we're on the road," shouted the rider. Iolo recognised the voice immediately it was that of Bob Stephens.

"Well, well, how are you? Big Bob," asked Iolo smiling at him.

"This cursed iron snake has been giving me gip since I started," complained big Bob with annoyance in his voice.

"Can I help?" asked Iolo as he tried to identify a problem with the journey, or Iron snake as Bob had called it.

"Let's have a look at it," said Iolo busily inspecting the journey. " Ha, here we are, looks like a cap has come off the wheel of a tram, the wheel must be floating on the stub axle making the tram jump off the track," exclaimed Iolo showing some excitement in his voice. "Big Bob, unload this tram and turn it out," ordered Iolo. "I'll get a blacksmith to come down the pit and sort it out for you," said Iolo, smiling.

"Thank you Iolo, boy; you don't want a job with us do you? I'll see the Overman and fix it for you," offered big Bob, grinning.

"Er, no thanks I've already got a job thank you," said Iolo as he walked away into the district.

"Mind the haulage ropes, Iolo we don't want to carry you out to the pit, injured," shouted big Bob, after Iolo.

As Iolo arrived at the coalface it became evident that something was wrong, supply men were busily carrying timber to the face; a few men stopped work and stared at Iolo, "he wasn't long about" said one of them meaning that he wasted no time in getting to the coalface on hearing of trouble, but the truth was, Iolo hadn't heard of any trouble. "What's the problem here, boys?" asked Iolo, wondering what was going on.

"There's a hell of a roof-fall on the face conveyor, the Overman's been trying to get hold of you all shift," said a supply man nodding in the direction of the coalface.

"This is the first time I've heard of it," said Iolo as he got on his knees and began to crawl up the face to where the roof fall was situated.

A stone the size of a small lorry was standing where it fell, on top of the chain conveyor stopping it moving in any direction. Beyond the massive stone other smaller stones were heaped along the conveyor. Joe Watkins Overman of the district was giving orders over the face tannoy "I want you to get any steel girders or rails onto the face," he ordered.

"How are you going to tackle the situation?" asked Iolo, naively.

"Well, first things first, we have to cover our backs, I've organised the men, they are dragging timber and steel up the face, I've got men rigging up a boring machine in readiness for drilling into this monster of a stone, with some luck, and a lot of effort we may get the conveyor going by tomorrow morning," answered Joe Watkins.

"Where's Bernard Thomas, deputy?" asked Iolo he hadn't seen him in the return road. Joe Watkins took out a pocket watch and squinted at it vaguely.

"Doing his rounds, I should think," said Joe as he replaced the watch into the pocket of a black waistcoat that was way too small for his ample frame.

"Does the Manager know about this?" asked Iolo wondering.

"Aye, as soon as we found out that the conveyor was bogged down with weight, I phoned him, I could hear him jumping about the office when I told him," said Joe, grinning. "He wanted to know where you were, I said that today, Thursday, you were due to make a visit here," reported Joe, grinning, he then proceeded to blow snobs into an old dusty handkerchief. "I think I've got a head cold coming on," he said. Iolo made a beeline up to the gate road he needed to speak to the colliery Manager.

"Yes Mister Mainwaring, Joe Watkins reckons he can get the face moving by tomorrow morning. We are going to need extra supports and I'll need to speak to the blacksmiths about organising some steel girders, they'll probably have to straighten reclaimed arch girders," said Iolo, he wrote in a note book as he spoke.

A little later, Mr Mainwaring made an appearance on pit top, word soon got around that the Manager was on the prowl, everyone was looking over their shoulders in case the Manager should be standing behind them watching their every move.

Outside the blacksmith shop Dai black-nail and a boy were busily using a reforming machine, Mr Mainwaring was standing nearby watching them straightening reclaimed arch girders. "How many can you do, Dai?" asked Mr Mainwaring, without waiting for a reply he suddenly looked to the timber supply yard, he could see no one there, then off he marched towards the timber yard in search of workers.

Friday 19th June 1970

At the Pritchard's household Ethel was listening to the radio, Iolo had been late getting home from work and was still in bed. Ethel listened to the news, her eyes widened as the news reader began to read the headlines. 'Edward Heath has become the new British prime minister after a surprise victory for the Conservatives in the general election. The result has confounded all opinion polls conducted before yesterday's election which had predicted a comfortable win for Labour.'

"Iolo, Iolo, Ted Heath has won the election," shouted Ethel as she ran up the stairs, she shook the sleeping Iolo.

" Iolo, Ted Heath has won the election," she shouted excitedly. Iolo stirred and drowsily looked up at Ethel. "Have we still got a donkey?" asked the sleepy Iolo.

"What donkey? Iolo, what are you on about?" asked Ethel, frustration in her voice.

"Never mind, Ethel, life will go on, you can be sure of that," Iolo groaned into his pillow.

Ethel lay beside Iolo, and placed a hand on his manly breast. He gazed at her and lifted up her dainty chin and kissed her gently on her pale unpainted lips. "I want you, Iolo," she whispered, he slipped off her thin dressing gown revealing her pale, appealing, and milky white skin. She quickly straddled him and gyrated until he was hard and ready. Iolo looked up at her and reached out squeezing her breasts as they stood proud and beautiful. With skilful, long silky fingers she guided him and then savoured his hardness as she worked gently at first, her eyes rolled revealing only the whites of her lovely eyes, and in a few minutes Ethel's trembling body had sated its self; she lay on his hairy chest her eyes looked up at him smiling in gratitude.

27s district afternoon shift

At 27s district it was grub-time and the men were sitting around on bits of timber discussing the events of the month. "Well we've got a conservative government now, I think Enoch Powel swung it for them," said Danny Wilmot as he finished chewing at a dusty sandwich.

"Aye, he said a lot of truth; rivers of blood and all that, what he said didn't go away did it?" said another.

Danny Wilmot sat in silence his craggy face looked stern as he thought about the politics of coalmines. "Did you know that from nineteen sixty-one we have had about ten different ministers of power, the civil servants were shutting our pits; there was just no continuity. Looks like Wilson had no control over anyone by the look of things," he said and the others nodded in agreement. "Aye, England lost in the world cup, rivers of blood, Norway's found oil in the North Sea," reflected Danny Wilmot.

Iolo and Ethel finally made wedding plans and today was the day that their plans were to come together.

Iolo and Ethel are sat in the waiting room at the Graig Ddu registry office. Ethel idly stares up at the lofty ceiling admiring the ancient looking cornices. In the background people are nervously laughing behind a large oak panelled door. Iolo stares blankly at the wall opposite thumbs twiddling idly. "I remember sitting here twenty-four years ago, staring up at the same old ceiling, studying the same old cornices, listening to the same old noises behind that same old door," said Ethel, her un-flickering eyes lowered to the floor. Iolo's mind was miles away he didn't hear her. David and Bethan, Ethel's daughter and son-in-law were sat alongside equally quiet, they too were married there. Suddenly the oak panelled door noisily opened and a wedding party emerged, laughing and noisily making conversation followed by the shy young bride nervously glancing at the bump under her wedding attire. Ethel glanced at the bride's prominent bump, she smiled at her politely, the young attractive and obviously pregnant bride nervously smiled back.

Iolo and Ethel had decided on a quick and informal wedding, opting for a small reception for their immediate families and friends at the Collier's Arms public house. Howell Davies, pub landlord, greeted the newlyweds at the door of his pub. "Congratulations on your overdue nuptials," he beamed a smile as he shook Iolo's hand vigorously and then hugged Ethel with equal enthusiasm. "Please have your first drink on the house, everything is set up and ready for your guests," he offered in his best polite voice.

"I'll drink to that, I'm as dry as a cork," exclaimed Caradog Pritchard who just happens to be Iolo's best man.

After the small reception had concluded and all had been said and done the wedding party began to enjoy themselves by ordering copious amounts of alcohol from behind the bar and from time to time well-wishers would come in and mingle with the guests. Dewi Brice, Iolo's old arch enemy came in and sat noisily on an old wooden chair, his large head lowered, he glowered at Iolo menacingly, his hair fell partly over his eyes, in his hands he held a half drunk pint glass of beer.

Caradog had noticed Dewi Brice sauntering into the room where the wedding reception had been: "Hello Dewi, have you come to wish the happy couple luck in their new life together, then?"

"I've been thinking about this so called wedding, and I've also been thinking about my old butty Maldwyn Evans, I just can't believe that he ran off with *his* old missus," growled the drunken Dewi Brice nodding in Iolo's direction.

"Take a tip from an *old un*, let sleeping dogs lay, it's their day, leave them alone," demanded Caradog, he stared fiercely at Brice. Others in the room had noticed that something was going on they also knew that Iolo and Dewi Brice had an altercation in the pub some time ago.

"I don't care, *him* by there had something to do with Maldwyn's disappearance," he shouted and pointed a nicotine stained finger at Iolo.

"Dewi, if you remember some time ago I said that I knocked the pair of them on the head, and then took them down the pit and buried them in the gob," said Iolo, grinning from ear to ear. Dewi Brice grew redder in the face his hands began to shake uncontrollably. Suddenly Brice rose from where he had been sitting, the wooden rickety chair fell awkwardly onto its side, and Brice lunged at Iolo holding the empty pint glass it shook visibly.

"Take it easy Brice, you've had too much to drink, give me the glass, don't be silly you'll go down if you use it," said Caradog, loudly. Brice lunged at Caradog with the empty beer glass, women began to scream; men shouted abuse at Brice.

"Kath call the police, quickly," shouted Howell Davies pub landlord. "Brice put the glass down, please, there's a good chap," said the irate landlord.

Brice realised through his drunken stupor that he had nothing to gain and dropped the beer glass to the floor sending shards of glass across the flagstone floor. Without warning he dropped to the glass strewn floor, sitting, hands over his ears, his evil blood began to pour onto the flagstones through baggy corduroy trousers.

Meanwhile not far away in Cwm Derw miner's institute, fondly called the *stute* by the people of the village another celebration was taking place, it was young Philip Jones' wedding. Philip had left the dark dismal colliery only a few weeks before William Thomkins, alias Bill Pumpy was cruelly killed by the dreaded black damp so called because it starved the miner's flame safety lamp of oxygen thus putting out the flame leaving the miner in the gloomy, black-ness of the mine, all wise miners knew what to look for in the confines of the flame safety lamp.

Word of the trouble involving Dewi Brice quickly spread like wild-fire. Young Philip was now twenty years old and had matured in both his out-look on life and his physical size; he wondered whether Dewi Brice would venture into the institute and cause more trouble.

Charlie Dicks, who worked as Onsetter at the Cwm Derw colliery, tottered into the long narrow hall where the wedding reception was being held. "Hello young Philip, I suppose you heard about our local trouble maker over in the Collier's Arms have you?" said Charlie slyly grinning as he always did.

"Yes, Uncle Charlie, that bloke ought to be locked up, the trouble he causes," uttered Philip; he frowned from behind a half drunk beer glass then proceeded to swallow the remainder of the contents.

"Looks like the police will take him away this time, I heard a copper asking about the mental health unit, perhaps he'll get sectioned with a bit of luck," said Charlie, grinning.

Philip and his young bride stood near the open door posing for photographs when Iolo Pritchard was heard to be heavily tramping up the marbled stairway. "I thought I had better come and offer congratulations to you and your beautiful bride, and wish you both the best of luck for the future," said Iolo slightly out of puff and smiling broadly.

"Thank you Iolo, and congratulations to you and your good wife," replied Philip as he hugged his blushing bride. "What has happened to Dewi Brice?" asked Philip looking a little worried.

"I think the police will try and get him sectioned under the mental health act. Every week he picks on someone or another. He tried to say I did something to his butty Maldwyn Evans, he won't believe me that Evans and my *ex* had run away together, so I said: 'I knocked them on the head, took them down the pit and buried them in the gob,'" said Iolo, laughing.

"Yes, very funny, and a good idea, they would never find them down there would they, Iolo?" said Philip, laughing. "I'm only kidding, mun, but who would think of such a thing? I mean you'd never get away with it would you?" Suggested young Philip; laughing not realising that he had heard the unspeakable truth.

"Look after your beautiful bride, and I'll see you when you get back from honeymoon," said Iolo as he tramped back down the marbled stairway and ambled towards the Collier's Arms pub.

As Iolo entered the pub the police were returning, and Ethel had a worried expression on her pale face. Howard Davies lightly tapped Iolo on the shoulder. "Dewi Brice has been banned from this pub while my name is above the door," he assured the worried Iolo.

A tall burly policeman called out "Is there a Iolo Pritchard in the building please?"

"I'm Iolo Pritchard what do you want me for?" asked Iolo nervously toying with small coins in a trouser pocket.

"I have to ask you a couple of questions; you can answer them here or if you'd prefer you can answer them at the police station in Graig Ddu," said the tall balding police officer holding his policeman's helmet under one arm.

"What do you want to know, officer?" volunteered Iolo.

"Is there another room where I could conduct this interview?" asked the officer looking for somewhere to hold an interview.

"You can go into our living quarters if you'd prefer," offered the landlord. My wife can help behind the bar for a while, she won't mind," he said as he briskly walked towards the living quarters.

Mrs Howells smiled meekly and strode by the apprehensive Iolo Pritchard and the interviewing policeman. The genial pub landlord ushered the pair into his abode and left them there.

After half an hour Iolo and the policeman emerged from the pub living quarters laughing loudly, clearly indicating that the policeman did not believe Iolo's entertaining tale of murder and mayhem concerning his former wife and her lover.

One week later.

Iolo and Ethel had decided on a very modest honeymoon seeing as they had both been married before and had been living in tally so to speak. Everyone who knew and respected the newlyweds thought it strange that Blackpool would be the honeymoon destination. Everyone being of the opinion that Blackpool was for boozing and seeing the lights from inside pubs and clubs. However, today was the day that they would set off with other Cwm Derw villagers to the pleasure grounds up North.

The villagers often held trips to the Blackpool illuminations and each street had its organisers, monies were saved up and looked after by the trip organisers. These trips were mainly populated by the womenfolk save for men who didn't like horseracing trips or could not get permission to take time off from work. Iolo had worked the miner's holiday fortnight, which meant that he had special permission to go on honeymoon when the time came. However, Iolo and Ethel had made other arrangements which involved staying in Blackpool a further week after the trippers had departed for home, they were to travel home on their own initiative.

Coaches were lined up outside the shops, the many Cwm Derw villagers excitedly jostled amongst them-selves hoping to share a seat with a friend, or maybe someone who might entertain them with clever stories about the world in general.

The coaches left Cwm Derw for the pleasure grounds of the Blackpool illuminations; life went on for the villagers who were left behind. Caradog Pritchard however began to prepare his vegetable allotment for the winter; digging up vegetation that had failed and buried it in specially prepared trenches for rotting down so that the ground had a ready-made source of nutriment for the following year.

Caradog and his lifelong butty Fred Morgan had built a sort of hut on the allotments, this hut of theirs was the envy of every allotment holder, he and Fred stored their tools there and had fitted a modest coal fired stove, they also installed a couple of armchairs from which they would lounge and sup copious amounts of home-made alcohol. This was one such day.

Most of the allotment holders had fled the village in search of other pleasures in Blackpool.

A cool wind blew the dust from the dry ground around the allotments, Caradog slammed the door of the makeshift gardener's hut and sat at one side of the hot coal fired stove, Fred sat on the other side supping homebrew from a thick glass handled mug, he shook his head as the biting brew attacked his taste buds." Good stuff eh Fred," said Caradog, grinning toothlessly.

"What strength is this then? It's got a kick like a pit horse," said Fred, grinning likewise.

"About ten per cent I expect, a lot stronger than the beer they serve at the workmen's club, eh," answered Caradog, reservedly. "We'd best take it easy then, we don't want to go home in a wheelbarrow, do we?" Remarked the grinning Caradog already feeling quite foxed.

Fred Morgan noisily shut the door of the makeshift hut, while Caradog slid a long thin bar through its brackets locking the bar with a solid padlock. Fred patted the door fondly as a chill wind blew the tail of his coat up over his back.

As the tipsy pair closed the allotment gate they bid each other farewell and went their separate ways as they lived on the periphery of the village. Caradog began to feel the full potency of the deadly homebrew he held on to his brown corduroy cap as the cool wind attempted to blow it from his greying and balding head. The retired old collier struggled with the cool wind with the added problem of controlling his dizzy legs. People grinned from behind partially closed curtains while others who met him exchanged their views regarding the current weather and chuckled at him openly. It seemed ages to Caradog as he struggled up the garden path to his house. Rowena his wife was alerted by the barking of the family dog an old and greying Jack Russell terrier. The door opened and Caradog almost fell through it. Rowena stood in the hallway arms folded high on her bosoms and a stern expression lined her aging face. "You've been drinking that homebrew again haven't you Caradog Pritchard?" she shouted angrily, her dark eyes narrowed at him, he struggled to get his words out." I...I only had one or two, mun... Things were quiet down the allotments so me and Fred thought...what the hell... everybody else's gone to Blackpool so why can't we have some fun," he drunkenly reasoned.

Chapter XIII

Christmas 1970

It was Christmas morning, Iolo sat in the comfort of the warm glowing open coal fire lazily gazing at flickering flames that licked at the sooty blackness of the fireplace. The aroma of a roasting turkey filled the whole house, Judy slapped her stumpy tail noisily on the lounge carpet, and from time to time she would look up head tilted to the side staring at her master and then return to a sleeping posture. Ethel busied herself, noisily clanging utensils and merrily hummed to Christmas carols being sung on the radio that stood on the cupboard in the kitchen.

Outside, children could be heard playing boisterously with their games of cowboys and Indians while others rode on brand new push-bikes shouting commands and playing up.

In the house of Caradog Pritchard things were equally festive and homely as Caradog prepared for Christmas morning at Cwm Derw workmen's Club. From the warmth of his comfortable abode Caradog looked out over the frosty fields that were interspersed with hedges and the odd tall tree that children climbed in summer-times past, now bare of leaf and fruit. He thought about his family now enjoying their Christmas' in faraway places Canada and Australia.

"Do you think Iolo will be in the club this morning?" asked Rowena,

 thoughtfully. "I haven't seen him for a while or Ethel for that matter, I hope they are all right, we must visit them after Christmas dinner, mind you don't have too much to drink," ordered Rowena unsmilingly.

Christmas morning at the workmen's club was always a colourful affair, with multi coloured cardigans and pullovers, along with pretty patterned socks filling brand new leather shoes. The air filled with the pungent odour of aftershave, and cigar smoke choked the non-smoker mercilessly.

Christmas was a time when some family members returned to their roots and was evident by faces that seemed familiar but no one quite knew what to say as they had not seen them for many a year.

Caradog stared with a questioning expression. Playing on the one-armed bandit by the bar was a tall man with wisps of ginger hair sprouting from a speckled scalp. The more he looked the more the face became familiar, he could not contain his need to make an enquiry, rising from his chair he strode to where the tall balding gingery man was playing on the bandit. "Don't I know you from some place?" asked Caradog, grinning toothlessly.

"I used to live around here I worked down the pit for a while," he replied, cautiously eyeing Caradog and resumed feeding the machine with tanner coins. Caradog thought for a moment, he wondered why the stranger didn't say his name.

"What's your name, butty?" he asked staring at him.

"Norman Stringer, is the name, you are Caradog Pritchard brother of Iolo Pritchard aren't you?" he replied quietly.

"That's right, me and Iolo are brothers," said Caradog holding out his hand. Norman Stringer limply shook the hand of his acquaintance. Caradog began to remember who this man once was. He returned to his chair and spoke to Fred. "Do you know who that bloke is, the one playing on the bandit?" he asked under his tobacco smoke tainted breath.

He looked at Caradog, and then at the stranger. "Do you remember Stephanie Powel?" whispered Fred turning and staring his butty in the eyes.

"That's what I was thinking but too afraid to ask," responded Caradog as it all came flooding back. "He's done his time then, they let him out, I forgot about the murder, I seem to remember people saying he was fitted up for it," said Caradog eyeing the ex con, wondering where he was now living.

As the morning gathered pace Fred Morgan, club's vice chairman took control.

"Gentlemen and the few ladies that are here this morning," he announced loudly, "we will carry on the clubs ancient tradition of community singing, I call on our good friend Caradog Pritchard to render the first Christmas carol here today," announced the vice chairman the choking cigar fumed room erupted in loud applause as the club's ancient piano sprang into tune with 'Hark the Herald Angels Sing' written by Charles Wesley.

Iolo studied his wristwatch as he remembered the previous Christmas he glanced at the telephone sitting silently on the lounge windowsill; the house was equally quiet, Judy sniffed the festive air filled with the appetising aroma of turkey, and stuffing. Bethan, David and the grandchild were due to make an appearance as they did in previous years. Suddenly the doorbell rang in a continuous loud ringing, Judy sprang to her feet barking excitedly, Iolo trotted smartly to the door and opened it. Standing in the doorway were the family, Bethan, David and Guto bach.

The festive meal was being enjoyed by all the family Iolo unconsciously maintained a listening ear for the telephone. Ethel stared at Iolo from time to time he seemed unusually quiet and had a moody expression on his pale worried looking face. "What's the matter Iolo, you've barely taken your eyes of the telephone all through our dinner," exclaimed Ethel her eyes narrowed at Iolo, questioning.
"It was this time last year, the phone rang and I answered it, do you remember?" asked Iolo putting down his knife and fork.
"Yes, I remember now! That man was gassed down the pit and the Manager telephoned you to let you know," remembered Bethan, unsmiling, she quickly glanced at the family one at a time. Ethel stared at Iolo a sorry cloud descended over her, as another episode in their lives had entered her greying head.
Iolo had chosen an untimely setting in order to express his fears for the future. "The year is coming to an end," he announced unceremoniously. "The Cwm Derw miners are building their confidences. Only about twelve percent of the colliery workers are under twenty-five years of age whereas I'm told nearly forty per cent are over fifty years old," he added, a serious frown engulfed his pale features. "The Wilson defeat of June put paid to the consensus in British labour politics," he confided, he glanced at Ethel and then at Guto bach. "Not only are our boys being made redundant but they are leaving the pits in droves, youngsters are not being trained anymore," said Iolo, gazing at son-in-law David who was still of the mind-set that mining was dangerous work. "I think the mining industry is working itself up for a fight with the Tory government, give it a year and we'll

all be out on strike," he said in a voice that said he knew what he was talking about. The festive air turned sullen and quiet as they all pondered their future.

Chapter XIV

1971

The year began with rumblings of trouble as the new conservative government planned their policy for domestic fuel. There was now a feeling of anger and frustration, expressed in unofficial meetings, disputes at local and area level and a new wave of militancy swept through the coalfields. Despite there being a moody atmosphere among welsh miners this did not stop them from enjoying their national sport. The sport of rugby football as it is called lives in the hearts of all Welshmen. whether they played for their local village club or indeed aspired to their ultimate goal running onto the turf at Cardiff Arms Park wearing the welsh red jersey.

Every year the management at the Cwm Derw mine dreaded the rugby season, scarlet fever was always rampant, low wages was not an issue as the miners saved for the biennial trip to the Wales Scotland match held at Murrayfield, Edinburgh. Each week they would save a hard earned pound handed over to a person in workmen's clubs and public houses so trusted that not a penny would go astray save for the bravest of scoundrels.

The first fixture of the five nation's cup was Wales versus England at the Cardiff Arms Park and Iolo Pritchard knew he was going to have problems getting men to work on a Saturday afternoon but luckily this year management postponed any work that needed an extended shift.

Saturday January 16th

Caradog Pritchard made sure he got his favourite seat on the edge of the bay window. The workmen's club was beginning to fill up with members and the atmosphere was alive with chatter. The television was positioned on a table sited on the low stage where everybody who came into the club could see the rugby match. Fred Morgan vice chairman eyed the chattering crowd of men adorning bobble hats and scarves of red and white. The beer was flowing, the air was full of good cheer and Lil the stewardess beamed a smile as she pulled the pints of amber liquid fit for a thirsting miner coming off shift. Iolo Pritchard smartly stepped through the green painted door followed by

Ianto Pugh eyes like a panda hair still wet and carrying a bag of dirty coal blackened washing under an arm. Iolo greedily supped the froth from the foaming pint while scanning the room for Caradog his elderly brother. A hand went up and Iolo scurried over to the bay window where Caradog was sitting quietly sucking on a briar that was fired with twist, the smoke twisted and billowed around him and Iolo coughed loudly as he sat on one side.

At the Arms Park the crowds had filled the ground to capacity a sea of red and white rippled as Welshmen and the England supporters rubbed shoulders and discussed the political atmosphere with English miners from Kent and the north. 'Aye the politicians have had an easy time,' they were saying, but first we settle our bets who would win this game we call *rugger?*

Back at Cwm Derw workmen's club the air vibrated, 'W*ales; Wales'* shouted the excited tipsy pack of villagers.
The club went silent as the toss was made and then the room erupted in a roar of encouragement *'come on Wales'* Iolo looked around as some of the men were on the sick list in readiness for the match against Scotland. He quickly forgot all about that, as he suddenly found himself engrossed in the battle between the reds and the whites.
Meanwhile in the Collier's Arms pub the air was equally electrifying as the bar staff battled with a sea of red and white, the English clientele made good natured gestures as this was the only time of the year that they did not stand shoulder to shoulder. Wales was winning as England struggled to make any headway. Surprisingly England had selected eight new caps for the opening match. Wales were out of sight by half time thanks to two tries by the brilliant winger Gerald Davies. Barry John began and finished the scoring with dropped goals as Wales recorded a comfortable 22-6 victory.

Monday morning

The Cwm Derw miners returned to their toil deep in the bowels of Fam Briddo 'Mother Earth.' The cold biting wind gusted unmercifully as the hardy miners tramped down the drive towards the pit head baths. Jack Williams under-Manager stood on the door of the officials-lodge eyeing the morning shift who were scurrying towards the upcast shaft in order to escape the unfriendly wind and he smiled as he returned to his grimy desk where the nightshift officials waited to be debriefed.

The morning shift on the return side of 27s district were having their grub-time as they called it. Big Bob, listened intently as his workmates relived the Welsh vs English match held the previous Saturday." Bah, grown men running after a bag of wind, they should be down here with us toiling in the bowels," he said loudly, sneering at his fellow countrymen.

"Come on, big Bob, that's not very patriotic of you, you're way out numbered here," exclaimed Terry Powel grinning at the scraggly haired figure sat next to him, big Bob had the appearance of a wandering tramp his scraggly hair hung down from under his pit helmet, a hooked nose seemed permanently devoid of pit dust as he was always stroking it with long bony fingers.

After the overlong discussions involving welsh-rugby-politics big Bob sniffed at the slow moving air as it flowed over the group of men." I smell a boss approaching, we'd better make a move…boys," he said in an urgent voice.

"What's all this then, Had kippers for your grub have you?" remarked Jack Williams as he rounded the corner of the junction. He pulled out a pocket watch and held it out at arms- length studying it with affected concern. "We were late securing the journey, we had to make it safe, see, we got a good record for safety, have we," stated big Bob the leading hand among the journey men. Joe Watkins accompanying the under-Manager stood over the sitting men, his broad hands resting on hips. Big Bob was first to get up from where he was sitting the others followed dutifully.

27s district was planned to run alongside the old 26s in the belief that the area over the old and new roadways would be de-stressed but this was not the case as the 27s return road suffered from floor heave, the Cwm Derw miners called this *pwkin up* pronounced (pooking up). As the floor of the mine roadway heaved the overall height was measurably reduced. This reduction in height caused problems when transporting supplies and increased the velocity of air passing along the reduced section of roadway.

Big bob made his way into the 27s district ahead of the journey of trams, stooping due to inadequate headroom. The velocity of air picked up the dust from the floor and stung the eyes of anyone following behind the journey, Terry Powel scrunched up his eyes as he slowly followed the passage of the clanging trams trundling along at a snail's pace through the restricted roadway. The journey of supplies crawled along at the pace of a snail, the edges of trams skimming the misshapen arch girders, big Bob stopped from time to time to observe progress. The trams abruptly came to a stop, the steel wired haulage rope rose sharply, and then slapped up and down violently against roof and floor raising clouds of coarse dust. Big Bob had guessed what had happened, quickly he grabbed the signal wire and pulled on it with all his strength. The all steel rope relaxed and lay on the dusty floor of the roadway. Big Bob in an unwise frame of mind crawled alongside the journey looking for the offending tram. About halfway he spotted a corner of a tram butted up against an arch girder. "Ha, here it is," he said to himself quietly. He shouted to Terry Powel "The tram's caught on a ring, the journey will have to be sent back towards you about two foot," he called.

"Ok get out of the way," ordered Terry, urgently. Big Bob crawled towards the leading end of the journey— on getting clear he shouted 'ok'. The signal wire shook three times. Terry had signalled to the haulage driver to draw the journey out bye slowly. The trams moved an inch and then stopped due to the driver having received the signal to stop the haulage.

Big Bob called to Terry to stand clear as he was about to signal for the trams to move in- bye. Inch by inch the trams began to move, suddenly the haulage rope tightened and then dropped to the floor then without warning it snatched and a loud banging noise was heard somewhere in the middle of the journey. Big Bob grabbed the signal wire pulling on it with all his strength. "Looks like the journey is off the track," he shouted to Terry on the other side.

Big Bob crawled to where the problem lay, the coarse dust blew into his eyes and stung them, one tram had derailed he had to find a way of putting the tram back on the rails. Between two trams lay pieces of timber and big bob had decided that it would be quicker to use the scraps of wood rather than go to the front and get the proper equipment, his eyes streamed with tears as he stretched himself into the gap between two trams in order to retrieve the scraps of timber.

Suddenly he remembered that he hadn't sent a signal of eight to the haulage driver which meant that the haulage must not be operated until the signal of eight followed by another signal to move the journey was received. It was too late the trams without notice moved violently. Big Bob screamed out, Terry had heard the piercing scream. He pulled down on the signal wire and hung on it. Quickly he scrambled on his knees to where big Bob was trapped between two trams." Oh my god, I'll get help," he shouted, big Bob had fell unconscious blood was everywhere. Terry struggled to make sense of what had happened he was torn between two thoughts, out-bye to the telephone, or in-bye to the face where a first aider was working.

It was a long 300 yards as he scrambled almost like a monkey to where the telephone was situated by the haulage.

Willy Smith the haulage driver trembled as Terry pushed him out of the way. "Out of my way Smithy, Bob has had it! You... you moved the journey without a signal from me," he stuttered, Terry picked up the ear piece and turned the magneto handle furiously trying to get the phone to ring on the in bye side of the district where he knew a first aider would be working. Terry turned the handle until his hands ached with fatigue. "Come on – come on," he shouted, sweat ran from his cleft chin he attempted to wipe it away with the rolled up sleeve of his shirt. "The phone wire must have snagged, it's broke, Smithy make sure that this haulage Isolated from the power, I'll have to go into the face for help," he said, his voice trembled and his eyes filled with sweat.

"What's the matter here Terry, why aren't you getting supplies into the face?" said a voice. Terry turned to face his inquisitor it was Bernard Thomas, deputy of the district.

"Am I glad to see *you*! Bob is trapped under the journey, I can't contact the first aider because the phone cable has snagged on the journey," explained Terry almost in tears.

Big Bob lay between the trams unable to move he drifted from unconsciousness to delirium due to loss of blood, he called out weakly unable to comprehend what had happened he had lost all sense of time a minute seemed like an hour.

"Ok Bob, we're here now, don't move," called a distant voice.

Clive Pugh district first aider crawled cautiously through the narrow gap between the offending steel grey, grimy trams and the side of the roadway. He could see Preacher's legs poking out between trams about half way of the length of the journey. The first aider called out to him, big Bob did not respond, the first aider called again, big Bob groaned. "Ok Bob, I'm going to give you something for the pain, do you understand?" he asked loudly.

"Give me anything! God what have I done to deserve this," he sobbed. "Oh God… oh God!" Then he screamed out "Eli, lama sabachthani?" That is to say. My God, my God why have you forsaken me?

Clive Pugh, first aider injected an ampoule of morphine into Preacher's thigh. By an act of parliament only certain trained and qualified miners were allowed to administer morphine below ground.

Big Bob went quiet as the morphine took effect the first aider did his best under the circumstances. But how could they get the seriously injured miner out from between the derailed trams. Ianto Pugh team captain and brother to the first aider took charge. He began by issuing orders to the various men waiting for an order from someone.

"OK boys, go into the face and get me all the lifting equipment that you can lay your hands on, any chain, any lifting jacks, and hauling equipment," he ordered. Quickly the men made their way in search of the asked for equipment and before long they returned with anything that was portable.

Ianto Pugh put his plan into action he ordered that all the trams must be, secured, all rails on one side of the track should be unbolted and dismantled. The volunteers put their backs into the physically demanding work, the ingenious idea was working, one side of the track was dismantled allowing for the trams to slip off the rails, the trams then hauled by a Tirfor until they were clear of the casualty. Clive Pugh and his brother Ianto gently eased the trembling Bob Stephens away from the trams and onto a pre made piece of conveyor belt, there was no room for a conventional stretcher. Inch by inch they dragged the belt along the low, narrow, tightness of gap between trams and side of the roadway.

"The doctor is on his way he should be with us in about ten minutes," announced Bernard Thomas.

Doctor Philips, a broad shouldered white haired man called to big Bob." What's your name, sonny?" he waited for a reply.

Kneeling beside his patient he made his examination, big Bob had stopped haemorrhaging he was very weak but could reply to questions.

It was a long slog carrying a seriously injured man on a conventional stretcher. Undulating and uneven ground underfoot made the trek to pit bottom and then up the shaft to a waiting ambulance on the colliery surface a daunting proposition. Big Bob groaned as the stretcher unintentionally tilted and lurched carried by caring and loyal workmates. Doctor Philips studied his patient and from time to time. He would order the stretcher party to stop and lower the injured man to the floor resting him between the rails of the tramway. After making an examination Doctor Philips decided to administer another dose of painkiller. The trek from the site of the accident to pit bottom was about one and a half miles of pure torture as the miners worried and fretted over every obstacle they encountered.

The heavy steel door opened wide, the stretcher bearers shielded their eyes from the winter midday sun now low in the heavens. The doors of the ambulance were wide open in readiness as the ambulance men relieved the grateful bearers of their burden. Doctor Philips accompanied by Terry Powel got into the sterile vehicle and gave comfort to the injured man, big Bob, to the miners of Cwm Derw.

10:00 am Tuesday Morning

Terry Powel paced back and forth out-side Mr Mainwaring's office door. He had been given compassionate leave due to the nature of the serious accident that had happened the day previous. Harry Carter Lodge chairman sat to one side of the door marked simply *Mainwaring*. The door opened, Mr Mainwaring's short and stubby secretary John Fairburn called to Terry to 'come in.'

Harry Carter, lodge chairman representing the shaking Terry cautiously walked in to the Manager's office they could not fail to notice the framed staring ex-Managers of Cwm Derw colliery. "Take a seat Terry," said Mr Mainwaring, gruffly. "Mr HG Darlington Her Majesty's Inspector of mines will want to ask you a few questions regarding the accident involving Robert Stephens. I'm sorry we have to drag you here especially after the horrendous events of yesterday. It is essential in my way of thinking, that we ask questions while the event is still fresh in your memory, get it over with, if you'll excuse the terminology," said the nervous colliery Manager.

Mr HG Darlington sat alongside the Manager on one side of the large table that doubled as an office desk.

"Terry, we need to know exactly what happened yesterday morning in twenty sevens' district, "asked Mr Darlington. He viewed Terry with concerned eyes. Terry began to relive the events guided by Harry Carter.

"How's that chap, the one they call big Bob?" asked Ethel looking at Iolo over a steaming cup of tea. Iolo looked up from reading a newspaper.
"I phoned his sister earlier this morning, she told me that the surgeons did what they could and it was up to Robert to make a good recovery he'll never work again by the seem of things. He's a hell of a character you never knew what he was going to say next," said Iolo as he resumed reading the day's news.
"Bethan's David will never make the decision to go underground to work, after hearing about what happened to the big Bob, bloke," said Ethel after taking another sip of the steaming tea. "And another thing I've been meaning to mention, I've been having dirty looks over the shops. I think people are saying we aren't properly married," she said after taking another sip of hot tea.
"How do they reckon on that, I did everything I could to find Anwen. I put adverts in the papers and I also had them signed by the Justice of the Peace. The only thing I didn't do was hire a private detective, the prices they charge who wouldn't blame me," said Iolo, chuckling, his wide shoulders heaved as he raised the newspaper to his face.

Saturday 6th February

Once again the dreaded scarlet fever hit the Cwm Derw colliery. To the management it seemed like half the workforce had contracted scarlet fever, the production of coal however was only slightly affected.
Iolo watched the build-up to the Wales Scotland match on the television he listened as the commentator described the scene on Princess Street, Edinburgh "The march of the Welsh down Princess Street is like a sea of scarlet there is nothing like it in the whole world, from here to Murrayfield nothing but a sea of red."
Every drinking establishment for the whole length of Princess Street rang to the sound of Welshmen singing, Cwm Rhondda.

Wales had secured a sixth grand slam and won the 5 nation championship meaning that they had routed England, Scotland, Ireland and France.

When the elation of the magnificent triumph had cooled down, miners began to get that feeling that something must be done about their poverty wages. Joe Gormley was elected as the NUM president, most miners thought he would be too right wing and would not do them justice.

Monday February 15th

Caradog Pritchard ambled through the door of Cwm Derw workmen's club briefly scanning the room for his butty Fred Morgan. "Early this morning are you Caradog, wet the bed did you?" said Lil, club stewardess, grinning broadly as she searched for Caradog's personal pint pot. The smiling Lil; dexterously poured the amber liquid into the pot, finally pulling on the pump with quick short tugs. Caradog eyed the foaming pint with suspicion for on a Monday morning the beer lines were cleaned and Humphrey the steward had just finished; the crashing of empty beer bottles could be heard as he attempted to sort them for collection by the brewery wagon.

Lil placed the foaming pint onto the bar and then announced, "That's ten new pence please Caradog," he pulled out of his pocket an assortment of coins and unceremoniously placed them onto the nearest bar towel, staring at them with wide eyes. Lil eyed Caradog her big brown eyes laughed as she fished out a ten pence piece from the mixture of old pence and the new-fangled new pence.

"I wish governments wouldn't mess with our hard earned money, we've had pounds shillings and pence for hundreds of years, why change it now?" moaned Caradog, Lil continued to laugh as she rang up the cash register and almost threw the coin into its designated compartment.

Caradog strolled towards his usual seat near to the bay window carrying his pint pot awkwardly, almost spilling the contents onto the newly polished floor. He sat himself down and winced due to the pain of arthritis in his hip and left knee, and at the same time placing the amber liquid down onto a laminate table. Lil came over and handed him the morning's newspaper. "Here you are Caradog, you can train yourself to handle this new-fangled money system, the papers are full of it," she uttered as she returned to the bar, muttering.

Caradog picked up the newspaper and instinctively turned to the racing pages he had done this since a teenager.

An hour had passed in an instant as every word in the racing pages was digested and each race in every meeting had the potential winner underlined in pencil. Caradog looked up as the main door slammed shut and Fred Morgan waved with an arm and ordered his usual tipple.

"Bloody decimalisation, let sleeping dogs lay I say, Callaghan should have left well alone," complained Fred as he noisily took a sip from his pint glass of beer and ambled towards where Caradog was reading the newspaper.

Everywhere in Cwm Derw people were trying to get their heads around the new decimal system most people had no problem but the elderly just didn't want the system and were vociferous in their views.

April 19th Dayshift 27s District

It was grub-time and the men who worked the road head began to settle onto makeshift seats on the floor of the mine. Danny Wilmot the leading hand and considered to be something of an old codger sat silently chewing on a jam sandwich, his lined craggy face showed the hardships of coal mining and continual harassment by his better half. "This country of ours is getting in a bit of a state, a brand new government, it insists on poverty wages, over eight hundred thousand unemployed, and we are sat here on bits of wood eating dusty jam sandwiches, perhaps it's a good idea shutting the pits, I stopped my boys from working down this hellhole," he said and most of the men agreed and nodded accordingly.

"They say the safety record is improving, it would if you considered that
For the last four years the last government had shut down one pit every week, and I also read that from January nineteen seventy, to now... a hundred and twenty men were killed in our pits and about nine hundred were seriously injured, I'm glad that my boys' are working in god's clean air away from all this filth that we are sitting in," he frowned as he said it and the men nodded in agreement in the darkness

of the mine. The conveyors started up, throwing up fine clouds of dust and the men grumbled as they rose from the bits of timber that they were sitting on and made their way to the workplace that was dripping water from the roof and it stank of the filth that filtered down from old workings above.

Word had reached Danny Wilmot and his butties that Mr Mainwaring was visiting the district and was somewhere on the coalface. Voices could be heard, Danny recognised the gruff voice of Mr Mainwaring colliery Manager as he emerged from the face edge, his probe stick tapped at the hydraulic supports and he commented on the alignment of the props saying "What's going on here, deputy? Why are these props erected in the fashion of a dog's leg; how would you get a stretcher through here if a man were to be seriously injured?" he snarled and Bernard Thomas the deputy of the district looked away in embarrassment. " I'll see to it straight away Mister Mainwaring...Jim, come over here and re-erect these posts in accordance to the Manager's support rules," he called to a man who was shovelling coal in the stable hole making room for the revolving disc that was noisily gouging out a strip of coal off the coalface.

Mr Mainwaring stood on the structure that was covering the stage conveyor he eyed the skill that was employed in the forming of a part of the tunnel called the road-head and remarked about the alignment of that section of tunnel that was slightly out of line." What's happened here then Danny?" he called.

"The face conveyor is creeping from left to right   Mister Mainwaring, we can't do anything about it until the face conveyor is shortened," answered Danny, the Manager stared out into the roadway and shook his head and muttered something.

The burly colliery Manager ambled out of the district pointing his probe stick at various items as he shouted to his under-Manager Jack Williams who was following behind him.

Meanwhile on the surface of the colliery where we would assume nothing much could happen things were going badly wrong, out-side of the fitting shop, riggers were busily unloading a brand new tunnelling machine familiarly called a Dosco. Colin Wilde, colliery chief mechanic was busily issuing orders to the various men who were standing around the powerful lorry that had transported the huge machine to the colliery.

"I'm not happy with that chain on the left rear end, it looks as though one of the links has spread," he shouted to the lead rigger, the rigger stared at the offending length of heavy duty chain quizzically, and then proceeded to drag another length of chain to replace the one that had a bad link. The damaged chain was heavy as the rigger struggled to lift it off the thick strong hook; he hadn't heard the shouts of 'stand clear' as the crane's engine roared into life drowning out the voices of the shouting men. Suddenly without much warning the huge tunnelling machine began to move, the rigger jumped backwards falling off the lorry and onto the concrete floor below striking his head as he fell.

Colin Wilde rushed to his aid, the rigger was motionless and ashen faced as Colin Wilde stooped down and examined him briefly. "Can someone phone the medical centre, tell the attendant that a rigger has fallen from a lorry and may have a fractured skull," men ran for the phone and first aid equipment. The chief mechanic examined the pulse from the wrist and said to a man who had knelt beside him," pulse is rapid and weak," and promptly took off his Donkey jacket and placed it carefully over the injured rigger.

It was only moments later the colliery Manager emerged from the box pit shouting abuse at the men who were gathered around. "Why did this accident happen who's in charge around here?" he asked, gruffly and almost ran to the accident scene.

"I think he's fractured his skull and concussed, the medical attendant is on his way and I presume that an ambulance is imminent," explained Colin Wilde the chief mechanic.

"How on earth did this happen, Colin?" Asked the Manager exasperation showed on his face his wide ginger moustache quivered uncontrollably.

"I don't understand it! the man was attempting to exchange a damaged chain when the winch started up and the machine moved, the rigger tried to jump clear but fell off the lorry," the mechanic tried to explain. Trevor Bayliss medical attendant hurried up to the casualty pushing everyone out of the way.

"Can everyone get back please let the injured man get some air," he ordered, the area around the injured man immediately cleared and Mr Mainwaring pulled Colin Wilde to one side and spoke to him quietly. Within a minute an ambulance arrived.

Chapter XV

November 1971

Monday morning

Iolo Pritchard studied the stubble of beard in the shaving mirror, "Bloody NUM overtime ban starts today," he muttered to himself. Meanwhile Ethel busied herself in the neat small back kitchen merrily humming to a melody being played over the radio.

In the house of Caradog Pritchard, things were somewhat livelier in as much as Caradog was up a ladder trying to hang wallpaper and being directed by his wife Rowena "It's not straight, mun, take more care, come down let me do it!" she ordered and Caradog didn't argue he slowly descended the ladder holding his arthritic hip cursing mildly.

Outside, the wind blew in gusts; the autumn leaves swept up in swirls and settled in an untidy pile against the garden wall. Men were hurrying by, on their way to the Cwm Derw colliery some held their coats close to them as they tried to escape the icy blasts of the wind blowing from the north.

Iolo's shift began on a quiet note as production in the coaling districts went without any major hitches 'the calm before storm' as Iolo would say.

Iolo glanced at the large wood framed clock that hung on the wall to one side of the dusty old desk, "Half past six, things are too quiet something is going to go wrong," he muttered under his breath. He picked up the telephone and dialled the number that would connect him to the switchboard that was situated in the powerhouse. Percy Higgins answered the telephone and just happened to remark about the 'absence of problems' belowground.

"Iolo I'll have to cut you off there's an incoming call and it's coming from twenty sevens district," remarked the operator.

"Yes, yes, I'll... I'll organise it right away." Stuttered the operator and immediately telephoned the officials-lodge office. After receiving the seemingly urgent message Iolo raced towards the box pit, his flame safety lamp swung wildly from his lamp belt.

"Turn the pit over to man-riding," ordered Iolo, the banks-man stared at Iolo quizzically.

"What's the matter Iolo, trouble?"

"Aye, I'll say there is— a man is buried in twenty sevens district apparently he's under a hell of a fall... stones as big as a trams" remarked Iolo, looking worried he handed his flame safety lamp to the banks-man for him to examine as he had to do so by law.

"Oh my god our kid works in twenty sevens," said the banks-man looking more worried.

Meanwhile on the return side of the coalface at twenty sevens' men were shouting, lamps flashed like beacons in the darkness. Furious sounds of shovelling could be heard. Bernard Thomas crawled out from the face, sweat streamed from his blackened chin he looked extremely worried as he made for the pit telephone. Bernard turned the telephone magneto handle furiously, and spoke to into the phone, "where's Iolo Pritchard, pit Overman?" he demanded impolitely. In the distance a lone figure could be seen hurrying; Bernard guessed it was Iolo Pritchard. Iolo approached Bernard the sweat- drenched Overman looked worried as he rushed by the deputy to the edge of the face.

"How are things looking here?" enquired the exasperated Iolo. Ianto Pugh team captain spat onto the dusty floor of the mine and spoke.

"There's a blutty big stone lying across his leg, we can't tell if he's alive or not as there's muck all around him, he's not responded to our shouts, we have to be careful as there are blutty big stones hanging like coffins, this side of the pit must be jinxed" said the team captain looking in the direction of the fall area. Iolo looked away as if to say he knew what was jinxing the west side of the mine.

Iolo crawled to where the miner was buried he looked up and studied the hanging stones. Face-men were noisily clearing around the fallen stones with shovels while at the same time keeping an eye on the imminent danger above them. The unfortunate miner lay motionless only a leg was visible beneath a large long stone. Iolo listened intently for any sound other than the sound of shovelling. "Quiet, quiet!" shouted Iolo, earnestly. "Did you hear anything?"

asked Iolo while carefully listening for any sound coming from beneath the huge pile of muck and stones. The men replied that they didn't hear anything but the expression on his face said there was life under that pile of muck.

Bit by bit the debris was being cleared and suddenly someone shouted that he could see a face. Iolo stared at the place being pointed at by one of the face-men. "Yes you're right it's his face," exclaimed Iolo excitedly.

After many minutes had passed and the trapped miner could be freed, the men organised a temporary stretcher eventually ferrying the unconscious miner out of the coalface.

Doctor Philips duly arrived at the coalface, staring down at his patient he quipped, "I'm spending more time down this mine than a bloody collier." He knelt and examined the unconscious miner "It's a miracle that he survived the weight of the fall of debris," he remarked, "his breathing is rather shallow, he may have some fractured ribs, let's look at his left leg Hmm compound fracture. I'll strap him up and then we'll get him out of the mine," he said and within a few minutes the unconscious miner was on his way to the bottom of the shaft and then on to hospital.

Iolo sat at his desk thinking, he was beginning to take on the idea that the mine was jinxed, and Anwen and her lover was to blame, hardly a year went by without a serious incident of one kind or another. His thoughts turned to Ethel he wondered whether she would come to some harm but the malevolence seemed to be contained to the workings of Cwm Derw colliery, but according to Sod's law things could change, he reasoned. Would he ever be found out? Would the ghosts of the dead lovers point fingers at him and Ethel, he laid his head in his arms and cried.

Chapter XVI

January 1972

British mining was in turmoil, an overtime ban had been in force since November 1971. Then on January 5th the National Executive Committee of the NUM rejected a small pay rise from the National Coal Board, who then 2 days later, withdrew all pay offers from the last 3 months.

Monday 10th January

Iolo marched through the colliery gates amid shouts and good natured jeers from the miners who were picketing the colliery gates. The National Executive Committee of the NUM called out all its members as from Sunday 9th. Iolo belonged to the supervisors union NACODS this union had not called upon its members to withdraw their labour. NACODS members were essential to the safety of the mine in as much as all mine airways and pumping systems were to be maintained. Serious flooding and falls of roof were to be guarded against at all times. The mine should fit and safe in order that production be restarted should there be a settlement from the National Coal Board.

At first the miners picketed the coal fired power stations, but then their attentions turned to all power stations, steelworks, coal depots and other bulk coal users.

For the first time in their lives many men were required to give personal details to the government in order to receive benefits to keep their families, however strikers were not allowed to make a claim for them-selves.

Iolo wandered around the colliery surface, things were unusually quiet in spite of the absence of surface workmen, Pit headgear wheels stood motionless crows cawed noisily above.

Meanwhile the deputies were belowground maintaining the pumps and inspecting airways.

The mine's senior officials were gathered in the box pit waiting to descend the shaft, the banks-man although a NUM member, was given dispensation due to the nature of his work he was considered a safety worker.

"This dispute could go on for some time, I hear the coal stocks are pretty high the government has prepared for this strike," said Jack Williams.

"This is a bit of a novelty for most of the NUM, there are a few who can remember the nineteen twenty-six strike. Times were even harder in those days. Caradog my brother remembers the strike and often reminds me of it," Chuckled Iolo as he remembered.

Iolo and the under-Manager strolled around the mine workings taking notes of potential hazards and problems. Iolo stopped suddenly he was at the mouth of the old 26s return road. "Are you all right Iolo you look as though you've seen a Ghost?" asked the under-Manager looking concerned.

"I thought I smelled something burning, it must be my imagination this district holds bad memories for me," answered Iolo, the under-Manager sniffed and shook his head slowly and carried on walking.

"You said twenty sixes' held bad memories for you, Iolo, was it the explosion?" asked the under-Manager, stopping.

"I expect so, but other men have reported strange things like smells and sounds," remarked Iolo as he took longer strides in order to catch up with Jack Williams.

"Yes, I seem to remember men intimating that they might have seen a ghost or something," said a sceptical Jack Williams stifling a chuckle.

The mine seemed very quiet as Iolo and his companion sat down on a pile of stone-dust bags, sitting quietly they both heard sounds that normally went unnoticed during normal working conditions every crick of the roof every rush of water in the pipe that conveyed nuisance water from the districts and elsewhere could be heard. It was warm and very quiet. Iolo began to close his eyes as he sat in relative comfort on the pile of stone-dust bags; his head nodded in short jerks and he rocked slowly to and fro unaware that he was falling asleep. Jack Williams slapped Iolo hard on one knee, Iolo woke momentarily startled.

"Come on we must make a move, it's too comfy here. I want to see the stable hole in twenty sevens," said the under-Manager as he got up from where he had been sitting.

Inside twenty sevens district deputies were sat around, discussing the strike situation. As the under-Manager and Iolo came into view, cap-lamps flashed all around. "Everything ok lads?" enquired the under-Manager uncharacteristically smiling at them.

"No problems as yet, but anything could happen as this side of the pit seems to be jinxed," answered Bernard Thomas nervously.

"You can get the notion that this side of the pit is jinxed out of your heads, if anything happens you can bet that a man had a hand in it," replied the under-Manager sternly. The deputies looked away as they were convinced that something was causing the accidents below ground. Iolo uttered under his breath "and a bloody woman." Iolo and the under-Manager slowly crawled through the quiet coal face and from time to time they would stop and discuss the on-going strike and the consequences the men would encounter on their return to work.

"If the men are out for any length of time we can expect problems with the hydraulic fluid in the Powered support system," remarked the under-Manager looking concerned. "The soluble oil will separate out from the water, we can expect rust problems in the system," he announced.

"Yes...I see," replied Iolo thoughtfully rubbing his stubbly chin." How do you propose that we can get around the problem then?" said Iolo, wondering.

I'll put the problem to Mister Mainwaring, he'll have to contact the NUM officials and ask them for special dispensation," said the under-Manager.

Chapter XVII

Picketing Power Stations

"It's around here somewhere according to our kid," said Ianto Pugh, peering through the windscreen at Uskmouth power station. "There it is over by there, it must be that old caravan," he quipped, and pointed to a dilapidated caravan with a notice stuck in the misted up window. "Official Picket Line," said Ianto chuckling to him-self. "I hope they've got brewing equipment, I couldn't stay here all day without a brew, big Bob you can be chief tea maker a nice and easy job for you," said Ianto as he parked his old banger of a car. Big Bob sat in the back of the car he had come along for the ride and spend some time with his old work butties. Billy Wilkins and Dai Philips had also come along, picketing at the power station.

Other men were there already picketing, the lead man was from another colliery and was the NUM chairman for that colliery. "How do boys, you are from Cwm Derw colliery are you?" the lead man enquired.

"Aye, how have things been, any problems to report," asked Ianto he studied a log sheet that was hanging on the back of the door of the caravan.

"No problems, we haven't had many lorries this morning as you can see from the log sheet. All you have to do is flag down any lorry attempting to gain access to the power station through those gates over there, ask the driver what he's got on his lorry. If you don't believe him ask him for permission to have a peek at the load. If you find he's carrying any coal you have to try and persuade him to return to his employer and say he's unwilling to pass picket lines, and above all, you must make a note of all the waggon's registration numbers that you stop," said the chairman. "By the way my name's Gilbert and you have to sign the attendance sheet that's pinned to the back of the log, and have a nice day. There's plenty of tea in the caravan, you have to bring your own sugar and milk," he said and smiled as he made his way to his car with the other picketers.

Big Bob shook his head as he searched for milk and sugar. "There's no milk or sugar in here, how am I supposed to make god's brew without milk and sugar?" he shouted out of the caravan. Ianto poked his head around the door and briefly looked around the squalid conditions inside.

"I'll have to find a shop or something," said Ianto as he got into his car, he drove off beeping the car's horn as he went.

Dai Philips' ears picked up the sound of a diesel powered lorry the driver noisily changed down the gears and rounded the corner suddenly coming into view. Dai rushed out of the caravan and stepped dangerously into the path of the oncoming lorry. The driver applied the brakes slowly coming to a halt he smiled broadly as Dai climbed onto the step below the driver's door. "What are you carrying, driver, coal is it?" he asked naively.

"Nothing important," the driver teased. "You can have a look if you want."

Dai strained his wide neck trying to look into the back of the lorry. All the lorry was carrying was a machine part covered by a dirty old tarpaulin.

"Ok, driver, carry on," ordered Dai in an assertive manner. Traffic came and went, the picketers diligently stopped each vehicle on merit.

Big Bob was in charge of tea making and enjoying every minute of it.

"I could do this job lying on my back, how long do you think this strike will go on for, Ianto, six months do you think?" asked big Bob, anxiously.

"I don't know, it all depends on the level of support we get from other unions, all coal goes into the power stations by rail, If the rail unions come on our side it might last a couple of weeks, we'll have to wait and see," replied Ianto; he went quiet and stared blankly out of the caravan's murky window.

6pm

Big Bob stood at the door of the caravan and listened to the sound of an approaching car, as the car rounded the bend and came into sight he could see the faces of Cwm Derw miners. Clive Pugh brother of Ianto climbed out of the car, he stared at big Bob with utter disbelief. "Bob I thought that you had finished work due to your accident, how come you are here picketing?" he asked, disbelief showed in his voice.

"I only come for the ride mun, and already I've been promoted to god's brew maker," he answered and grinned.

"I thought so! The injuries that you sustained would have kept most men in bed for the rest of their lives," remarked the colliery first aider.

"Aye, it is only pain killers and good butties that keep me going," said big Bob smiling.

The shift change-over was executed after the exchange of news and Ianto briefed his brother to the ins and outs of picketing. It was now dark and the picketers sat in the caravan listening to a battery powered radio, but in the distant the sound of shipping could be heard as the night was very still even for the sound of distant machines working hard in the PowerStation.

The evening was long and dreary, the paraffin heater warmed the dilapidated caravan some of the picketers nodded and dozed while others whiled away the time with stories about the pit.

Wednesday 9th February

Iolo sat at the kitchen table listening to the radio, Ethel worked noisily at the kitchen sink while humming a tune and from time to time she would stop and stare at her husband. "Iolo I've been meaning to talk to you about..."

"Hush, the news is coming on," he commanded.

'The government today has announced that it is to introduce a three day week;' Iolo and Ethel listened intently to the news bulletin the idea of a three day week grabbed Ethel and unnerved her. She stared at Iolo her lower lip quivered she wrung her long elegant fingers nervously as she sat on a chair opposite her husband.

"Ethel what is the matter dear?" he asked as he turned his attention away from the radio.

"Yesterday I went to the doctor's...I've been meaning to speak to you since yesterday...I've got something to tell you," she said quietly. Iolo stared at her intently he went pale and his fingers trembled as they lay across the kitchen table.

"Ethel you are ok, are you? It's nothing serious is it?" He asked nervously. Ethel's lower lip quivered,

"I'm...I'm expecting," she blurted, her eyes filled with tears.

"You're expecting... what?" asked Iolo in an exasperated voice.

"I'm having our child," she shouted at him.

"Oh my god," screamed Iolo as he got off the kitchen chair and hugged and kissed her. Ethel wept and put her slender arms around his ample waist.

"Six weeks, I thought I was menopausal I'm only forty four, maybe god has blessed us," she whispered and Iolo lifted up his head stared up at the ceiling then closed his eyes in thanks.

The weeks went by; Ethel was again the talk of the village and she didn't care. The strike has ended and the miners were amongst the highest paid manual workers in the country.

Monday 28th February

Monday morning the colliery drive thronged with men returning to work after a seven week absence. In the pithead baths men complained loudly about the lack of heating, some of the men's working clothes were still damp from lack of heat inside the lockers. John Evans, bath's superintendent marched up and down taunting the miners. "you lot haven't worked for seven weeks, and you expect the heating to be on, it takes three or four days to get the system back up to temperature. You'll just have to grin and *bare* it," he said grinning broadly. The men continued to grumble and the air filled with the dank smell of the miners clothing.

Meanwhile in the officials' lodge the deputies and over-men were being debriefed by the under-Manager, Jack Williams. "Boys...this is the position as of the end of the night shift. The coal faces in general has stood up well during the last seven weeks, most of you inspected the faces so you know what to expect, but before you go down the pit... a word of advice… don't let the men leave the lamp stations until you have briefed your team captains as to what they will encounter when they get to the coal faces. The captains have had their orders in writing which were issued on their lamps in the lamp-room. They will discuss tactics with the team members while travelling." Explained the under-Manager, he knew the men and had the greatest of confidence in them.

The Cwm Derw mine had recovered from the hardships caused by the striking miners but the officials still had concerns regarding the jinx which seemed to reside in the west side of the mine.

Late March

Caradog Pritchard sat in the hut on the allotments he had been working leisurely preparing the ground for planting vegetables. It was warm and cosy, the coal fired stove glowed kindly, his tired head nodded in the warmth of the hut. A couple of flagons of home brew lay at the side of his comfy armchair. Suddenly someone rapped loudly on the heavy wooden door, Caradog sat up quickly. Fred Morgan stood at the door a brand new pint glass held firmly in his large fist he, grinned at his butty. "Fred, mun I thought the under-Manager had caught me nodding off," he joked. Fred sat in the armchair on the other side of the glowing stove. Caradog reached for a flagon of home brew and began to fill Fred's brand-new beer glass.

Fred held up the glass of beer and peered at it with concerned eyes, "clear as a summer's day but a tad warm," he criticised.

"Aye, I'll have to find a way of keeping the beer, cool," said Caradog unsmiling and deep in thought. The day passed by peacefully as the tipsy pair drank the warm homebrew.

The evening was dark but the nights were drawing out as the drunken pair attempted to lock-up for the day.

Curtains twitched as people peered out at Caradog stepping two forward and three back. The heavens opened up as Caradog slowly made his way home. Rain gushed down the gutters, raindrops as large as garden peas bounced off the pavement. Caradog was soaked to the skin; the pensioner was tired, drunk, and far from home as he staggered onwards towards his house. He tried to grab a fence post and fell heavily onto the rain sodden pavement. He attempted to get to his feet but it was too much he collapsed and laid still on the pavement, the rain hammered down relentlessly.

Ethel studied Iolo with concerned eyes as he put on his raincoat and whistled to Judy his faithful and aging cocker spaniel. "There must be something wrong with your head going out on a night like this!" scolded Ethel, Judy sniffed at Iolo's heavy raincoat excitedly.

"I like walking in the rain it clears my head said Iolo, any way Judy hasn't been for a walk for a couple of days, it's about time we went," said Iolo as he opened the door and studied the down pour.

"Be it on your own head and remember your unborn child," said Ethel, she wrung her fingers nervously and watched as Iolo and Judy disappeared into the torrential rain.

Iolo whistled a tune as Judy sniffed at garden hedges her stubbly tail wagged as she went from garden to garden. Suddenly as if she had disturbed a wild rabbit she yelped excitedly and barked at something that looked like a pile of old rags. Iolo grew concerned as Judy never yelped or barked when walking the streets. Iolo stooped and examined the bundle of soaking wet rags that lay before him. Looking more closely he could see that the bundle of wet rags had grey hair. He called to the crumpled figure there was no answer, gently he turned the body onto its side and swept away the grey hair from its face. The craggy face stared up at him with pleading eyes. Iolo looked more closely, it was the face of his brother— his lips moved as if to say something. "Caradog, oh my god!" shouted Iolo, he shouted for help but no one heard him, he had to do something fast. The life of his brother was at stake. Iolo looked up through the rain that ran off his worried brow there was a light in a window he had to get help somehow.

Iolo hammered at the wooden door with all his might. A voice called out. "All right I'm coming," door bolts were being undone with urgent metallic slams. The door opened and a face peered through the gap." What do you want?" the man asked. Iolo recognised the face it was that of Billy Parfit who at one-time hated the colliery bosses. "Oh, it's you Iolo, what is the hammering for?" he queried.

"It's my brother he's fallen down drunk, I need to get him inside, can you help?" pleaded Iolo, his eyes said more than pleading words. Mrs Parfit came to the door clutching her woollen cardigan close to her.

"Oh, it's you Iolo Pritchard! What do you want, what is the matter? She asked sternly.
"Caradog has fallen down drunk and I need to get him inside out of the rain, can you help?" he pleaded again.

"We have no phone here, you'll have to go over to the village and use a public telephone box," she said and pushed Iolo out of the way and hurried to where Caradog had floundered.

"You two, come and give me a hand and get this poor man inside the house," she called in a demanding voice.

An ambulance duly arrived and Caradog was taken to the infirmary at Graig Ddu. Mrs Parfit waddled through the heavy rain her short legs hurried as fast as they could carry her. After one short tap on the door of Iolo Pritchard's house the door flung open and Ethel stood in the doorway. "Oh, I thought it was Iolo, he left his keys on the kitchen table," she said in a surprised voice. Judy ran in and almost knocked Ethel over. "Where's Iolo?" asked Ethel in a panicky voice.

Mrs Parfit explained everything to Ethel. The two anxious women went and gave the bad news to Rowena and offered comfort.

Rowena Pritchard stood on her doorstep wringing her hands as Ethel and the wife of Billy Parfit hurried up the garden path to the front door. "Hello Ethel, you haven't seen my drunken husband have you?" she asked, the worrying showed in her eyes. Ethel ushered her indoors and sat her down on an old shabby sofa.

Ethel began to unfold the events that led up to the accident that befell Caradog. Rowena suddenly straightened her narrow back and sat bolt upright. She quickly folded her arms and began issuing a tirade of abuse at her absent husband. "That no good son of a colliers shovel will pay for this when I catch hold of him," she hissed, the other women could see and feel her anger. Then a gleam appeared in Mrs Parfit's eyes as she remembered her husband, Billy, telling her of the 'overheard' conversation on the coach returning from the miners outing to the races some time back.

"Aye, he's never been any use to you girl, even during the war years he had an eye for the ladies and a half empty beer glass in one hand," informed the treacherous Mrs Parfit. Ethel looked away sheepishly as she remembered Iolo telling her the story and how her sister had a narrow escape from the lecherous Caradog Pritchard. Mrs Parfit had delighted herself in telling the story of Caradog's wartime philandering and now Rowena had an English stepson she never knew she had.

Rowena sat on the sofa her lip trembled she attempted to say something but she couldn't get her words out, Ethel put an arm around her and comforted her.

"I'm always last to know anything, nobody says anything to me they just snigger behind my back," she blurted out loud. Mrs Parfit grinned slyly but the grin slowly disappeared and a sorry gaze filled her eyes. The consequences of her action began to take hold. Rowena had broken down and sobbed uncontrollably.

Mrs Parfit quickly left the house of Mr and Mrs Caradog Pritchard leaving Ethel and Rowena in the now quietness of the house just waiting for something from Iolo.

Chapter XVIII

Caradog recovers

Caradog Pritchard recovered from his drunken predicament, doctors warned him that he must cut down on his alcohol consumption or next time he may not be so lucky. Rowena confronted the hapless Caradog about his wartime philandering, he thought that it was fate that exposed the existence of a son. Rowena suggested contacting the woman concerned and see what would follow.

Ethel was now into her sixth month of pregnancy, doctors had told her that all was well considering her advanced age of forty four, and the talk in the village was that she might be carrying twins.

Iolo stared intently at the brand new aneroid barometer that was fastened to the wall of the officials' lodge office. He raised his right hand and tapped at the face of the glass, the pointer moved fractionally Iolo gave a faint grin as the pointer indicated a rise in atmospheric pressure. Miners dreaded a fall in atmospheric pressure none had forgotten the explosion of the 3rd May 1968 not least Iolo. He put on his donkey Jacket after informing the power house attendant that he was about to go down the mine.

Iolo pulled on the door lever that released air pressure allowing him to enter the airlock, on entering the low pressure side he was met by the banks-man who held out his hand, Iolo handed him his flame safety lamp, the banks-man examined the lamp briefly and then began to blow around the glass checking for leakages. He had to do this according to mining law: if the flame contained behind the glass had flickered whilst being blown by the breath of the examiner the lamp would be condemned and the user would have to seek a replacement via the lamp-room.

Iolo was the sole rider in the cage, and every sort of unusual noise un-nerved him, the carriage swayed and clicked as the guide ropes crashed against the friction boxes bolted to the corners of the steel carriage. The dank odour from the mines workings wafted up in the warm air current, Iolo was immune to the smells of the mine as he had many years of experience, most smells generally went unnoticed except for the ghostly whiffs of Anwen and Maldwyn, lovers long dead in the gob of 26s.

Iolo ambled along the return airway on the west side of the mine hands behind his back and taking mental notes as moseyed inwards, he sniffed the air like a dog, it was now a habit.

In the distant a cap-lamp seemed to hover, Iolo covered his cap-lamp lens with a hand, the light ahead stayed motionless he had satisfied his curiosity it was not a reflection of his own lamp on a distant sign or glass-sight aperture on an electrical transformer. Iolo walked onwards slowly, he deliberately kept the beam of his lamp to the floor of the mine. However the distant lamp stayed lit and motionless, he wondered who it could be, perhaps it was Bernard Thomas deputy of twenty sevens district.

As Iolo fixed his eyes on the lamp the light suddenly disappeared only the darkness of the mine remained. Iolo was dumfounded he could not explain why the mysterious light had vanished he walked more quickly hoping to catch up with whoever or whatever it was.

Iolo sat on a makeshift seat and wiped away the sweat from his brow, then suddenly he heard the doors in the crosscut opening and closing he waited in anticipation as to who it could be.

"Oh, it's you Iolo!" said Bernard Thomas. "I wondered who was going through the crosscut doors in front of me," he remarked quietly.

"I haven't been through the doors!" replied Iolo with some indignation "I thought it was you!" he accused.

"When I entered through number one door I heard number two or three door closing. It wasn't caused by shot firing because I'm the only official this side of the pit issued with detonators, so who *did* go through the crosscut doors?" asked Bernard, a thoughtful expression appeared on his dusty face. He then removed his spectacles and began to clean them.

"Yes, very queer, it must have been the man who walked in front of me earlier said Iolo as he began to explain what had happened as he walked up the return roadway.

"What man was that?" wondered Bernard Thomas; out loud." No one has informed me that they wanted to come into my district, not even one of the services bosses," said Bernard his face took on a mesmerised expression.

Bernard and Iolo never discovered the phantom miner, and the episode was soon forgotten about.

As Iolo travelled 27s gate road he kept a bosses eye on the fast flowing coal being transported on the belt conveyor. Iolo smiled to himself as he always did when things were going smoothly, but today things were not going to be so straight forward as one might think. He was noticing tell-tale marks on the conveyor belt, long thin black lines of small-coal stretched as far as the eye could see in the darkness, Iolo's face took on a worried expression the brisk ventilation had slowed, the ambient air seemed warmer, he began to perspire as he had previously been cool due to the ventilation being efficient. Iolo began to quicken his step he had guessed correctly at what had happened; suddenly he was faced by a wall of coal spillage a large lump of coal had jammed between pipes and the fast moving conveyor belt. Iolo had no idea of the extent of the spillage, could it be twenty or thirty yards or so? He pulled sharply on the signal pull-wire the conveyor should have stopped abruptly but it carried on moving, by now the volume of air in the spillage area struggled to pass over the blockage, the wind whistled as it now tore itself through the very narrow passage over the conveyor belt. Iolo raced out-bye towards the conveyor drive pulling hard on the signal wires as he passed them. Nearing the mouth of the gate road he screamed at the conveyor attendant to stop the belt. Sweat ran down his broad features as he raced to the pit telephone, he cranked the magneto handle vigorously but he failed to get a response.

Mikey Thomas the conveyor attendant commonly called 'button boy' was sent into the tail road of 27s, he was to inform the district officials of the mass spillage. Communication was broken somewhere under the spillage, there was no way anyone could contact the people at the face as the telephone cable was probably broken.
Meanwhile at the coalface the team captain vainly cranked the telephone the experienced miner guessed what had happened as he shone his cap-lamp along the conveyor he could see that the conveyor belt had risen up on one side, big lumps of coal had pushed the belt over to one side. Within minutes men were at the scene shovelling away at the spillage trying to get the conveyor moving in a flat and even kind of manner. Lamps flashed like beacons as the miners tore at lumps of coal, an electrician ran a temporary signal wire over the

spillage area he had to try and get it all working satisfactory so as men could work in safety.

Eventually the miners managed to shovel the huge spillage back onto the conveyor belt the ventilation then improved and a possible methane gas build up was prevented.

Iolo sat on a pile of stone-dust bags near the tail end of the coal face he was talking to Bernard Thomas. "Nothing seems to go well in this district, it's like the place is jinxed," remarked Bernard he frowned as he said it.

"Aye you can say that again, but Jack Williams wouldn't agree with us," said Iolo, he grinned faintly, just then a loud bang was to be heard. "Dagnabit the panzer chain has snapped yelled Iolo the men in the stable hole stopped the Panzer conveyor. The name panzer is derived from German and in mining it refers to an all steel chain conveyor. This was another episode in the catalogue of jinxes attributed to the west side of the mine. Iolo stayed at the coal face for a while and then gave a verbal briefing to senior management via pit telephone.

Meanwhile at Iolo Pritchard's house Ethel was experiencing abdominal pains she wondered whether it was the beginning of labour pains as she was nearly 38 weeks gone. Daughter, Bethan was due to call and Ethel was worried that she would be late, the pain was getting worse. Ethel heard the doorbell ringing loudly and guessed that it might be her daughter, Bethan, slowly and painfully she made her way to the door and let Bethan in.
"Mam, are you ok you're not in labour already are you?" she probed.
"I'm not sure, thirty-eight weeks and something's going on, I may be in slow labour, what should I do?" Ethel Asked looking very worried.

"I'll phone the hospital at Graig Ddu," said Bethan in an urgent sort of voice. Bethan phoned the hospital and asked for advice.

An ambulance arrived at the Pritchard's household, Ethel went on her way and Iolo was informed of the position regarding Ethel's 'labour'.

Chapter XIX

Iolo bach

Iolo and the family visited Ethel in the maternity ward at Graig Ddu hospital, Iolo glanced out of the window the sun shone brightly and for the first time in a while Iolo felt pleased about something. Ethel held Iolo bach close to her; the ward was warm and smelled nice and clean.
 Big Iolo held out a large finger Iolo bach seemed to grip it firmly, Ethel smiled and said. "He's got all his fingers and toes, and the doctor said that he could find nothing wrong," she looked to where the 'new father' was sitting and smiled broadly at him. "Our life's perfect now," she said quietly and kissed Iolo bach fondly on the forehead. Iolo thought for a moment, the past suddenly flashed before his eyes Ethel noticed that something was going on in that big head of his, she almost guessed that it was the murder of Anwen Pritchard and her lover Maldwyn Evans.
 More than a week had passed Ethel and her baby were discharged from the maternity ward at Graig Ddu hospital.

Meanwhile Iolo had started back to work at Cwm Derw colliery and was greeted by one and all as big *daddy* and offered him sweets and chewing tobacco, the chewing tobacco was always refused as Iolo could not stand the stuff.
 Mr Mainwaring called Iolo into his office and Iolo naturally thought that he was to be congratulated on the birth of his son Iolo bach, but it was not to be.
 "Iolo you've probably been wondering why I've called you into this office today," said Mr Mainwaring in a quiet sort of voice. "As you know the west side of the pit has been letting the side down, the east side of the mine has been carrying twenty sevens for some time now and the men there are saying why should they be carrying the pit. The west side should pull their socks up so to speak," he said as he paced the floor of the office. "Iolo, I've heard about the so called jinx that the men say is plaguing the west side of the mine, Jack Williams is adamant that the problems are of the men's doing, and not some jinx. I need your input on this, I spoke to Jack Williams this morning and he suggested that we call a consultative meeting between the face men

and the officials of the west side of the pit. This is anticipated to be a Saturday morning or a time best suited to the men. Can I have your thoughts on this?" asked the troubled Manager.

Iolo stared at the Manager, he had to give his opinion and decided that he should give his opinion in no uncertain terms.

"I'll speak to the face captains and arrange for a meeting here in this office on Friday next between shifts," said Iolo, loudly. He turned and left the Manager's office closing the door behind him. Iolo acted fast, he marched to the lamp-room and spoke to the head lamp-man, the afternoon team captain's lamp was to be stopped and he was to receive written information that he was to see Iolo Pritchard senior Overman before going down the mine.

Iolo waited patiently for the day and afternoon shift team captains to make an appearance. They duly arrived coincidently together. Ianto Pugh and Dickey Watts stood at the desk of Iolo Pritchard. "You wanted to see us did you Iolo?" asked Ianto looking concerned.

"Aye," answered Iolo eying the captains. "Mister Mainwaring is concerned that the performance of twenty sevens is disappointing, he needs to find out what is causing the delays and mishaps that seem to be plaguing the west side of the pit, he is saying that the men on the east side of the pit are complaining that they are carrying you lot on the west side. So he is calling a meeting in his office on Friday next at twelve noon," said Iolo smiling faintly.

"It's that blutty jinx, mun, we're being plagued by that blutty jinx, nothing has gone right since the explosion, it's like the ghosts of all those men killed come back to haunt us," explained Ianto Pugh.

"Aye that's more like it," said Dickey Watts, frowning.

"Jack Williams blames the men working on the west side of the mine," said Iolo.

"We'll see about this on Friday, something is going on and it's not our fault," hissed, Ianto. "Come on Dickey, I want to say something but not in front of an official," urged Ianto.

Outside of the officials' lodge, Ianto Pugh gathered all the available men who were about to go down the mine. "Gather round, boys, we seemed to have been blamed for all the problems on the west side of the pit, it's like this, see, old Mainwaring the Manager is intent on putting the blutty fault on us, regarding the lack of production, he has called a consultative meeting for Friday afternoon between shifts, me and Dickey Watts will be standing on the blutty big wide belt that he calls a carpet. He expects answers and he'll not hear a word about blutty ghosts and jinxes. So, boys we'll give him some facts, we'll discuss it when we go down the pit, walls have ears I can see some ears flapping already," remarked Ianto as he thumbed in the direction of a window.

The banks-man watched as the pit cage began to lower, the men on board were shouting and swearing oaths, the voices were getting fainter as the cage descended into the darkness of the pit shaft. Meanwhile Charlie Dicks On-setter, pit bottom, commonly called the hitcher listened as the men were continuing the argument. As the cage landed he grinned at the arguing miners. "Trouble is there, boys? Sounds like they'll be shutting the pit before long, the west side of the pit is not pulling its weight so I hear," he said; and grinned as he said it. The men brushed by the On-setter and his insidious remarks, still arguing and shouting.

Manager's office Friday afternoon

Ianto Pugh and Dickey Watts paced back and forth outside the general Manager's office. Dickey Watts caught sight of his own reflection in the glass covered notice board. "Good god, mun, I look a sight. I've only half washed my face, a bloody panda is me by the look of it!" He said in exasperation.

Ianto grinned at him and said " that's going to be the least of your troubles if we don't persuade old Mainwaring that the problems of this pit is his own doing... then we're finished," said Ianto as he put an ear to the Managers door. The Manager's door opened abruptly and the short stubby frame of John Fairburn the Manager's secretary looked round the door." Ok, boys, the Manager is ready now," he said and beckoned to the captains to come into the office. Ianto and Dickey went through the door, in front of them were two chairs set back from the Manager's hefty old table that acted as a desk.

"Sit down boys, is it tea or coffee?" asked John Fairburn as he went over to the window where a large tray of steaming coffee and tea was waiting. After a few pleasantries and the captains were settled; Jack Williams came into the office knocking loudly on the thick wooden door, he sat alongside Mr Mainwaring and promptly took a large sip of coffee from an ancient looking mug.

"Right, boys, you must know why you are here," said the Manager where- upon the captains pulled up their chairs and placed them right next to the table. Mr Mainwaring grinned faintly he knew he was in for a hard time.

"Mister Mainwaring," said Ianto his face took on a seriousness that belied his voice. "This pit has had its problems, what with the explosion in May nineteen sixty-eight and the number of serious accidents that has happened recently, the men are quite rightly jumpy when things don't go the way they planned." said Ianto taking his time and thinking like a chess player.

"Now, boys, please don't expect us to believe that jinxes are at work in the west side of the mine, when things don't go to plan you can bet a human being had a hand in it at some-time or another," said Jack Williams, looking serious.

"If you remember, mister Williams, the twenty sevens district replaced the successful twenty six district, the reason that twenty six district was successful was that the whole installation was brand new except for the so called self-advancing supports. Yes, the brand new face chain broke from time to time, so did the power loader but we overcame the problems of logistics and such. As for the present twenty sevens district the whole installation was second-hand, it was paid for by some other pit up in England I shouldn't wonder," said Ianto becoming irate at the thought.

Mr Mainwaring's bushy moustache bristled as he countered the statement made by Ianto Pugh team captain of twenty sevens district.

"Now look here, Ianto Pugh, that chain was inspected and tested at NCB engineering works before it went down the pit— are you insinuating that a jinx or something weakened it?" Countered the Manager; using accusing tones.

"No! — We're saying, that the NCB were expecting a cheap installation with the added potential of the old twenty six's performance record, and I speak for all the men on the west side of the pit," said Ianto, staring intently at the red faced Manager. The Manager thumped hard on his desk with a large freckled fist.

"There's nothing wrong with twenty sevens equipment, maybe you are trying too hard, trying to get the machinery to do work that it isn't designed to do," said the Manager raising his already loud voice.

"Mister Mainwaring, loud voices have never frightened me, and I still say that we are working with blutty inferior machinery, if there are jinxes then the jinxes are the work worn equipment its self," said Ianto trying hard not to get ruffled. Mr Mainwaring began tapping the desk with the end of a pencil he looked to where Jack Williams the colliery under-Manager was sitting.

"What's your thoughts on the matter, Jack, do you think that we installed inferior equipment?"

"I have always stated that there is no jinx at work on the west side of the mine, when something goes wrong you can bet a human had a hand in it, and we must educate the workforce in this respect," stated the under-Manager smiling faintly. Ianto was not to be out done, he reached inside his jacket and pulled out a dog eared notebook he opened it to the first page.

"When I was appointed a team captain some years ago I began to keep a diary of events and such, this note book contains entries that I made when twenty sevens district was in the development stage, and twenty sixes was coming to the end of its working life. This is what I wrote. 'Trams are being loaded with panzer chain, most of the chain is already work worn, a lot of the couplers have spread and worn almost flat, trams are marked for twenty sevens district.' Here is another entry that I made, 'I see that flat trolleys have been loaded with face side pans some have been salvaged from elsewhere.' That is only the first page or so... I can go on if you like," said Ianto with a gleam in his eye.

Mr Mainwaring gripped the pencil tightly, nervously tapping on the table with it; it then snapped in half, Ianto grinned and turned to Dickey Watts tapping at the ankle of his colleague. It was Dickey's turn to make a statement or two, and he began to speak his mind.

"About those accidents, the ones that seriously injured our colleagues, some men said that the terrible accident that big Bob Stephens suffered was an accident waiting to happen," blurted the irate miner. "The planners of twenty sevens plotted one roadway, to run too close to its neighbour, that's what caused the floor heave... the district should have been stopped for repairs," he blurted again. "And another thing, when that man got buried on the afternoon shift, *that* could have been avoided, the hydraulic props were faulty, they were 'giving off' they were reported on the pre shift inspection sheets but nothing seemed to be done about it," explained Dickey Watts. Mr Mainwaring looked down at his desk thinking and then he looked to Jack Williams his under-Manager.

"Jack can you dig out the mines and quarries records for twenty sevens district," asked the Manager. The under-Manager left the office in search of the relevant records regarding the accidents that occurred in twenty sevens district.

Chapter XX

Christmas 1972

Miners were enjoying the rewards of the last strike and it was reflected in the way that Christmas was being celebrated, the best Christmas in years.

Meanwhile at Iolo Pritchard's house, Ethel and daughter Bethan were busy in the kitchen preparing the lunch and humming to Christmas carols that were being sung on the radio. Iolo and stepson in- law David were looking after the children Iolo bach and Guto bach by playing and showing the children the merits of various toys that littered the lounge floor.

Meanwhile at the house of Caradog Pritchard all was not as well as previous years, the master of the house was under orders, wife Rowena had not forgotten the drunken incident earlier in the year. "You know you're getting older, you just can't take the booze the same way as you used to, do you think that you could take your time for once in your life, and remember you- are –an- old age- pensioner," she scolded, arms folded high on her bosoms.

"Ok love, I'll do my best... I'll have no more than four pints of ale and come home stone cold sober," said Caradog he looked at his wife with sheepdog eyes as he put on his coat and went quietly through the door.

The door of the Cwm Derw workmen's club opened, Lil the stewardess turned her head just as Caradog stepped through the door; she grinned broadly and shouted: "Look who's here boys it's homebrew Pritchard," The members applauded loudly as Caradog stood by the bar grinning toothlessly. Men came up to him and patted him on the shoulder saying 'long time no see' Fred Morgan called to his lifelong butty and Caradog wasted no time in getting to his once usual seat in the bay window.

Time seemed to stop as Caradog tried to take his time, to others who knew him well, he looked miserable as he took tiny sips of beer from his personal beer glass and as usual the club began to carry out its time honoured tradition of carol singing. Caradog looked up at the clock that hung on the wall above the bay window. "One o'clock and already I'm on my third pint," he said to Fred who looked at his butty with some concern.

"One or two pints won't hurt you, mun, why don't you have a drop of short with your next pint," said Fred trying to be helpful and Caradog took on a frightened look.

As the cheered drinkers were leaving the workmen's club Caradog and Fred exchanged Christmas greeting cards. It was a long time since Caradog went home from the workmen's club almost sober, the thought of his wife Rowena never left his head or the consequences of going home drunk especially on a Christmas day.

Twenty sevens district prematurely came to the end of its working life, the coal face suffered from geological faulting making it impossible for the west side of the mine to make any viable headway. The mine was now totally dependent on its productive east side. Three-shift coaling was introduced.

Mr Mainwaring was transferred to another coal mine somewhere in England. Cwm Derw now had a new general , Mr Cledwyn Jenkins who had a reputation for being ruthless.

Development on the west side of the mine was stepped up, the push was now on and the new colliery Manager pushed men and officials as hard as he was allowed to under mining law.

Mr Jenkins put pressure on the development teams and their officials, wanting progress reports every half hour. Iolo Pritchard was now down the pit every day as the general Manager wanted no down time regarding the supply of equipment. Iolo was busier than ever organising and keeping up to date with production news from the east side of the mine and speaking to management whenever he could.

At the intake side of the of the twenty eight district now under development advancement was going well, only ten yards to go before the face of the drivages' would meet hopefully on the centre line.

March, one Monday morning

The miners of Cwm Derw had been under extreme pressure from management it had been, make or break time. If the miners had failed to respond to the pressures of management the colliery would have been deemed *doomed to failure* and yet another colliery closed; but the men were made of sterner stuff. Working around the clock the miners pulled out all the stops, the new installation was almost complete and the new general Manager Cledwyn Jenkins was visiting the twenty eights district prior to the commissioning of the new installation.

Ianto Pugh turned his attention to the cluster of lamp lights that flashed around the new machinery. Although the new general Manager and his companions the NUM lodge officers,' under-Manager Jack Williams and deputy Manager Fred Bishop were some distance away, their voices could be clearly heard by Ianto as he waited to meet them. "Not a bad job here, mister Bishop, shouldn't be long now before we can begin coaling," said the Manager, loudly.

"Yes, the men responded well to the applied demands made by management," replied the deputy Manager. Harry Carter NUM lodge chairman said: "Aye, we saved the colliery and hundreds of jobs." Mr Jenkins general Manager eyed Harry Carter cautiously.

"We are not out of the woods yet, this district and its men have yet to prove themselves. We have a lot of lost time to make up for, time is now of the essence," he said in a voice that sounded gruff and serious.

"Refurbished chocks and a brand new armoured face conveyor is just what we needed, it's a pity that it wasn't a consideration when the old twenty sevens was planned and installed," said Ianto who was never afraid to speak his mind.

"Yes, we'll leave all that in the past, we must now concentrate on the future of Cwm Derw colliery, this installation has placed a heavy burden upon us all, we must now begin to repay our dues," said Mr Jenkins.

By the end of the week, twenty eights district was ready to make its first cut of coal, the engineers had finalised the fitting of embellishments to the two— bi -directional power loaders the first of their kind at Cwm Derw but had been in use in most of the English coalfields for some years. Iolo Pritchard senior Overman was sent to twenty eights to oversee the first cut of coal.

The armoured face conveyor was running smoothly the power loading discs were spinning, intermittent thunderous churning sounds filled the air, the power loader operators began to move the huge machines. The spiral discs started to gouge out a strip of coal and the armoured face conveyor began to be filled high with coal— like a long mountainous carpet. Iolo stood at the tipping point, the point where the coal emptied onto the wide belt conveyor, Iolo and the district Overman Joe Watkins grinned at each other as the coal made loud thumping noises as it tipped onto the belt.

After watching the results of a few months toil and perspiration Iolo went to the pit telephone and informed Mr Jenkins general Manager that the face started up with no problems, coal was coming thick and fast and out-side bunkers were ready and waiting for the deluge.

The out-side bunkers were capable of storing up to two hundred tons of cut coal. The massive hydraulic drives hauled the heavy duty chain inch by inch, creaking and groaning; the coal packed the high metal walled storage machine. The only drawback now was the shaft's capacity to wind coal by the ancient and time honoured tram filling. The installation of automatic skip winding was planned for the summer when the miners would be taking their annual holidays. Skip winding would increase the production capacity by many hundreds of tons, eliminating the need to tediously fill the unreliable supply of trams.

Twenty eights district was proving a success and was breaking production records only a few weeks after its commissioning. Cwm Derw was on the road to recovery and its future was guaranteed for the foreseeable time ahead and skip winding would put the icing on the cake.

August 1973

Traditionally the Cwm Derw miners took their annual holidays on the last week of July and the first week of August. Iolo and his family had decided to take the holiday at a later date due to the massive amount of work that was to be carried out namely the installation of automatic skip winding in the downcast shaft and Iolo was ordered to work during this period as he was to see that no work underground would cause any impedance to the on-going works.

The installation company had good weather on their side which was unusual for Cwm Derw as it seemed to be always raining.

Iolo and Ethel along with Iolo bach had booked a holiday in Rhyl, north Wales and Ethel was looking forward to going away for two weeks as she had relatives living in Rhyl and had not seen them for many years.

Monday morning two weeks later

The pithead baths was hive of activity as the miners filed through the doors carrying their sacks of fresh work clothes. Men were busy loosening the hardened small-coal that had accumulated inside their working boots by banging them hard on the concrete floor. New socks had replaced the tattered olds ones, a few men now sported an old suit that stood out as they looked more like Managers than face workers and the like.

On the pit yard out side of the box pit or upcast shaft, men gathered all fresh faced and ready to face the uncertainties of underground work. Jack Williams the under-Manager stood outside the officials' lodge office watching the men coming down the steep long steps from the pithead baths. Some men were curious and wandered over to the south or downcast shaft to take a look at the new automatic skip winding system. "They tried this system at another pit and they shut it just after," said a man wearing a newish suit some men agreed and muttered as they walked away.

The pit hooter blew a long blast sounding like an ocean going liner, the blast echoed up the valley and could be heard in Cwm Derw village. Jack Williams shouted to the men, "come on you eager beavers, down the pit please we have a new skip winding system to pay for," some men shouted back in good humour 'ten bob a week should see us through a few years then' some men laughed loudly at the aside.

As the weeks rolled from summer into winter the miners were grumbling yet again, they were falling behind in the wages league; from first in 1972 to eighteenth in 1973, inflation was eating away at their income. The mining unions saw that the poor economic situation might be used in their favour as the Arabs and Israelis were at war and was the cause of soaring oil prices. Relations between the industrial unions and Government were strained as the government were attempting pay freezes and economic restraints to help the country.

Cwm Derw miners were now being asked to vote in favour of industrial action. Many men were mindful of the consequences of withdrawing their labour as the colliery was going through an economic transition. Tremendous costs were imposed on the Cwm Derw mine as it attempted to pull out of the impending closure caused by the failing twenty sevens district.

Iolo held out his newspaper at arms-length and read out the headline news. "Miners vote for strike," he said in a quiet voice. Ethel listened as she held a spoon to Iolo bach's mouth.

"Will it be like the last strike?" asked Ethel with a worried look in her eyes. "I was very nervous as you being on another union NACODS," she added.

"This government has probably learned from the last strike I expect," said Iolo arms out stretched.

"You need your eyes tested; this time next year your arms will be too short to read any newspaper by the look of you," said Ethel, grinning from ear to ear.

The miners once more voted to take industrial action if their pay demands were not met. The government would not give in to the union's demands, so on the 9th February 1974, the miners came out on strike. This strike lasted four weeks. A state of emergency and a three-day working week were once again declared. The Prime Minister, Edward Heath, called a General Election hoping that the electorate would support the Government's attempts to deal with the deteriorating industrial situation, but the Conservative Party was defeated. The new Labour government reached a deal with the miners shortly afterwards.

Colliery canteen

Iolo Pritchard stared down into the steaming mug of hot tea; he began to play with the swirling froth with a spoon. "A penny for your thoughts," said a female's voice, Iolo looked up it was Maureen sister to Anwen, Iolo's first wife. She sat down heavily on a plastic chair while clutching a mug of tea in both hands. "We don't see much of you in here, Iolo, is everything all right?" she enquired while gazing at him with eyes that seemed to say there's something wrong. Iolo looked up from staring into the mug of tea.

"Er, hello Maureen how's the family?" he said trying to dodge her question.
"The family is fine, our Marion is getting married in June, but you worry *me* more than my kids," she said, staring at him.
"I have a lot to think about what with the pit, Ethel and Little Iolo and things in general," answered Iolo. Have you heard anything from Anwen lately?" asked Iolo trying to be clever.
"I still wonder about our Anwen, we were quite close at one time, before she bothered with… that Maldwyn Evans. It's strange that she hasn't been in contact with me," said Maureen after taking a sip of her hot tea.
"She must be feeling guilty I expect, after all the people she hurt in running off like she did," said Iolo trying to sound like the innocent party. Maureen eyed Iolo with accusing eyes and then said.
"You didn't tell us you were getting married again, we didn't know that you were a father until I heard the gossip in here from the men," she said, " they say gossip spreads like wild fire in a small village," she remarked sarcastically as she rose from where she had been sitting and made her way to behind the canteen counter. Iolo was feeling very nervous as he had no answers to give his ex-sister-in-law. He drank the remainder of the tea and hastily made a retreat to the pithead baths saying 'ta ta' as he quickly disappeared through the double swing doors.

As Iolo descended the last of the steps from the pithead baths he saw that Jack Williams was walking across the pit yard towards him.

"Iolo" he called, waving a piece of paper in the air. Iolo walked towards him cautiously.

"What's the problem mister Williams," asked Iolo, eying the under-Manager's worried facial expression. Breathlessly he stopped and faced his Overman.

"Mister Jenkins general Manager is having a reshuffle of the men... he seems to have the opinion that the east and west side of the pit is out of balance," he wheezed.

"Out of balance?" questioned Iolo as he took off his helmet with one hand and scratched his grey head with the other hand.

"Aye, he's been going through the manpower records and he seems to think that because the colliery has been losing men to other industries due to strikes and low wages, the skills *equilibrium* has been disturbed," he quoted.

"So what happens now?" asked Iolo as they began to walk to the officials' lodge office.

"What it means is, the east side will lose some of its men to the west side and vice versa. Some men are more skilled than others, we lost some very good men over the last couple of years," said the under-Manager.

"What about the NUM what do they make of it?" asked Iolo. The under-Manager sat at his desk before attempting to answer Iolo's question.

"They are having a meeting right now... god knows —what the outcome will be!" answered the under-Manager a thoughtful expression appeared on his lined face. Iolo went and sat at his own desk and began to wonder about the financial aspect of Cwm Derw colliery, was he being told the truth about its viability.

Chapter XXI

Fight-back

A notice was duly put up in the pithead baths inviting the miners to attend a special meeting—redistribution of manpower.

The miners of Cwm Derw reluctantly accepted the management's recommendations that the workforce be redistributed about the mine due to many miners leaving the industry consequently subjecting the mine to a skills shortage.

Although welsh mines had been closing at a phenomenal rate the overflow of surplus skills did not top up the skills shortage of other working mines. Men were now fed up with strikes and low wages, the never ending cycle of transfer after transfer, young men in particular were now seeking work in fledgling industries and the ever expanding steelworks.

Meanwhile at the house of Caradog Pritchard things were quiet. Caradog sat on a chair outside the house watching children playing among the distant trees, he felt comfortable and at ease as he sucked on his briar putting a thick finger over the bowl and then gently blowing tobacco smoke through the side of his mouth. Rowena stood on the door and watched her husband alone but happy smoking his pipe. She tapped him on the shoulder and then pushed a five pound note into his hand. "Here you are cariad," she said and patted him on the shoulder. Caradog stared at the five pound note and then stuffed it into the top pocket of his coat.

"Bless you love, I'll take my time, I promise," he said as he stiffly got out the chair. He fondly kissed his wife and wasted no time in making his way to the workmen's club.

Iolo ambled, slowly walking into the gate road of twenty-eight's district taking mental notes as he went. On reaching the coalface he sat down on a piece of dry timber and wiped away the perspiration from his brow with the back of a dusty hand. "Hello there stranger!" said a voice, it was Ianto Pugh, team captain. Ianto knelt on the dusty floor next to Iolo; he slapped a big bony hand on Iolo's knee. "Iolo, can I ask you a question?" he asked, and stared at Iolo with piggy like eyes "do you remember the old south west one?" he asked. Iolo looked down onto the dusty floor of the mine and then looked at Ianto as he remembered.

"Yes, I remember working on that face as a young collier. I also remember you working on the ripping lip in the gate road. I lost some good butties on that face, do you remember Will' Probert working next to me?" asked Iolo as the memories came flooding back.

"Aye, I can name all the men who worked on that blutty face, but do you remember what closed it down?" said Ianto. He spat tobacco juice on to the dusty floor and watched as it rolled into a dusty grey globule.

"The water broke into the district on the night shift," answered Iolo, quietly.

"Iolo... where do you think all that water went to," asked Ianto as he began to draw a plan of the mine on the dust. "The old south west one ended up two miles from the bottom of our pit shafts, the twenty-eight's district is now approximately one and a half miles from pit bottom. If my memory serves me right all that water is still there; the district was stopped off. I pray to god every day that the survey department will get their measurements right, I also pray that the survey department of twenty odd years ago —got their blutty measurements right, also," said Ianto, looking worried.

Iolo stared at Ianto a cold shudder raced up his spine. Had the so called jinx disappeared only to re-appear some-time in the future. Iolo decided that he had to make a visit to the survey department on the next day. Iolo worried for all of the remainder of his shift and even mentioned it to Ethel who seemed to worry over the littlest of things.

Walking briskly down the colliery drive all he had on his mind was the visit to the survey department.

Steve Parker head surveyor stared out of the window at Iolo walking briskly down the path and entering through the main door.

"What can I do for you Iolo?" asked the portly head surveyor he wondered what the senior Overman wanted.

"I'm a little worried, the question of the old south west one came up recently and I am wondering about the old plans for the district," said Iolo, loud and confident.

"Ha, yes, a workman came in the other day and asked the very same question, the old south west one!" answered the head surveyor confidently. "Come into my office I'm still studying the situation," he said, he reached for the rolled up copy.

The portly surveyor rolled out the mine plan of the district onto a large desk and placed an up to date transparency over the plan. Iolo studied the situation thoughtfully. "How far does the twenty-eight's district have to travel before we have to pre bore as a safety precaution," asked Iolo, he studied the surveyor, waiting for an answer.

"Twenty-eight's district has quite a way to go, there's no need to worry just yet. The Manager has been informed of the workman's query considering that he has knowledge of the old district", said the surveyor and he smiled as he said it.

As the weeks turned into months Iolo worried about the potential of an inrush of water; he still held the belief that the west side of the mine was jinxed even though the productivity of the mine had improved and no serious injuries to any of the workforce had been reported.

It was a sunny but windy Monday afternoon, Iolo descended the steep steps that led the way from pithead baths to the colliery yard. Jack Williams called to Iolo as he stepped off the last step. "Iolo, a word please," he beckoned with a long finger. "The Manager has decided that he intends to store enough pipes and pumping equipment in the return side of twenty eight's district just in case there are problems as the district approaches the old south west one district. Men are deployed enlarging the roadway making room for the proposed stage one of the Manager's schemes of work," he explained. Iolo gazed at the tram loaded with a white painted multi-stage centrifugal electric pump, new shiny pipes were loaded on pallets ready to be loaded up onto special trams. "Jenkins isn't wasting any time getting things together," muttered Iolo quietly.

As the days went by Iolo continued to monitor the Manager's scheme of work in regards to the precautions against inrushes regulations. Cledwyn Jenkins general Manager was taking no chances as the colliery had already experienced minor inrushes of water from old workings. The Cwm Derw Miners had driven an advanced roadway in front of the coal face and set up machinery in respect of the Manager's scheme of work.

Iolo sat at his large time-ravaged desk thinking about the old south west one district. Suddenly the telephone rang out making Iolo sit up, he picked up the handset. "Iolo Pritchard," he spoke loudly, he listened to the voice intently and by looking at Iolo's features you could tell it was the colliery general Manager on the other end of the phone. "Ok Mister Jenkins I'll be with you at three o'clock sharp," said Iolo he stared at the phone's handset and gently replaced it.

3pm at the Manager's office

Iolo walked down the corridor to the Manager's office, he saw that Jack Williams was locked in a deep conversation with NUM chairman Harry Carter. "I worked in the old south west one more than twenty years ago, and that hell hole was never drained of its water, it's been sitting there patiently waiting for us to make a mistake and I fully intend to make my voice heard on the matter," said the NUM chairman, loudly. Suddenly the office door opened and Cledwyn Jenkins beckoned them inside.

"Take a seat please, gentlemen. The sooner we start the sooner we can put our plans to work," said the Manager as he silently counted the men taking their seats. "Just, Joe Watkins to come, and then we'll make a start," he said, just then Joe Watkins district Overman for the twenty eight's district put his grey head around the door.

The Manager had put his scheme of work to the assembled officials and invited them to make comments as to the workability of the scheme.

"I'm concerned about the quality of workmanship in regards to the men who will be putting this plan of yours into practice. Where will the men be coming from, will it be from the existing workforce or recruited from other pits," asked Harry Carter NUM chairman. Cledwyn Jenkins momentarily stared at him and he began to explain the workability of his scheme. "There are a number of suitably experienced men already working at Cwm Derw. I intend to introduce a three shift system of production on the east side of the mine and then take a shift off the twenty eight's district, we must not let this district run ahead of us as we need to drive a water heading to-wards the suspected water logged old south west one district. I have planned this 'water heading' to drive into the deep for three hundred yards and then bore up to where we suspect the main body of water to be. If we are lucky enough to penetrate this body of water, we will then drain it off and let it stand in the water heading where we can pump it out to the pit bottom standages and then to surface, out of harm's way so to speak," explained the Manager, smiling. The officials went into serious thought trying to think of anything that might go wrong.

"Do you have any idea of how much water the district might be holding?" Asked Iolo, he gazed at the drawing of the Manager's scheme of work.

"Colliery records of the time suggest a figure of two thousand tons or so, with water making from collieries closed during the twenties and thirties," answered the Manager his eyes narrowed at the drawing of the affected districts.

"Phew! I never realised that there was that amount of water in front of us," said Iolo his face paled as he considered the consequences of an accidental inrush of foul water.

After the meeting regarding the Manager's scheme of work Iolo decided that he should visit the work in progress.

In the box pit the heavy steel door slammed shut behind him he held his arms out stretched inviting the banks-man to make his statutory search for contraband; the banks-man grinned as he patted a pocket in Iolo's donkey jacket. "Ha, what have we here," he uttered; he then dipped his fingers into the bulging pocket of Iolo's coat and fished out a white bag. The banks-man gave a horrified wide eyed stare into the offending bag, pulled out one of the contents and promptly popped it into his mouth and began to chew on it.

"Ok Whitey, hand them back," said Iolo, grinning like a drain. The cheeky banks-man grinned likewise and then relieved Iolo of his flame safety lamp and began to blow against the glass of the lamp after making sure that the locking mechanism was working as it was designed to do.

The pit cage descended into the darkness of the brick lined shaft, water dripped onto the garland drains that collected the water from the warm air that turned into condensation and ran down the wall of the shaft. As the pit cage descended the shaft, rattling of brass boxes seemed to get louder the cage speeded up. Iolo suddenly had that feeling that something was about to happen, then suddenly the cage seemed to travel faster than its passenger. Iolo grabbed a handrail the cage came to an abrupt stop then recoiled and fell again in ever diminishing repercussions. Iolo found himself on the floor of the cage he struggled to get to his feet, with one hand on a handrail he perched on a checkrail and waited for something to happen. It seemed ages for something to happen there was no communication between the rider of the carriage and the surface, Iolo had to wait patiently for something to happen he looked at his watch. "Five o'clock," uttered Iolo quietly, he sat on a checkrail and listened to the sound of voices coming from the bottom of the shaft. Fifteen minutes had passed and nothing had happened the far away voices had vanished all that could be heard was the constant dripping of water onto the garland drains that were set into the wall of the brick lined shaft.

Iolo looked at his watch, twenty five minutes had passed and the cage had not moved, not even an inch. Then from below, the sound of the shaft signals rang up the shaft, Iolo got to his feet and held onto to a handrail and the cage began to move slowly upwards and Iolo prayed in earnest.

On reaching the surface a crowd of faces peered into the ascending cage.

Trevor Bayliss medical attendant studied the hapless colliery official and grinned slyly, Iolo seemed to be in good shape considering the situation that had detained him in the dark, damp pit-shaft.

"Well, Iolo you get into some scrapes fair play for you... by the way the Manager has stopped you from going underground until you have been checked out at the hospital at Graig Ddu," said the medical attendant, still grinning.

Ethel met Iolo at the hospital in Graig Ddu, the husband and wife were sat on a long wooden bench gazing at the many notices that happened to be dotted around the buttermilk coloured walls. A tall well-built nurse pushed open the door of an examination room and began walking briskly towards Iolo and Ethel. "Iolo Pritchard?" asked the nurse staring at the sad looking Iolo.

"That's me," answered Iolo, raising a hand.

"Cubicle three please the doctor will see you now," she said loudly. He followed the nurse into the cubicle only to be confronted by a short, turbaned man who seemed to be humming a tune that didn't sound like any tune that Iolo was familiar with.

"What is your name please?" asked the doctor, smiling.

"Iolo Pritchard," came the inevitable answer. The doctor stared into his patient's eyes and moved a finger from side to side. Iolo's eyes followed the finger as if by instinct.

"You are a coal miner are you not?" the doctor asked but before the patient had time to answer he said: "Why are you here in this hospital?"

"I had an accident in a mine shaft, and the colliery Manager insisted that I came to this hospital to be examined," explained Iolo wondering what the doctor would ask next.

"How deep is the mineshaft that you are speaking about?" asked the doctor, the incessant smile started to disappear.

"Almost half a mile," answered Iolo his eyes lightened as he saw the bewildered expression on the doctor's face.

"Please hold out your hands I wish to examine them," ordered the doctor. The doctor stroked his greying beard before taking his patient's hands in his own, he turned Iolo's hands over looking for cuts and bruising which would be consistent with an accident in a mine shaft. "You are looking wonderfully healthy for a man who tries to fly in a miner's pit-shaft," remarked the doctor, wide eyed. Iolo began to grin as he suddenly realised that the doctor thought that he had tried to throw himself down a mineshaft.

"Doctor, I think you must have misunderstood what I had said, I was in a cage descending the mineshaft when the cage came to a violent stop half way down," explained Iolo still grinning.

The turbaned doctor began to see the error of the statement made by Iolo and began to laugh loudly, the well-built nurse rushed into the cubicle wondering what was going on. "I advise you to take a day or two away from your duties, I will be writing to your mine Manager to say that I have found no physical injuries but the trauma may affect you mentally," explained the doctor. "Can you please give the name and address of the mine that you are working, to the nurse outside," said the doctor as he rinsed the suds from his hands after washing them.

Following day

Mr Cledwyn Jenkins colliery general Manager was down the pit making his inspection of the twenty eight's district, along with his deputy Manager Mr Fred Bishop and Jack Williams. Hands firmly held behind his back he watched as Pete Price's face grimaced; he and an assistant pushed hard against a compressed air boring machine. "Stop boring please," he shouted and banged his probe stick loudly on a hydraulic pit prop. The men promptly stopped the compressed air coal borer. "Why are you men using a conventional coal borer?" asked the Manager angrily.

"This is the only machine we've got, except for another one in the other road," answered Pete Price. The Manager turned and asked for Jack Williams, under-Manager. "Williams come here this instant, I want a word with you," shouted the Manager as he turned and made his way out into the roadway away from the ears of the workmen.

The men watched from the coal face as Mr Jenkins tore a verbal strip off his under-Manager. Jack Williams went to the pit phone and turned the magneto handle furiously. "I want to speak to the head store keeper, now!" shouted the irate under-Manager. The men watched as the under-Manager's arms seemed to illustrate his anger he didn't like being bollocked by the Manager in front of the workmen.

"Boys, when you come to work tomorrow, you will have proper equipment to work with. I expect to see this new equipment working when I next visit this district. Carry on working, do what you can!" said the Manager as he turned and began walking out of the district and on to the next place on his agenda.

Mr Jenkins, stood at the mouth of the water heading studying the arch lined tunnel for alignment and then began walking and pointing with his probe stick at various objects. Men inside the heading watched as flashing cap-lamps panned about and people pointed at various things. On reaching the face of the heading the general Manager stopped the on-going work in order to speak to the men who were busy erecting an arch girder. Glyn Hopkins the leading hand stopped what he was doing and waited for the Manager to speak. "How many more yards of advance before we abandon work and prepare a site for exploratory borings," asked the Manager uncharacteristically smiling at the workmen?

"About twelve yards I expect or about a week's work if we work weekends," answered Glyn Hopkins, grinning. The Manager smiled as he knew the men had a good reputation for speed and quality of their work.

"There's more than two thousand tons of filthy water up there and we don't intend to break into it accidently, time is of the essence, if we fail we drown, if we fail it's also the end of Cwm Derw," remarked the Manager, he looked down to the wet and fragmented pile of stone beneath his feet. "Carry on men we don't want to hold you up any longer, speed is of the essence," he said and beckoned to his officials to start walking out-bye. As he walked he tapped at the rails like a blind man a worried look taunted his face; he stopped and looked back into the heading and muttered, "I should have mechanised this drivage …too late now!" Jack Williams looked at the Manager with concern but dared not say a word; he feared the Managers wrath twice in one day.

Iolo Pritchard found it hard to relax; his mind seemed to be continuously at the colliery, he wondered about the potential for an inrush of water. Ethel knew he was a one to worry.

" For god's sake Iolo why don't you go and speak to the Manager about going back to work," shouted Ethel angrily. Iolo got out of his chair went to the door, looked out and then promptly put his hat and coat on; he slammed the door and made his way to the colliery.

Iolo knocked loudly on the thick wood panelled door; a few seconds later John Fairburn secretary to the general Manager opened the door. "Ah Iolo, we were just talking about you," said the secretary, smiling," come on in".

Iolo had spent an hour talking to Mr Jenkins about the colliery in general. Mr Jenkins had decided some time ago that his senior Overman is a conscientious official and could be trusted to make good decisions on his behalf. Iolo had won him over and had permission to resume his duties at the colliery, with the proviso that he visited the medical centre and informed the medical attendant of the history concerning the last couple of days and was fit for work.

He wasted no time in getting back to his duties the men he met in the pithead baths teased him about the pit-cage incident, he always took any teasing in good humour and dished it out with equally fervour.

Word from the twenty eight's district suggested that the coalface line was within fifty yards of the old south west one. Iolo was itching to get involved in the exploratory borings.

Stepping onto the pit-cage he instinctively held onto the handrail, and waited for the shaft signalling to begin. As the pit-cage began to lower and the lights of the box-pit disappeared, the cage picked up speed; the brass boxes rattled on the guide ropes and began to whine as they rubbed against the tightly twisted strands of the thick wire ropes.

Iolo's knuckles blanched as he grasped the hand rail tightly, waiting for something to happen. Had the jinx been following him around causing things to happen? The cage began to slow and the brass boxes rattled once more, sounds from below gave a clue to what was happening, the clashing of trams coupled with shouts from men working on the pit bottom. Iolo gave a sigh of relief as the cage landed softly onto the heavy wooden baulks that absorbed the impact.

Charlie Dicks, hitcher, grinned slyly as he lifted the cage gate onto a safety hook. "Had a nice ride did you Iolo, we haven't had any problems since your last ride down this pit," he remarked. He turned away from Iolo and gave a sly grin.

Chapter XXII

Silt

Iolo never failed to stop and sniff the air whenever he passed by the old twenty sixes district, sometimes he thought he could smell rotting flesh other times there was nothing at all.

At the junction of the water heading, supply men were busily working trying to get a journey of trams around the turn, Iolo watched until the trams had rounded the turn and began disappearing down the inclined water heading, he followed behind chatting to a rider who was supervising the rumbling journey of trams from behind.

The journey of trams had reached inside of the dead end, Iolo went and spoke to the men who were engaged in the preparation of the boring station, this is the site where surveyors would direct the aim of the drilling rig with the intention of hitting the body of water somewhere above in the disused workings of the old south west one.

Two days later

"Silt, just silt," uttered big Doug; he held his hand under the trickle of water feeling for grains of stone. Iolo studied the situation before making a comment.

"We must be on the periphery of the water by the looks of things, have the surveyors plotted a second borehole?" asked Iolo looking around for markers.

"They are on the way with their equipment so I'm told," answered big Doug.

"Hmm, I think I'll have a look at the situation in twenty eights, if anyone asks for me would you tell them where I am," said Iolo, he turned and began the walk uphill and out of the heading.

At the advanced heading of twenty eights district Iolo watched through a dusty haze. The workmen were busy operating the boring machine ordered by the Manager on his last visit. The orange glow of the men's cap-lamps caused by the swirling coal dust gave an indication of the conditions the men were working in. The high pitched sound of the machine suddenly changed, a low growling sound of the boring machine filled the air. "We've hit something," shouted Pete Price, He struggled with the borer's controls; water spurted out from the borehole. "Looks like we've hit the water, we'll have to shut it off before something happens," shouted Pete, excitedly. Iolo watched though the dust blown up by the exhaust of the compressed air borer. He could see something happening, a fine spray of water sprang out around the circumference of the stuffing box, the stuffing box began moving, it was being pushed by immense pressure of the captured body of water, within seconds, water gushed out from the now gaping hole made by the pressure of dirty foul water. Pete struggled vainly with the compressed air boring rig, but by now the water had flooded the advanced heading, men began to scream as they tried to escape a tidal wave of foul water. Pit props and timber that had lain on the side of the roadway was now being washed away under the immeasurable weight of water. Some men climbed onto trams trying to escape the monstrous avalanche of moving water and wooden pit props, but it was all in vain— trams were quickly filled with water there was no escape for some.

    Iolo had managed to scramble up the coal face but there was no escape from the tidal wave that shoved him along the coalface conveyor, he tried vainly to grab a piece of machinery; but the force of the onslaught of water was too much. Eventually he was carried to the gate road where he managed to scramble miraculously uninjured onto an armoured staging above the chain conveyor. He rested and watched the torrent flood the roadway, suddenly he heard someone shouting; it was Pete Price, the boring machine operator. Pete struggled to get onto the staging but the powerful force of water would not allow him to get near the staging occupied by Iolo.

    After many attempts to gain a hand grip Iolo managed to grab one of Pete's hands and successfully hauled him onto the heavy steel staging. "Thank god, I thought I was a goner. I can't thank you enough Iolo," gasped Pete, he struggled to get to his feet. The exhausted miners watched the torrent of black coal dust saturated water flow by them, they shone their lights out into the roadway trying to assess the extent of the inrush, but it was hopeless, there was nothing that they could do but watch helplessly.

It seemed like hours as they waited for the water to become still. Finally Iolo decided to get into the blackened foul water; he gingerly began wading to the pit phone. Slowly but surely he managed to reach the phone. With water up to his chest, he cranked the magneto handle furiously, but the phone was dead." Dagnabit," yelled Iolo," what do we do now?" He screamed in desperation.

We'll have to wait a bit longer, when the water stops flowing," suggested Pete as he eyed the flowing stream of foul water.

Time had passed and the water had finally stopped flowing, Iolo and his colleague had decided to try and wade to the mouth of the district.

Using a stemming stick Iolo prodded the water in front of them searching for hidden dangers, after a stressful half an hour probing the murky waters they came to an abrupt stop. The water ahead was up to the roof of the roadway there was a dip. Iolo knew the district and guessed that they would have to travel underwater for about twenty yards or so. "Sod it," shouted Iolo it's too much, we'll have to go back. The two miners then retreated to the metal platform.

The staging measured six feet by eight feet and enough room for them to lie down.

Chapter XXIII

The Rescue

Meanwhile on the surface, men and management battled to get survivors up the shafts. The mines rescue brigade was on the way, and a control room was being prepared for the rescuers.

Mr Jenkins colliery general Manager, waited outside the office buildings for the first of the rescue vans to arrive, he paced backwards and forwards impatiently.

Meanwhile a crowd of pit villagers had gathered at the colliery gates after hearing the pit hooter sounding long continuous blasts. They were anxious for news of their-ill-fated menfolk.

Once more Ethel stood shoulder to shoulder amongst the worried womenfolk of the village, she had that feeling, something would happen soon. Had Iolo's jinx manifested its self once more? The worried villagers gazed in awe as the first of the black rescue vans arrived, accompanied by police cars and ambulances,' sirens blaring. The evening sky filled with blue flashing lights; emanating from the emergency services vehicles.

On the bottom of the down cast shaft, engineers were desperately trying to assess the extent of the massive flooding, they waded through foul fetid water up to the knees, but they had one cause in their favour, owing to the nature of skip winding the water had found an escape route; it had flooded part of the shaft from the skip landing point to the standages below.

Meanwhile on the bottom of the up-cast shaft other engineers were trying to assess the severity of the inrush and the possible consequences. Colin Wilde, chief mechanic, worried about the main pumps that were situated on the bottom of the up-cast shaft they might have been overwhelmed by the sheer volume of unexpected water.

"I need a volunteer to come with me, we need to examine the situation at the main pumps, I hope to god that the water hasn't damaged the electrical equipment," shouted the chief engineer to a group of other minor engineers.

"I'll come with you," volunteered young Billy Smith an enthusiastic but inexperienced young apprentice. The engineer stared at him anxiously.

"Come on then, follow me, take your time it's very slippery under feet," shouted the engineer. The young apprentice followed his boss through a hole in the stage landing; a nauseating smell wafted up from the sump below, Colin Wilde tried not to breathe in the stench. The steep steps to the sump below were wet with slime, and from time to time he lost his footing as he tried to keep an eye on his young colleague. The chief mechanic carefully stepped around the foul smelling water- filled sump. Water was only a few inches deep around the big centrifugal pumps, he went to the pit phone and cranked the magneto handle and listened for any sound that may come from the ear piece. *"Hello, who's ringing pit bottom?"* A voice from the telephone called out.

"It's Colin Wilde, engineer," he answered and told the voice on the other end to replace the receiver. Next duty was to inform the general Manager of the situation concerning the condition of the pumping station. He cranked the magneto handle in one continuous rotation until he heard the powerhouse attendant's voice. "Get me the Manager's office it's urgent," barked the engineer. After a while Mr Jenkins colliery general Manager came to the phone.

"Yes, Wilde, where are you now?" barked the Manager.

"I'm at the main pumping station under the up-cast shaft," answered the engineer sounding pleased with himself.

"You are where!" remarked the Manager with anger in his voice.

"Under the up-cast shaft," repeated the engineer in a naive voice.

"Get out from that place now! before I sack you, the ventilation officer has not sanctioned that place as free of gases, get from that place now and retrace your steps do you hear me?" he bellowed down the telephone.

"Yes mister Jenkins, right away," said the engineer looking worried. He led the young apprentice back up the slime covered steps to the landing stage where he was met by Pete the ventilation officer, known as Pete the vent by the miners of Cwm Derw.

"So you spoke to the Manager then?" said Pete grinning at the naive engineer.

"Yes, he tore a strip off me, I suppose I'll be suspended now," said the dejected Colin Wilde.

"You should have known better, and you... colliery chief mechanic as well," remarked the ventilation officer, grinning. "The Manager has asked me to take you with me on an inspection of the ventilation system, we need to know how the districts are affected especially the mouth to the standages," he informed the engineer.

Iolo studied his watch, "eight o' clock, I wonder if the water has gone down?" he said to his companion. Iolo dipped the stemming stick into the now still water and marked the water level with a piece of wet chalk pulled from a soaking wet trouser pocket. "I'll check in half an hours' time to see if the water is receding," suggested Iolo as he eyed the chalk mark.

"Aye, that's a good idea, anyway, how's the ventilation here?" Pete asked, while scanning around for a flame safety lamp. Iolo felt for his own flame safety lamp which should have been on his lamp-belt.

"Dagnabit, it must have come off my belt when the water swept me up the face, I expect," squealed Iolo; he wondered how he could examine the air for gas. Pete's worried eyes gazed at Iolo with concern, he respected the senior Overman and now his life might depend on his experience. Iolo swept up a handful of dry stone-dust from the staging and threw the fine grains of dust into in the air; the pair watched intently as the minute grains fell to the water below and was not carried any distance at all by the still ventilation.

"Looks like we've had it, we've no lamp to examine for gas or oxygen deficiency," said Iolo looking dejected. The trapped miners stared out into the arch lined roadway praying for someone or something to come and save them from the impending suffocation.

Half an hour had passed, and Iolo decided to make an examination of the depth of water using the stemming stick. Iolo eyed the watermark it matched the previous chalk mark the water had not receded not even by a half an inch.

"I think I'm slipping into delirium said Pete he stared dead ahead not even blinking. I keep imagining that there is a light under that coat hanging on a piece of lagging about twenty yards away," explained Pete wide eyed and quietly spoken. Iolo instinctively studied the roadway where Pete had suggested that he could see a light.

"I think I can see a light too, under that coat over by there," said Iolo, he pointed with a thick finger and began to enter the water, and he slowly waded over to where he thought he could see a light of some kind. Iolo lifted the coat that was dry because the water had not reached it and to his great surprise a workman's lamp greeted him, with a bright yellow flame. "Pete I've found a workman's lamp and it's lit, under normal circumstances the workman would be sent up the pit to see the Manager but this time he's excused!" shouted Iolo excitedly, he picked up the lamp and held it tightly to his chest he dared not drop the lamp into the water.

Iolo returned to the staging and held out the shining lamp to Pete who grasped it tightly with both hands. "Ok, I'll hang the lamp on a brace just above our heads there isn't much methane in the general body just yet. Just study the flame from time to time. There's one thing in our favour the barometer was fairly high when I came down the pit this afternoon, so if luck is on our side for once, we shouldn't be bothered by it, blackdamp may be our undoing," said Iolo cautiously.

Meanwhile in the rescue control room David Grimshaw Mines Rescue first officer studied a working plan of the colliery workings. Fred Bishop colliery deputy Manager pointed to various positions on the plan." I know most of that area from previous training visits with your own rescue teams," said the rescue first officer. "The permanent rescue teams should have established a fresh air base by now, and be assembled waiting for instructions, I now know how to proceed," said the officer, he quickly marked on two small waterproof copies of the main plan and promptly left making his way to the downcast shaft. At the fresh air- base, rescue teams were assembled and were waiting for instruction.

"Gentlemen of number one team there are miners missing, management believe that these men are trapped, somewhere on the west number twenty eights district, on the intake side, your mission is to find them, you have your mine plan of the area where we believe these men are— Number two team will examine the return airway and proceed to in-bye of twenty eights return road so marked on your mine plan. Gentlemen good luck," said the first officer, a serious look never left his face. The two teams of sixteen men in total made their way to their respective places of inspection.

"It's nine o'clock, let's check the water level it might have gone down a bit," suggested Iolo, he looked at Pete and Pete looked up at the flame safety lamp that was burning brightly on a low flame in order to conserve fuel. Iolo gently lowered the stemming stick into the water and then retrieved the stick and marked the top of the wet part with a piece of chalk. "No change," uttered Iolo sounding gloomy.

"Why do you think that the water is not going down, Iolo?" asked Pete in a quiet kind of voice.

"Well, we already know that there is a dip outside we've seen it, the water was up to the roof, as for the return road, well I can only guess that all the timber supplies, and coupled with the vast amount of debris lying on the floor of the district, the massive weight of flowing water swept it all up and formed a dam across the roadway, I think it's the dam that's stopping the water from flowing away to the pit or into that water heading that's just been driven," suggested Iolo, he stared at the still and murky water almost wishing it to start moving.

Mike Thompson captain of number one rescue team signalled to his men to halt. They had only travelled fifty yards into the gate road when they were met by the body of water.

He examined each of the bulky self-contained breathing apparatus worn by his team; he studied the mine plan. Mike showed the plan to the rest of his team members; they read what he had written on the bottom of the plan, each member of the team signalled with a 'thumbs up' that he understood that they had to pass through the body of water and out the other side. The team made an examination of the ventilation and wrote down their findings.

Mike Thompson examined each of his team members, making sure that they were each attached to the safety line, he looked into the eyes of his brave men, and he could see that they were very uneasy about venturing into the dirty foul water. They had trained in a swimming pool wearing blacked out goggles.

The team were now wearing their watertight goggles, he signalled to his team to move forward, each man paid notice to the life line as it was carried along by the captain into the foul water. Inch by inch they waded in until the last man disappeared beneath the murky, foul water, all that could be seen was a tell-tale trail of bubbles from the air that was given off by the self-contained breathing apparatus that they were using. It was black as night. Mike felt about the side of the roadway gingerly feeling his way about the icy filthy water. Bits of timber floated over his head and from time to time a piece caught him on the face causing him to wince in pain.

After a while the team emerged from the blackened water, thankfully they could not smell it due to them wearing breathing apparatus.

Once they were all on the other side of the body of water Mike Thompson studied his team, he counted the men and re-examined them again, and detached them from the life line. All present and correct. The team marched onwards.

Pete was sitting up staring dead ahead as if he were day dreaming, "I think I'm hallucinating again," said Pete, still staring dead ahead. Iolo looked to where Pete was sitting on his haunches.

Suddenly there came the sound of squeaky hooters, the rescue team had spotted signs of life.

"It's the 'rescue' we're saved," shouted Iolo excitedly. The sheer joy lit up their faces they shouted to the rescuers and waved their cap-lamps wildly.

Mike spotted the flame safety lamp hanging on a brace above the metal staging he wasted no time in examining the atmosphere, his eyes lit like beacons when he discovered that the body of air that had supported the trapped men only contained about two per cent of methane.

The rescue captain promptly decoupled his equipment and turned off his supply of oxygen, he studied the gauge, he had ample supply of oxygen in reserve.

"Ok, decouple and turn off your supply valves," ordered the captain, he studied the miners and asked them questions regarding their health and fitness as they were being asked to traverse a body of water.

The rescue team and the survivors had now reached the body of water. Mike had to make a decision; the procedure was not a tried and tested one, as it concerned using the reviver, which was used to keep a rescued man alive in an irrespirable atmosphere.

Mike studied Iolo, briefly, "Listen, butty, do you think you could use this breathing apparatus if I showed you how?" asked the team's captain. Iolo eyed the piece of apparatus which consisted of an oxygen cylinder a corrugated tube and a face mask with built-in essential valves. Iolo turned to where Pete Price was watching proceedings.

"Aye I'll give it a go, show me how to use it," answered Iolo his head started to fill with images of Ethel and Iolo bach.

Iolo held the black and white oxygen cylinder tight to his chest with one hand while holding the breathing mask to his face with the other hand although the mask was secured to his head with straps. The team captain ordered two rescue men to stay with Pete while he and the other rescue men patiently guided Iolo through the cold and murky water.

Iolo waded into the icy water, he began to tremble as his head went into the water and for the first time in his life he became aware of his own breath. Inch by inch the brave Overman blindly followed the life-line, praying that he would come out the other end alive. Suddenly a waterless space appeared ahead, and he sort of laughed. Iolo was now aware of his head emerging from the icy cold water; he opened his eyes and pulled down the face mask of the breathing apparatus. Mike motioned to him to put it back on, and pointed in the direction of the junction ahead. Iolo almost ran to the roadway junction.

At the junction of the intake roadway Iolo pulled off the face mask that had saved his life, and promptly dropped to his knees with nervous exhaustion. It was now the turn of Pete Price.

Mike turned off the supply of oxygen to the reviver and returned to the body of dirty, icy water once more.

Iolo sat in a manhole a coarse brown blanket wrapped around his shivering body. The remaining rescue men had examined the atmosphere, and they were satisfied that it was safe for the time being.

After a while, Mike, captain of the rescue team emerged once more from the body of water with Big Pete Price in tow. The men were now safe and they began making their way to the surface and then on to hospital.

Number 2 team had located the other miners that were missing but it was too late to save them, they were washed along with the debris and were embedded in a wall of muck and timber.

On the surface outside of the main gates the villagers had remained steadfast and waited for news of the missing men. Ethel and Iolo bach wrapped up tightly against the cold wind waited. The crowd of mainly women hushed as Fred Bishop hurried up the driveway to where the crowd was waiting for news.

Ethel's eyes began to stream with tears as Fred Bishop, colliery deputy Manager stared at her. He then began to give some news, but not all of it; he began to read from a piece of paper. "The mines rescue brigade has— recovered two men from twenty eights district. They are Iolo Pritchard and Peter Price. Ethel wept as she heard the news that Iolo was alive.

At the hospital in Graig Ddu Iolo and Pete Price were being examined by doctors, they had been referred by Doctor Philips who had been called out to the incident at the Cwm Derw mine. Iolo sat in a cubicle waiting for a doctor to appear, he began to recall the last time that he had cause to visit Graig Ddu hospital.

A brown hand swept open the curtain that had afforded some sort of polite barrier against prying eyes. The doctor stared at his patient with disbelief. "I am thinking that we have been here before, I believe the last time was, when you had an accident in a miner's shaft, and now they are telling me that my patient nearly drowned that in that same pit shaft," exclaimed the doctor, his eyes were wide and staring. After the doctor examined Iolo he began offering some advice to his blackened patient." My advice to you is… you must give up this job of yours, which involves yo-yoing in mine shafts and trying to swim in stinking water, do you understand what I am saying to you?" stated the doctor, earnestly staring at Iolo.

"Yes doctor, I think there is a sort of jinx hanging around the mine," answered Iolo grinning.

"This jinx that you talk about, seems to be hanging around your neck," I will be writing to the Manager advising him that you are accident prone and he put you on light duties for a while," said the doctor, sternly, he turned away and began washing his hands in a small hand basin.

Chapter XXIV

Christmas 1974

Iolo Pritchard had not returned to his job as senior Overman. Ethel had placed enormous pressure on Iolo to accept a job in the colliery stores, whereby he would not have any responsibilities regarding the supervision of underground personnel. Iolo spent his working hours learning the ropes of store keeper in readiness for when the head storekeeper retired in the coming new-year.

Christmas in the Pritchard's household hadn't changed much over the last couple of years, except for the arrival of Iolo bach who was now more than two years old and a handful to manage. The family were sat around the dinner table enjoying their Christmas dinner. Ethel was preoccupied she continually stared at the telephone that sat on the windowsill nearby and from time to time she turned her head and nodded politely to various family members. Suddenly the telephone rang out loudly Ethel dropped the fork that she was eating from and stared at Iolo the look on Ethel's face echoed the Christmas when Iolo received the news of the accidental death of Bill Pumpy who had been overcome by the blackdamp while servicing a compressed air pump. Iolo got up from the dinner table and went to the phone he slowly put the handset to his ear and spoke quietly into the phone. "Iolo Pritchard speaking who is it?"
"Oh...Oh, I am sorry I must have dialled the wrong number!" replied the anonymous female voice. Iolo gave a sigh of relief and put the handset back on its receiver and promptly returned to the others who were also relieved by the misdialled number.

Christmas had come and gone without any bad news and now a new-year was on the welcome- mat and Cwm Derw colliery had new goals to achieve after the massive inrush of water almost closed the beleaguered coalmine, for good.

It was early January the cold weather chilled the nation, and miners were cheered by the news that OPEC (Organisation of the Petroleum Exporting Countries) agreed a ten per cent rise in oil prices the Cwm

Derw miners were feeling a little easy, any planned closure of their colliery might be delayed due to the agreed new price of oil. February saw the announcement that nuclear power stations were to be built at Sizewell on the Suffolk coast and Torness Point near Edinburgh. Edward Heath prime minister resigned as Margaret Thatcher won her first ballot. February also saw the miners accept a thirty-five per cent pay rise, and the National Coal Board announced a thirty five per cent increase in prices.

Danny Wilmot chewed at a corned beef sandwich while staring straight ahead; his eyes glazed he then revealed what he had been thinking. "Well, I didn't think that we would be here sat around still chewing dusty sandwiches after what this pit went through, anyhow who would give me a job at my age sixty next birthday," he recalled, still staring dead ahead.

"Aye, this is my fourth pit and the last by the look of things, I've had a gut full of hopping from pit to pit. I might not *escape* the Cwm Derw jinx, it might get *me* next time," said Dai Evans grinning like a drain. The others laughed loudly and went back to their places of work.

Iolo was busy in the colliery stores learning the ropes prior to Ted Morgan retiring from a working life. He missed the underground visits and often wondered what was happening below ground, sometimes an underground official would phone an order to the stores and Iolo would take the call, a conversation would be struck up and Iolo would be told of the gossip from around the colliery. Iolo felt safe in the confines of the stores, what could possibly happen there, the jinx was confined to the west side of the mine and as yet it had not manifested itself anywhere on the colliery surface save for the lightning strike that caused the explosion way back in May 1968.

Out-side, the February sun shone low in the heavens and Iolo shielded his eyes from the blinding glare as he walked away from the colliery stores and towards the steep steps that were leading to the pithead baths.

Iolo raised his head and stared at a lone miner sat on a wooden step at about three flights up; plucking up the energy he began to make the steep climb towards the pithead baths, the lone miner had not moved and seemed to be waiting for Iolo. "Hello old timer, trying to get your wind are you?" shouted Iolo from a short distance away.

"I'm buggered now Iolo, I haven't enough wind to fart now days," exclaimed Charlie Dicks trying to grin. "I'm certified as having ten per cent dust... more like fifty per cent right now," he said as he tried to get up from the step that he had been sitting on. Iolo eyed the miner with concern. He was obviously stricken by what miners called pneumoconiosis, or black-lung. "I haven't worked on pit bottom for all my working life, I was a collier for thirty years," explained Charlie, he began to cough violently and spat out blackened phlegm onto the side of the steps.

"Charlie, I remember you working on the coal in the old west one district more than twenty years ago," said Iolo. He held out a hand, Charlie reached out for it and managed to get to his feet.

"Aye, that district was the worst district that I ever worked in, how I never got drowned, I'll never know. I'm lucky to be here, now but look at me...almost finished," said Charlie with a wry look on his grey and lined features.

"How old are you Charlie? Asked Iolo who was by now wondering if there were many years between them.

"I've got six more months to go and then I'm on the stute steps with the other old uns," replied Charlie. He gasped for air as he slowly began climbing the steep steps to the pit head baths. Iolo glanced at the construction work that was on going. The coal board had started to build a tower; housing a pair of lifts and Iolo began to think that it had come too late for Charlie Dicks, On-setter.

Life had been hard for four generations of miners the daily struggle of climbing the steep steps to the pithead baths had seen many men leave the colliery. Youngsters raced up the steep flights of steps while the old ones shouted to them: 'You wait till the black-lung gets you!'

Eventually, Iolo and Charlie had gratefully reached the baths and the quietness of the building was broken save for the water rushing out of the two showerheads being used by one or two miners.

Summertime was inevitable and most miners tended their allotments and if they were lucky they had a garden. Caradog Pritchard was no exception he had a modest back garden, and an allotment! He loved going down the allotments and meet up with life-long pal Fred Morgan. The little makeshift hut stood out as it was the only one on the allotments and the envy of all the miners that gazed upon it. A haze of smoke lazily billowed from an old galvanized pipe that served as a chimney. Inside, the two old timers were sat in their respective armchairs supping homebrew. Caradog drained the last of the potent homebrew from his favourite pint glass and rested the empty glass on one knee. "Another pint is it?" asked Fred eying the empty pint glass.

"I had better not, I promised the wife that I would leave the homebrew alone. I haven't quite been forgiven for the last time," said Caradog, remembering the incident.

"One more won't hurt you, mun, go on have another drop, one for the road as my old man used to say," said Fred, grinning from ear to ear.

The alcohol began to feather the brains of the tipsy pair of retired miners, outside a wind began to pick up dust that had lain undisturbed. Caradog listened to the wind as it whistled around their makeshift hut; he eyed his beer glass and took a long lingering sip until the very last of the brown fluid had gone. The old codger stiffly raised himself from his cosy armchair and opened the door; the potent wind was as strong as the homebrew and snatched the door out of Caradog's once strong grip. He groggily regained his hold on the door and closed it tightly." Good god, I think I'll wait until the wind dies down, there's no sense in going home in that sort of weather," he exclaimed and promptly sat back in his cosy armchair.

"Aye, there's no sense in going home wind swept is there butty?" said Fred as he reached for a flagon of home brew. The tipsy pair continued to swap village gossip and guffawed loudly as they reminisced about old times down the workmen's club, and Cwm Derw colliery was being reworked in the minds of a pair of old codgers pickled by homebrew.

Chapter XXV

Autumn 1975

Cwm Derw miners saved the mine from closure with the help of a lot of luck and very hard work. Men had continued to leave the mining industry as other opportunities appeared from time to time, some emigrated to Australia or Canada and others had found opportunities all over Great Britain.

Iolo Pritchard had eventually taken on the job as head store keeper as Ted Morgan had now retired. Things at the colliery stores were generally quiet compared to underground work as Iolo was beginning to feel bored with the lack of real challenges. He began to find spare time and often walked around the colliery yard talking to various people.

Colliery washery

A major breakdown had occurred at the colliery washery the washing of coal had now come to a stop as a main mineral crushing machine had broken down and all coal bunkers had been filled to capacity. Engineers were busy dismantling the breaker/crusher, Colin Wilde chief mechanic ran about barking orders at the various fitters who were using compressed air tools undoing the many nuts and bolts that had held the machine parts together.

Iolo had been called to the scene as the Manager had ordered that new machine parts were to be made available along with the many nuts and bolts and other equipment.

Colin Wilde shouted orders and pointed manically as a compressed-air winch raised one of two gearboxes that had once driven a breaking machine. This had crushed large lumps of coal and hard stones into small manageable sizes ready to be washed and separated into saleable coal; debris was to be sent to the mountainous slag heap.

Iolo Pritchard left the colliery stores and made his way to the washery where the fitters were attempting to dismantle the failed large lump breaking machine. Iolo moved with a sense of urgency he began to hear the sound of men shouting and a compressed air winch screamed and snorted as it tirelessly tugged at a huge coal blackened gearbox; its hardened chains shook as it took up the slack.

Iolo stopped in his tracks; he sniffed the air expecting to experience the odour of gearbox oil but another sort of smell invaded his sensitive nostrils. Iolo shook his head in disbelief: 'the stench of rotting flesh! *it just can't be*,' said a voice inside his head. Iolo shook his head and began marching to where the fitters were working. A short, stout and balding fitter wearing ragged overalls gestured to Colin Wilde who was operating the winch. Suddenly the huge gearbox swung wildly as if an unseen hand had tugged at the heavy machine sending it spinning in Iolo's direction. The short statured fitter was sent reeling to the concrete floor, he screamed in agony as others wrestled with the very heavy gearbox in an attempt to halt it from swinging further. Iolo froze mid stride, the air seemed to fill with the stench of putrid flesh. He watched as the few fitters sniffed at the air and grimaced. The Cwm Derw jinx was now haunting him on the surface of the colliery and now Iolo was convinced that the jinx was that of Anwen Pritchard or her lover Maldwyn Evans.

Iolo seemed quieter than usual, Ethel was concerned and she too believed that Iolo's ex-wife and her lover were haunting the Cwm Derw colliery with a vengeance. What would happen now? How far would the ghouls venture in their quest for revenge?

Tales of the stench of putrefied flesh reached the ears of the Cwm Derw villagers every-one was now saying that they could smell the stench of death, tales of Dracula circulated the village and the youngsters joked about it, but it was no joke to Iolo and Ethel.

Chapter XXVI

Christmas 1975

Christmas had come around once again but the Pritchard household were apprehensive as ever, Iolo and the other members of the family were sat around watching television as Ethel prepared the Christmas dinner but this Christmas she seemed very quiet, didn't even hum a Christmas carol and no one seemed to notice. She momentarily stared blankly out of the kitchen window, a familiar face stared back at her, a face from the past. Ethel screamed and threw the potato peeler to the floor, Iolo and the others rushed to her aid. She trembled violently as Iolo held her tightly in his arms, she whispered to him.
"It's...Anwen...I saw her in the window...she was staring at me!" Iolo closed his eyes tightly, was there no escape! The Cwm Derw Jinx was all around them.

Ethel took to her bed for a few days, Bethan nervously ran the Pritchard's household for a while as her mother struggled to regain her health.
This coming evening was New Year's Eve, the family gathered round sipping copious amounts of alcohol waiting to welcome in the New Year. The television played loudly, Iolo chatted to son-in-law David, and Bethan eyed her mother watchfully. Ethel sat in front of the glowing coal fire; she studied the pale yellow flames flickering from between the hot and glowing coals, never taking her eyes from the fire grate. Bethan looked on with concern for her mother as she never believed in ghosts and ghouls.
Ethel steered her red and tired eyes away from the coals, she became fixated by the big ticking clock sat on the mantelpiece. "Five minutes to midnight," she said quietly, Bethan and Iolo stared fixedly at Ethel, they were anxious for her but only Iolo knew what was going on in her head. "One minute to midnight," uttered Ethel, her eyes widened and she sat upright in her chair; the room went silent except for the television, the sound of Big Ben began to chime out through the TV set. Suddenly a loud banging came from the chimney breast. Red-hot soot billowed out from the fireplace, Ethel gave a blood curdling scream, Bethan screamed and ran upstairs to where the little boys were

soundly sleeping, and luckily the midnight mayhem had not disturbed them. Downstairs Ethel sobbed uncontrollably while Iolo and David sprinkled water onto the smouldering lounge carpet. The fire brigade was on its way as concerned neighbours had called them from the local call box.

New Year's Day was manic as all the neighbours seemed to want to know what had happened at precisely twelve o'clock midnight. Ethel seemed to spend the whole day sobbing as friends and neighbours tried to comfort her. Ethel dared not reveal her true thoughts about the matter. Iolo remained reticent and was now dreading returning to his place of work.

The month of April was now visiting the good people of Cwm Derw, gardens were being turned over and the men who were lucky enough to have an allotment plot, toiled from morning to dusk getting it ready for planting.

Ethel's health was failing fast and Iolo didn't know quite what to do, he was now dreading every waking moment, he continually sniffed the air no matter where he happened to be.

It was a fine dry day on the allotments as Caradog Pritchard busily put his tools away for the day and was looking forward to a drop of homebrew with his butty Fred Morgan.

Caradog held out his favourite pint glass as Fred held the flagon of homebrew at an angle, the potent amber brew began to flow and gurgle. Caradog eyed the full pint glass greedily and gently raised the glass to his pursed lips. Just as he took his first long sip of the day he felt the ground beneath his feet,' move,' his eyes widened and he took another long sip from his beer glass. Fred Morgan had also felt the earth beneath his feet shudder, the makeshift hut rattled and the stove pipe became dislocated from the quivering stove. Caradog dropped his pint glass despite it being almost full. He collapsed into a chair; it swung around ninety degrees and back to its original position. Fred's face had taken on a terrified expression his mouth gaped, he clutched at his chest and fell back into his chair which promptly swung back and forth in the limited available space. Caradog eyed his butty with astonished eyes; the experience over whelmed him as a vice like grip grabbed him around the chest; he gasped for breath and tried vainly to get out of his chair but an unseen hand threw him back into the shuddering chair. Fred Morgan sat in his chair, eyes bulging, his worn out frame motionless.

In the house of Iolo Pritchard things were quiet as Ethel did her best around the house. Iolo worked on the family car giving it a basic service and a good clean. Bethan visited from time to time just to make sure her mother was coping.

Iolo stood back admiring his handy-work, and then put his tools and equipment away. A voice called to him from a distance, he looked to where the voice was calling from. Charlie Dicks gasped as he struggled to get to where Iolo was waiting. "Iolo something has happened to Caradog, the police are investigating," he gasped trying to catch his failing breath.

"Come into the house," said Iolo as he led him to his door. Iolo shouted to Ethel to make a cup of tea.

"I was quietly working on my plot at the allotments; I could hear noises from Caradog and Fred Morgan's hut. I thought nothing of it at first, and then I went and banged on the door. Old Caradog and Fred liked a drop of home brew. I thought that they had overdone it a little bit. When I opened the door I had the shock of my life... the pair of them were sat in their armchairs...the expression on their faces...well ...I could only say that they had seen a ghost or something!" explained Charlie, his eyes were wide and staring a bewildering look shrouded his pale and craggy face.

"Did you call the police?" questioned Iolo, anxiously.

"As you Know Iolo, bach, I've got ten per cent dust...my legs get tired if I try and rush things," he explained again. "I managed to get to a working phone by the Collier's Arms. I phoned the police...and told them what I saw and where I saw it, then I put the phone down," said Charlie, still trying to catch his breath. "The police were pretty quick about it. I could hear the siren blaring just soon after." Iolo's face momentarily lost its colour.

"Can you look after Ethel for a while? She's not been very well lately," remarked Iolo, Ethel came into the room with two cups of tea on a tray, she looked a little bewildered as Iolo hurriedly made for the door.

A policeman stood at the gate that opened onto the allotments. Iolo halted; blind panic gripped him as his mind flashed back to that fateful Friday night in December 1967. What could Iolo do? he dared not turn and walk away, he had to take the bull by the horns and explain to the policeman that he was the brother of Caradog Pritchard one of the men who the police were investigating.

Police Sergeant Ivor Edwards sat on a comfortable couch in the Pritchard's lounge sipping a cup of hot tea from Ethel's best china tea service. "From our investigations it appears that there was an altercation between your brother and a Mr Frederick Morgan," explained the round faced policeman. "From our enquiries we found that they were life-long friends," he went on to say. Iolo and Ethel were anxious that no foul play would be suspected as a thorough investigation might delve too deep and expose the murders perpetrated by Iolo Pritchard and witnessed by Ethel Probert as she was known at that time.
"We have spoken to a Mr Charles Dicks a retired coalminer, and we are satisfied that no other persons were involved in the altercation," stated the policeman; a faint smile momentarily appeared on his rotund features. " It appears that they had been drinking copious amounts of potent homebrew, which contributed to their deaths."
"Will there be an inquest, constable?" asked Iolo. The policeman curiously, eyed Iolo.
Aye, almost certainly, they were coalminers so the law says their remains must undergo a post-mortem," answered the policeman. He then promptly replaced his notebook into a tunic pocket and then handed the empty teacup with saucer to the nervous looking Ethel and smiled saying: "I'll see my-self out," and promptly left the Pritchard's house.

Chapter XXVII

July 1976

Iolo and Ethel had just returned from the inquest of Caradog Pritchard and Fredrick Morgan held at Graig Ddu. Iolo sat in his armchair staring up at the white painted ceiling he suddenly went into deep thought. "I don't think even for minute that Caradog and Fred had drank themselves legless and started fighting, they had drunk beer together all of their lives and never fought each other before!" Remarked Iolo, thoughtfully.

Things seemed to quieten down for a while as the Cwm Derw jinx seemed to have sated itself with the death of a loved one. However, Ethel and Iolo worried about the rest of the family, Bethan and David, Guto bach grandson to Ethel and four year old Iolo bach.

Iolo had now returned to his place of work and was dreading the events that he was now sure would be inevitable, but at least the jinx might stay at the colliery and not torture the family of Iolo Pritchard with ghoulish doings and untimely deaths.

Everyone working in the colliery stores had noticed that their boss was unusually quiet. Iolo seemed to be in a state of continuous thought.

Brian Webb knocked loudly on Iolo's office door, "Come in" shouted Iolo without even looking to see who it was. Brian entered the modest but dingy office, carefully holding a large mug of steaming tea.

"Here you are boss, a steaming hot mug of tea for you," said Brian as he set it down on the edge of the desk. Iolo looked up and thanked the small statured stores-man. "The Manager has been telling us that the colliery needs to cut costs and was thinking of sending you down the pit for a couple of days," remarked the stores-man eyeing Iolo and waiting for some kind of reaction.

"Why would the Manager want to send me down the pit?" asked Iolo, looking puzzled.

"My best guess is! You know the colliery and the bad habits concerning the underground officials," answered the stores-man.

"Yes, I understand," said Iolo. There's a lot of material lying about the sides that could be used up before anything is ordered from stores. I'll inform the Manager that I intend to make a record of anything above and below ground that can be recovered and I'll try and put a cost on it," said Iolo as he reached for the office telephone.

Tuesday morning 9:00 am

Iolo stood on the bank in the box-pit waiting to descend the shaft along with other men and varied officials of the mine. The banks-man gave the appropriate shaft signals and waited for a reply from pit bottom. The reply came promptly and the waiting men were searched for contraband (smoking material) by the banks-man's assistant before they were allowed to enter the carriage.

As the carriage began to descend the shaft Iolo had sudden flashbacks of times when the pit winding gear had problems. His face had an expression of fear.

Iolo listened to the guide-ropes rattling the spark-proof brass boxes that were attached to the sides of the carriage, they began to hum as the carriage picked up speed and the riders began to exchange idle gossip regarding their working shift. The carriage reached pit bottom and settled gently onto the stout baulks that spanned the bottom of the pit-shaft. Iolo felt a sense of great relief as nothing had happened he was spared this time but what about the return journey?

Men had remarked to Iolo about the inrush and explosion, and asked how they had affected him but Iolo put on a brave face and said: 'I'm out of it now except for the occasional underground visits demanded by the management.'

All went well as Iolo made entries in a ledger concerning reusable material and material that had not been used at all, and stuff that was in transit and in the wrong location being re-routed by unscrupulous officials for their own districts.

The mouth of the old twenty six district was only fifty yards ahead and already Iolo felt very uneasy. He continually sniffed at the mine air, the blocked off roadway was heavily stone-dusted and a seat of wood was placed on one side of the junction. Iolo nervously sat down and began to write a note in the large ledger that he carried under his arm. He began to feel very sleepy and struggled to keep both eyes open; he shook his head and unhooked the flame-safety lamp from his belt. Lowering the flame of the lamp he watched intently at eye level for a pale blue cap of methane gas, the testing flame was unchanged. He then lowered the lamp to near floor level still the flame burned as normal. Smartly he raised the testing flame to a walking flame and quickly made his way in-bye feeling that *something* had made him tired and sleepy.

Iolo had stopped at the mouth of the twenty eights district and was about to use the pit telephone he needed to asked the district deputy for permission to enter his district as required by mining law. A flashing cap-lamp could be seen approaching someway from the mouth of the roadway. The sweating Bernard Thomas duly emerged and greeted his old-time Overman. "Well, well, Iolo what brings you down the pit you haven't lost your job in the stores have you?" joked the smiling deputy.

"The management have requested that I make cost cutting visits around the colliery and yours is the first one to receive my meticulous attention," answered the grinning head stores-man. Iolo had not had an occasion to laugh or smile for many weeks.

After making notes and recommendations for management regarding twenty eights district, Iolo received a message from Jack Williams asking him to meet at the west twenty nine's development drive-age.

Waiting at the mouth of the return drive-age was Jack Williams; he beckoned to Iolo and sit beside him on a piece of timber that doubled as a makeshift seat. Iolo sat beside the unshaven under-Manager and listened to what he had to say. "They're almost ready to fire a round of shots off, sixty holes I expect," he remarked as he pulled out a dusty notebook from a pocket. Iolo could see a cluster of cap lamps in the drive-age and guessed that a shot-firing operation would be imminent. The cap lamp wearing men disappeared into manholes in order to escape any stone that might be propelled at great speed and so land at some distance from the face of the drive-age. A distant voice shouted 'preparing to fire' a few seconds later the voice of the shot-firer shouted "**Fire**" and then a- ear-shattering explosion followed by another and then another for five whole seconds a series of explosions. Iolo counted the explosions "Ten" he said.

"We'll give it a quarter of an hour or so, that' give 'em time to sort things out," said the under-Manager. He smiled wryly and then began a conversation with Iolo regarding the gathering of information concerning materials that were considered re-usable or lying in waste.

After a while when the under-Manager had considered that the men who were *up* face of the drive-age had secured the face of the heading, he and Iolo walked into the place and began an impromptu discussion about what the findings were concerning the state of affairs regarding the unnecessary wastage of mining material.

At the face of the drive-age men had begun clearing the vast amount of fragmented stone that had been removed by the use of powerful explosives, Iolo sniffed the air as mounds of shattered stone passed by him on a conveyor belt, the pungent smell of spent explosives drifted up from the moving conveyor and was absorbed by the ventilation.

Iolo and the under-Manager watched as the machine driver skilfully manoeuvred a hydro-electric track driven bucket loader. The under-Manager spoke to a workman who nodded enthusiastically while keeping an eye on proceedings. The pair of officials along with the deputy in charge walked out of the drive-age chatting and stopping from time to time.

Iolo had completed one shift of cost cutting and now he stood at the bottom of the up-cast shaft waiting for the On-setter to give permission to the waiting riders to board the vacant and waiting pit carriage.

Once again Iolo listened to the sound of the guide-ropes humming contentedly in the brass boxes, the carriage slowed as it neared pit-top and then abruptly stopped with a jolt. The riders began to shout angrily as the carriage swayed gently right next to the fan-drift. The ventilating fan's job was to draw up mine air from around all parts of the mine that the law stated had to be ventilated. Vast quantities of stale-mine-air whistled as it passed between the stopped pit carriages and entered the gaping entrance to the fan-drift.

The riders shivered uncontrollably as the restricted entrance caused the passing air to rapidly cool.

Ten minutes had passed and the carriage had not moved; the men were very angry and shouted abuse at the men on the pit-bank who were trying to shout out reassurances. Men could see the anxious expression on Iolo's blackened but pale face and could sympathise as they knew he had suffered being trapped after an inrush of water and had been ensnared after an explosion.

Twenty minutes had now passed and no news of when the winder would be expected to be operational. Men were cold and angry; however some men had arrived at pit bottom with wet clothing and were shivering with cold. Iolo heard the sound of the signalling system and immediately thought that all would be well. Then the carriage began to be raised inch by inch, all of a sudden the carriage dropped like a stone, the guide-ropes screamed as the friction built up and the screaming of the men sounded like all hell was being let loose. On the pit bank, surface officials shouted and pressed the emergency stop button. Immediately the winder stopped, the brakes were applied after it had travelled at more than thirty feet a second. When the pit rope stopped, the fast descending carriage's momentum continued until the pit rope could not be stretched any more. Grown men continued to scream until the carriage recoiled and dropped by ever decreasing amounts, then it finally halted. Some men laughed nervously others wept openly, thinking that they were to meet their maker. Within a minute or two the carriage began to make a very slow ascent. Some men openly prayed for the first time in their lives. Iolo Pritchard had prayed more than any man on that seemingly doomed ride to the surface of Cwm Derw colliery. Was Anwen Pritchard responsible for the many mishaps at the jinxed mine or was it merely fate?

After the management enquiry regarding the over-wind in the upcast shaft Iolo began to dread each and every day. Ethel was beginning to put enormous pressure on Iolo; she urged him to end his lifelong employment at the Cwm Derw colliery, and even suggested emigrating, but Iolo was made of sterner stuff and was determined to stick it out.

The summer of 1976 was one of the driest on record. Cwm Derw villagers were using water drawn from standpipes, the colliery struggled on regardless. The natural water table was being drawn off by the Cwm Derw underground workings and in turn would be pumped to the surface by powerful underground pumps and then used to wash the newly extracted coal, but the water table was being depleted no rain came to restock the water baring rocks.

Chapter XXVIII

Christmas 1976

The Pritchard family were dreading another Christmas like the previous one, but time had marched on and Christmas had finally made an appearance. Children played noisily in the cold of the morning but Iolo bach and cousin Guto were not allowed out of doors as Ethel was convinced something evil would happen to them.

All was solemnly quiet at the Christmas table no one even thought that the phone would ring as Iolo no longer worked as a Colliery Overman. Things began to lighten up as the festive meal was being eaten, the boys began to chatter loudly and Ethel smiled at their impish antics. Iolo turned on the radio and tuned into the Queen's speech. The Monarch began her Christmas message while Ethel listened with quiet interest; her mind was now at peace she idly looked up at the mirror above the mantelpiece a familiar but haggard face glowered down at her. Ethel put both her hands to her mouth and stifled a cry. Iolo quickly looked up to where Ethel had been looking, and saw the ghoulish Anwen; an ugly, satisfied look on her fading haggard facial image. Bethan hurriedly ushered the boys away from the distraught Ethel and little Iolo cried as he could not understand why his mam was crying.

Another Christmas was destroyed by the spectre of Anwen Pritchard. The Pritchard family were distraught what could they do?

Ethel and Iolo considered telling the family the whole history behind the apparitions but the risk was too great— Iolo a double murderer— maybe the only answer was exorcism.

Ethel began spending a lot of time away from the marital home. She often visited the grieving Rowena Pritchard, wife of Caradog, Iolo's elder brother.

Ethel walked awkwardly and slowly to the front door of Mrs Caradog Pritchard— her sister-in-law. She stopped briefly before knocking on the solid green painted door. The door opened just as Ethel was about to use the brass knocker. "I saw you walking up the road, you've slowed a bit these last few months, is every-thing all right?" asked the concerned Rowena as she ushered her worried looking visitor into the best room.

"I just don't know what's happening to me. I think I'm going insane," blurted Ethel, a tear began to form in an eye, Rowena sat her down and listened patiently as the story of the last year unfolded before her.

"Have a word with Father Donovan, Ethel; perhaps he can shed some light on what's going on… yes that's what I would do, take the stubborn Iolo with you," said Rowena as Ethel emerged from the best room and into the light of day.

"Ta-ta then Rowena, me and Iolo will visit Father Donovan," said Ethel as she tottered on high heels down the path to the gate.

Iolo and Ethel sat around the kitchen table, she had not yet told Iolo of what she had said to her sister-in-law. "Iolo…I visited our Rowena this afternoon; I told her about the apparitions of Anwen…I said I might be going insane imagining seeing Anwen… all over the place. She suggested visiting Father Donovan the Catholic priest and see if he can help us," recalled Ethel, eyeing her troubled husband.

"We are not Catholics and Father Donovan would wash his hands of us… he'll probably try and convert us to Catholicism, any-how, I rarely pray now-days except when my very life is threatened," said Iolo uncharacteristically smiling. "We'll have to think of something else, in any case, if we were catholic we would have to confess our sins and there's no way that I'm going to tell anyone about the things that I have done not even to a Catholic priest," retorted Iolo, the expression on his face said it all.

Weeks had passed and nothing untoward had happened, the Pritchard family had unwisely thought that the bad old days were gone and forgotten.

Iolo and Ethel were more relaxed and started to visit Cwm Derw workingmen's club where they enjoyed drinks and entertainment, along with games of bingo. Iolo being a member was entitled to join the club's outing to the races as he had been to race meetings before.

"Iolo I think it would be a good idea for you to get away from the village for a day, it will do you no harm, it's a pity that Caradog is not with us any-more," said Ethel, she saw the look of despair in his eyes and wished that she had not mentioned his deceased brother.

More weeks went by and it was time for the annual trip to the races and Iolo was looking forward to it. Groups of men bustled around the local shops on the sunny Saturday morning. Iolo was leaning against a lamp post reading a newspaper. Ethel and Iolo bach were spending the day with daughter Bethan.

The coach laden with colliery workers and others seemed to rattle and roll as it made its way to the races. The race-goers chatted loudly among them-selves, most of the punters were miners some were steelworkers and others were from emerging new industries. Iolo sat next to the almost crippled big Bob Stephens and they talked of 'old times, down the pit'. The sun shone through the big wide windows of the coach as it steadily made its way along the motorway, keeping pace with the other traffic that seemed to be going some-place or returning from somewhere. Lorries sped along overtaking the other slow moving traffic and from time to time the coach swayed as a lorry overtook the coach-full of joking, laughing miners and their friends.

The coach duly arrived at the race course and its passengers hurriedly made their way through the hustling throng of eager punters willing to part with their hard earned cash. Iolo however accompanied big Bob, he moved slowly but surely, eventually gaining a good spot from where they could see the winning post. Big Bob reminded Iolo of the time that he had his wallet stolen by a young man called Beaky. Iolo winked while patting a thigh and smiled, big Bob winked and returned the smile. Most of the day had gone without Iolo or big Bob having backed a winner. The last race was about to get ready for the off, Iolo was eager for a winner as it was his last chance to make his money back.

"THEY'RE OFF" shouted the race commentator and he began his excited on-going account of the last race. After three quarters of a mile the horses hooves thundered as they hurtled past the excited punters, 'come on' they cheered as two horses stretched their necks for the winning post and the commentator announced the winner, Iolo frowned with disappointment, big Bob patted his comrades back and paid his commiserations.

As the Cwm Derw race goers boarded the waiting coach Iolo was delighted in the knowledge that he and big Bob were not the only ones, not to come away without having backed a winner.

Ray Chapman the club's burly chairman steadily made his way up the aisle of the coach counting the heads of men who were chatting loudly. "All present and correct he said and smiled to himself with a look of contentment.

The coach duly made its way to the motorway and gently lulled its passengers into a pleasant state of slumber. Next stop was Bodsworth Workmen's Club and Iolo remembered that it was here that Caradog had learned that he fathered a son during the Second World War.

The coach slowed and gently turned into the rough ground called a car park. Iolo looked out of the window at the now improved clubhouse; one part of the buildings was now demolished leaving a single Nissen hut joined to a brand new brick-built and much larger modern unit. The Cwm Derw race goers entered the brand new clubhouse the smell of newness filled their nostrils but few members turned out to greet them. However, the 'beer was good' said some punters and they soon settled down to some serious drinking. The night eventually broke into song and joviality. The club slowly but surely filled to capacity on the news that a good night was to be had at the workmen's. Iolo and big Bob were enjoying the convivial atmosphere, the beer settled comfortable on their stomachs and a free buffet was offered on a table by the wide stage. Iolo noticed a slender hand resting on his shoulder. Quickly he turned his greying head to see who it was. A slim silver haired woman smiled down at him and spoke softly.

"I remember you from your last visit, I see you are you enjoying yourself," she remarked while still smiling softly. Iolo suddenly remembered who she was.

"Yes thanks, it's been a great night and thank you for remembering me," said Iolo returning the smile.

"I've been wondering about the gentleman who was with you on your last visit to us, is he here tonight?" she enquired politely. Iolo thought for a moment before he answered.

224

"The gentleman was my older brother, Caradog," he replied with equal politeness. "But I'm afraid to say that he passed away earlier this year," said Iolo and a sadness filled his eyes which was quickly noted by the woman who had now lost her warm smile and was replaced by utter concern.

"Oh...I am sorry... no one informed me...I had no idea!" she blurted and dragged an empty chair and sat beside Iolo. He explained the death of Caradog as best he could. Big Bob noticed that Iolo and the slim silver haired woman were getting on together and left them chatting together all night.

The night finally came to an end and Iolo bade the woman farewell as he boarded the coach heading for home.

The coach once again lulled the tipsy race goers into a pleasant slumber. Iolo and big Bob were sat in a seat behind the portly coach driver, they slept, heads nodding, as the coach hurtled towards Wales on the now not so busy motorway. Iolo opened an eye and sleepily gazed at the road ahead. Slowly a haggard face seemed to be forming on the windscreen in front of the driver, Iolo began to wake up, and he strained his eyes at the now fully formed face. "*ANWEN*," Iolo screamed, and then the coachman's eyes saw the apparition, he froze in his seat, eyes bulged. He quickly regained his senses and struggled with the swerving coach but it was too much; he lost control on the wide dark carriageway. The vehicle skewed onto its side and tumbled—into a drainage ditch. The coach's belly faced the night sky and the roaring diesel engine spluttered and finally cut out.

The smoking wheels continued turning and all became silent for a brief moment. Drunken Cwm Derw miners climbed through shattered windows shouting the names of their comrades. Up on the motorway vehicles came to a screeching halt and stranger's voices called down to the injured men below.

Iolo wiped the streaming blood from his tortured features and vainly tugged at the lifeless body of Bob Stephens.

People shouted orders while others saw problems where none existed; a small fire began in the engine compartment and was quickly put out by one of the men who had stopped to help the ill-fated race-goers. Iolo rolled his companion onto his back and began to give artificial respiration. Blood dripped from his bleeding nose mixed with perspiration and it seemed a lot worse than it actually was. Big Bob gave a gasp of air and batted his bloodshot eyes; he looked up at Iolo and screamed loudly at the terrible sight of the bloodied Iolo Pritchard. Big Bob eventually came to his senses and sat on the grassy bank above the drainage ditch. In the distance, sirens blared out and the sky lit up with alternating flickering flashes of blue light. Seconds later a fire engine arrived on the scene and firemen raced around the stricken coach while other professionals doused the engine compartment with fire retarding foam.

More ambulances eventually arrived at the scene and the injured men were ferried to a local hospital with accident and emergency facilities. Iolo sat in the speeding ambulance as it raced along the motorway and daybreak began to show in the east.

Big Bob coughed— pain was evident on his bloodied face and an ambulance-man reassured him while the equally bloodied Iolo Pritchard looked on with concern.

At the hospital doctors examined the injured race-goers and Iolo held his head in his hands while waiting to be examined. His mind became twisted with thoughts of Anwen. A doctor had noticed Iolo's behaviour and became concerned. The tall balding doctor stared with piercing dark blue eyes at the man holding his head in his hands. "Can I help you?" he asked in a loud voice. Iolo looked up at him through bloodied eyes and answered.

"I suppose so, I've stopped bleeding now, where have you taken my butty ?" answered Iolo in a faraway voice.

"He's been taken care of and is in good hands now," answered the doctor, he examined Iolo where he was sitting.

Ethel wrung her hands nervously as Iolo had not returned home from the daytrip to the races it was now seven-thirty early morning and no one had yet received any messages regarding the whereabouts of the Cwm Derw race goers. Bethan continued to reassure her mother that all was well and the coach must have broken-down somewhere.

8:00 Sunday morning

The front door echoed loudly as someone banged on it, Bethan raced to the door opening it with a flourish. Police Sergeant Ivor Edwards stood on the doorstep holding his police helmet under one arm. "I'm looking for a Mrs Ethel Pritchard, her neighbours said she may be staying at this address," said the policeman. Ethel listened intently from the living room as the police sergeant explained what he had called for. Ethel hurriedly came to the door.

"It's Iolo isn't it?" she blurted: "he's had an accident hasn't he?" The look of terror on Ethel's face somehow mystified the policeman. Little did he know of Ethel's shocking well-kept secret.

"Mr Pritchard...he's all right, the coach that they were travelling on overturned on the motorway, the entire party is being kept on observation and we are letting the relatives know what has happened," explained the police sergeant, a smile appeared on his wrinkly features.

David Morgan, son-in-law to Ethel was given the task of taking Ethel to a hospital somewhere in Bristol. Meanwhile the motorway police were holding an investigation and would want to question the coach party regarding the road traffic accident.

By Sunday evening Iolo had been discharged from the hospital and was being transported home by David in his car with the faithful Ethel at his side.

Ethel fretted as she waited for a member of the police force to come and interview her husband, the apprehensive Iolo Pritchard.

The day came soon enough as Iolo was taken to the Police Station at Graig Ddu for questioning in regards to the motorway accident.

Iolo sat at a large table, situated under a high narrow frosted window which allowed some natural daylight to penetrate the magnolia painted room. A stern-faced; woman Police Constable stood at the heavy door, it suddenly opened quickly and noisily. Police Sergeant Ivor Edwards and a burly balding Police detective swiftly entered the room and noisily sat down on wooden chairs. Sergeant Edwards began reading from a note book.

"Are you Iolo Pritchard of number three Herbert Road Cwm Derw?" asked the policeman in a loud tone of voice. Iolo eyed him momentarily and answered back.

"You damn well know who I am," retorted Iolo.

"Just answer the question Mr Pritchard," said the Detective in a low tone of voice.

"Yes, I *am* Iolo Pritchard of number three Herbert Road Cwm Derw," said Iolo, arms folded as if he was protecting himself some kind of harm.

"Mr Pritchard, on the sixteenth of July nineteen seventy seven you were among a party travelling on a coach owned by Evans coaches of Graig Ddu. When on the M4 motorway it overturned subsequently landing on its roof injuring all of its passengers. We have spoken to the driver Mr Henry George James who said, and I quote: 'the bloke behind me must have been drunk and out of his mind, he screamed the name *Anwen* and pointed to my windscreen, I turned my head to see what was going on and then I lost control.' Was this man's account of what happened; correct do you think?" recounted the policeman. Iolo stared dead ahead, arms folded and he thought for a moment.

"I don't remember much about it. I'd drunk a bit more beer than normal and fell asleep. I think I had a nightmare; you see I have this recurring dream about my ex-wife. Her name's Anwen," answered Iolo. He wondered what would happen if he said he and Ethel had often seen apparitions of Anwen.

"Tell us more of your ex-wife, she sounds like an interesting personality," ordered the detective. He leaned back in the chair, folded his arms, crossed one leg over a knee, and began to study his interviewee. Iolo thought long and hard about putting a story over, there was no way that he would reveal the truth.

"Anwen left me for another man," Iolo answered slowly and deliberately the detective smiled and then sat upright in his chair and posed another question.

"When did your wife run away with this lovely man, then?" asked the detective still smiling.

"About November nineteen sixty seven… I think," replied Iolo he rubbed his nose profusely, "my damn nose keeps itching it's a sign that my injuries are healing," remarked Iolo with a faint grin.

"Who was the lucky man then?" asked the inquisitive detective. A worried look appeared on Iolo's face and the policemen saw it.

"Someone called Maldwyn Evans, everyone in Cwm Derw knew about it except me and his missus," recalled Iolo, earnestly.

"Did you ever discover their whereabouts? Did they go and live somewhere local?" asked the detective staring at Iolo deliberately making him very nervous. Iolo's brow began to break into a sweat. The detective retreated to his previous sitting position and silently watched the man before him squirming in a chair while the uniformed policeman recorded his every word.

"No one has seen hide or hair of the pair," said Iolo. He put his chin in cupped hands and rested his elbows on the wide, long table. Both policemen sat up and took a renewed interest in what Iolo was trying to put over. "Anyhow, what has my ex-wife got to do with the coach crash?" asked Iolo beginning to show signs of annoyance.

"You have told us that you suffer from recurring nightmares, your ex-wife apparently is a star of the show so to speak," remarked the detective, and Sergeant Edwards gave a crooked smile. "What we want to know is, what happened in the dream that so violently woke you up and caused you to scream out in the manner that you did?" said the detective.

Iolo was in a corner, he struggled to give an alternative account as to what happened and wondered why the coach driver hadn't said he saw a woman's face emblazoned in the windscreen of the speeding coach.

"I can't remember, I'd had a drop to drink but in previous dreams she came to me with a knife in one hand, her other hand held the head of her lover by his hair. Maybe this was the same sort of dream; I'm trying my best to remember," exclaimed Iolo trying to feign a reaction. The policemen studied Iolo with great suspicion and began writing in their notebooks.

Iolo was allowed to go home pending further enquiries, Ethel worried incessantly and Iolo was showing great concern for little Iolo bach. If he was convicted of a double murder the child would be unmercifully bullied for the rest of his life.

An autumn Saturday

The days came and went, an autumn wind blew multi-coloured leaves around Cwm Derw village, and Iolo went hunting rabbits on the foothills of the mountainous slagheap.

Iolo held onto his brown corduroy cap as the wind desperately tried in vain to wrench it from his greying head. The aging Judy sniffed while weaving through dampened leaves drying out by a whirling breeze. Sheep grazed lazily beneath the stark hedgerow that led to a five-bar gate at the entrance of the great black slagheap fondly called the *tip* by the Cwm Derw villagers. Iolo stood at the gate and scanned the brown decaying bracken for signs of movement indicating that a rabbit might be traversing among the decaying brown fronds. Judy sniffed and snuffled as she slowly ploughed her way making trough like paths through the undergrowth. "No luck! must have gone on," Iolo muttered to himself. Judy however picked up a rabbit's scent and weaved expertly to and fro, moving faster than Iolo could manage through the thick lifeless bracken. Further on, Judy obeyed whistle commands from Iolo and waited for her master to catch up.

In the distant of the cold morning, a man sat on a banking; his warm breath turned into a steaming cloud, the man never moved, a black sheepdog sat at his side silently watching for something. Iolo whistled to Judy to come to him she obeyed his command and came trotting tongue hanging to one side, Iolo quickly fastened a chain to her collar and then led the faithful, panting dog, around to the flank of the lone and silent man sitting on a muddy bank waiting for something to happen. Iolo recognised him as the son of Fred Morgan the lifelong friend of his deceased brother, Caradog Pritchard.

The man continued to stare from the muddy bank while his black sheepdog began taking an interest in Judy, Iolo's faithful cocker spaniel.

"You're Fred Morgan's boy aren't you?" enquired Iolo, he gazed at the homemade hemp nets placed over the various mouths of a rabbit warren, large wooden pegs had been hammered into the moist earth deep enough to restrain a bolting rabbit.

"Aye, I'm the son of Fred Morgan, what's it to you?" he replied curtly.

"Your father and my brother were life-long butties, do you miss him?" asked Iolo who was now wondering what to say. He watched solemnly as a rumbling, bumping, sound came from beneath their cold muddy feet. The man quickly raised a hand, the eager dog posed ready for the inevitable pounce. Loud squealing of a terrified rabbit came from beneath the feet of the waiting men poised above. Suddenly a ball of fur hurtled from a hole thus instantly ensnared in the hemp netting. The man dropped his hand and instantly his black sheepdog pounced and held the squealing rabbit firmly between its paws. The man quickly got to his feet and grabbed the struggling rabbit freeing it from its hemp enclosure; he expertly killed the squealing animal and quickly put it in a large pocket inside his brown overcoat. He replaced the hemp net over the hole and went to where he had been sitting previously. At his side was a stout wooden box big enough to comfortably house an albino ferret which was marginally smaller than the polecat kind. Judy sniffed at the mysterious box and sneezed loudly, then turned away and concentrated on the bumping noises beneath her wet paws.

In a matter of minutes the man had netted two more unfortunate rabbits, he began to relax and spoke to Iolo. "You say my dad and your brother were butties, from the Cwm Derw workmen's, was it?" remarked the man." By the way I'm Byron, I just can't believe the rumours that my dad and your brother, Caradog, were fighting after drinking homebrew. They had been doing that for...donkey's years, drinking homebrew, that is," said Byron breaking into a faint smile. "Anyhow my dad had never hurt anyone in his life. Yes, it's a bit of a mystery isn't it?" remarked Byron, he stooped and grabbed a white albino ferret from behind its head and promptly put it in the stout wooden box, he began clearing away evidence of his visit to the warren at the foot of the mountainous, ugly slagheap. The sheepdog continued to sniff at Judy the cocker spaniel and Iolo watched carefully." I'm off home now, it'll be rabbit stew for a couple of days I should expect," said Byron, he smiled broadly and made his way to a well-worn pathway that led to the five bar gate at the entrance to the black mountainous, heap of mining spoil.

Iolo continued on his expedition hoping to shoot a rabbit or two. It was some time later that Judy had managed to raise a rabbit but Iolo was too slow, the rabbit disappeared before he could raise his shotgun.

At the end of the day Iolo returned home empty handed, the rabbit population had lost only three members but Fred Morgan's boy would be back for more of them.

Once again time marched on and the spectre of Anwen Pritchard seemed to have gone away, but rumours began to circulate the village, people were saying: 'Iolo Pritchard is being investigated.' Ethel dreaded shopping in Cwm Derw and was now catching the bus into Graig Ddu, but even there she could not escape knowing looks and whispers. Meanwhile Iolo had returned to his workplace at the colliery stores, men there were more cooperative. The workforce seemed to understand that Iolo had been through hell and high water. Few men however posed him any problems save for some who had transferred from other collieries.

Once again Christmas had caught up with the ill-fated Pritchard family. It was Christmas Eve; Ethel dreaded getting out of her comfortable fireside chair. However she made a tremendous last minute effort and began the preparations for the following Christmas dinner. Iolo had gone to Bethan's house, and then a visit to Cwm Derw workmen's club.

All was quiet at the workmen's club. Iolo stood at the bar talking to Lil and Humphrey the club's steward and stewardess. "It's very quiet tonight," remarked Iolo, "not many members in attendance," he stood at the bar surveying the thinly populated room.

"Yes, everybody's dressing-up tonight, every house a Father Christmas, but roll on tomorrow you won't be able to see for new socks, cardigans, and cigar smoke," remarked Lil, grinning at her husband.

"I'm off home now, I said I'd be home at ten," remarked Iolo as he briefly glanced at the clock that hung above the bay window. He quickly drank the last drop of beer from his glass and bade the other members' farewell.

The wind began to waft up the remaining leaves of autumn, a gust of wind suddenly lifted his cap and he quickly grabbed it with one hand while clutching the front of his overcoat with the other. He shivered as icy blasts tried to prise open his black Melton overcoat. Iolo hurried head down against the prevailing icy twisting wind and from time to time he raised his head as to judge how much further he had to go. In the distance he saw a lone woman hurrying, tottering as if on high heels. The windswept woman shouted; Iolo could barely hear her through the howling icy wind. "Iolo, Iolo," he heard the woman shout as she came within ear-shot. Iolo looked up and was amazed to see the bedraggled Ethel.

"It's her, Iolo, she's come back, she's in the house," cried the terrified Ethel. The howling wind whistled and malevolence was in the stirring air, a dark nightmare was beginning show itself once more.

"What did you say Ethel?" shouted Iolo, he only heard the word '*she*.'

"It's Anwen, I saw her in the kitchen sat at our table she was naked and horrible," shrieked Ethel above the shrieking and whistling wind.

Iolo and his bedraggled wife struggled against the breath-taking icy wind.

Iolo pushed open the old rickety gate; all was in darkness although Ethel had vacated the house in one hell of a hurry, the door was shut tight. Gingerly he opened the creaking door and feebly felt for the light-switch—the light failed to come on, "dagnabit, the lights have fused," screeched Iolo. He dared to breathe as he felt for the door handle that opened the door to the cwtch. He fumbled for the flashlight that he kept for such emergencies. The terrified man began to rummage for a stepladder suddenly the stench of rotting flesh filled his nostrils, he recoiled in horror and dashed for the front door. "What's the matter Iolo, what's wrong?" screeched Ethel, her hair windswept and face streaked with smudged makeup.

"It's that rotting smell again," shrieked Iolo, he grimaced. Recovering his senses the frightened man went back to the cwtch. While holding his breath he quickly grabbed the wooden stepladder and placed it under the fuse box. His hands trembled uncontrollably as he fumbled with the wire fuse. He managed to turn on the light; suddenly a thunderous noise came from an upstairs bedroom. Iolo courageously rushed to the scene, what he saw bewildered him; the large iron bed had been turned upside down revealing rusting steel springs. Ethel stood behind her husband and gasped at the sight of the upturned bed that had now exposed its tarnished bedsprings. Iolo didn't know quite what to do; he and Ethel dreaded the prospect of staying the night in their own home and it was Christmas-eve after all.

Chapter XXIX

January 1978

In the Morgan's household things were not themselves. "I'm very worried about my Mam, every Christmas it's the same thing, she sees things that are not there, it must affect Iolo bach, and even Dad's acting strange. What's the matter with them?" Exclaimed Bethan, her eyes began to fill with tears. David stared at her with penetrating eyes he too wondered what was going on.

"I suppose you've heard the rumours going around the village, the police are taking an interest in what people are saying considering what went on last summer," said David, he chewed at his thin bottom lip and looked at Guto bach with concern.

Iolo was at work, Ethel is busy cleaning the house and from time to time she would stop and listen for any strange noise. At the bottom of the stairs she busied herself cleaning, suddenly she shook with terror as a loud rapping came from the front door. Gingerly she opened the door and peered through the narrow gap. "Mrs Ethel Pritchard?" asked an aging policeman, it was Police Sergeant Ivor Edwards from the Graig Ddu constabulary.

"What do you want?" demanded Ethel?" unwisely. The policeman looked puzzled as only criminals asked 'what do you want?'

"Can I come in, it'll only take a few minutes?" he replied.

"I suppose so!" she retorted, I expect it's about the coach crash is it?" she enquired looking nervous.

The policeman looked down at the carpeted floor and then up at Ethel. "It's not the police' business to respond to chit chat and village gossip, but the rumours are consistent and seem to relate to the coach crash of last summer.

"Oh yes! Iolo's at work right now, perhaps you could call later when he gets home," suggested Ethel, her eyes were wide and pupils pinpointed. The policeman could see she was ill at ease, he hadn't started to make an enquiry. "I wanted to ask you about the rumours, you must have heard about them, have you not?" asked the policeman. He studied Ethel for any reactions, she began to stutter.

"I...I've heard that people have been saying that this house is haunted, things go bump in the night so they say," recalled Ethel. She nervously laughed and looked around the hallway, he eyed her every move.

"How well did you know Anwen Pritchard?" asked the police sergeant.

"Let's have a cup of tea, shall we!" invited Ethel, as she led her inquisitor to her kitchen. "I used to live next door when Anwen lived here, she used to *potch* about, you know," informed the now relaxed Ethel.

"You say, 'used to potch about," he questioned. "I take it potch means to play around have affairs and so on," he suggested and a knowing smile lit up his wrinkled features.

"Yes, that's it, Iolo and the other man's wife were last to know anything about it," confirmed Ethel.

"So where did Anwen Pritchard and her lover go to when they eloped so to speak," asked the policeman. "what was his name and where did he work?"

"He was a bit of a rogue, he worked underground in Cwm Derw colliery, his name was Maldwyn Evans," reported Ethel and a great weight seemed to lift from her narrow shoulders. "No one knows where they went to; Iolo tried to find out so that he could get a divorce and we could marry. I was a widow, my husband was killed down the pit," answered Ethel. She began to gaze into the kitchen window; suddenly she began to shake violently as thoughts of an imminent apparition came to her,"

"Are you all right Mrs Pritchard?" asked the policeman. His eyes showed concern.

"I'll be ok in a minute, I must be coming down with the flue," she answered. Ethel eventually recovered but dared not look out through a window or stare into any mirrors while she was being interviewed by the inquisitive policeman.

"I'll see myself out," offered sergeant Edwards." Tell Iolo I'll be getting in touch in a day or two," remarked the sergeant as he closed the door behind him with a slam.

At the colliery, Iolo idly studied the clock that could be clearly seen through the office window. "One hour to go till home time, I wonder how Ethel is getting on?" mumbled Iolo, quietly.

Outside in the stockyard men worked noisily loading trams with supplies of Steel arches called rings, and timber for the various coal faces and developments. Iolo listened to the sound of a machine groaning and chugging and then the rumble of timber as it was dropped into an empty tram, men near-by shouted as they attempted to communicate their ideas over the noise of the machine.

A group of underground workers stood at the bottom of the steep steps that led to the pithead baths. Their eyes stared up at the towering building that housed a pair of lifts.

"Nearly two years to build this white elephant, too late for the old ones, I bet they're turning in their graves now," remarked a middle aged miner as he stared intently up at the white tower.

"Aye, you can bet on that! They'll close the pit just one week after they get everybody riding in it," remarked another miner.

These lifts would ease the pain of laborious work that had seen generations of Cwm Derw miners' struggle with aching limbs and gasping lungs; ascending countless steps up to the bathhouse after heavy work and a tiresome walk from the coalfaces and other distant places of underground work.

The official commissioning of the new lifts would happen soon ,and all the local dignitaries' would be in attendance.

Iolo Pritchard strolled across the colliery yard he stopped to admire the tall white painted structure that towered above the colliery surface buildings, crows cawed and circumnavigated the winch housing high above the colliery yard below.

Halfway up the steep flight of steps two aging miners had stopped to catch their breath, one held onto a handrail while the other sat on a damp, cold, wooden step, his hands were clasped and his shoulders heaved as he desperately struggled to get air into his dust burdened lungs. Iolo stopped and began a conversation with them. Danny Wilmot had worked under Iolo's supervision when Iolo was Overman on the old twenty six' district. Danny was considered to be a bit of an old codger and had a long memory of the colliery and would tell stories of times gone by and the conditions men had worked in.

"Iolo boy, you haven't got a decent pair of lungs in your coat pocket have you?" asked Danny in a breathless voice, he sort of grinned when he said it.

"I left a good pair of lungs over a chock, but I just can't remember which one!" Joked Iolo and Danny joked likewise. Iolo was not in any particular hurry and began to climb the remainder of the steep steps with the two gasping miners, stopping and starting as the need arose.

The air filled with birdsong the distant patchwork fields seemed greener than ever as Iolo strolled through the local lanes that led to the numerous farms that were dotted around the locality. His mind meandered like the narrow tracked lanes. He leaned on a wooden style looking across the newly ploughed fields. The air smelled fresh as a light wind fluttered the leaves of beech trees that lined the lane behind. Cwm Derw village majestically sat on the horizon, thin wisps of smoke disappeared into the blue sky and Iolo momentarily forgot the many problems that had dogged him and Ethel for a few years now. He glance at his wristwatch: "Twelve o' clock nearly time for lunch," he muttered loudly and began a leisurely walk back to the village and into the unknown.

Iolo studied the hot meal that Ethel had laid before him. "I hear that the Mayor of Graig Ddu will be opening the new lifts down at the pit on Monday afternoon. Perhaps the Cwm Derw jinx will get him," quipped Ethel, she quickly gave a lopsided grin, Iolo noticed it and returned a knowing smile and began tucking in to his delicious homemade steak and kidney pie with a fresh bottle of his favourite brown sauce standing in the centre of the gingham tablecloth on the kitchen table.

Monday afternoon

Mr Cledwyn Jenkins colliery general Manager looked out of his office window which overlooked the colliery yard, surface workers were busily sweeping up loose debris with square mouth shovels. Half-filled trams were lined up ready for the receiving of the sweepings. On the colliery drive other workers were sweeping up and helping the surface dogsbody tidy up the gardens and various lawns that made that area pleasing to the men who would notice them on their way to the pithead baths.

From time to time the Manager's secretary, John Fairburn would come out and inspect the work that was being carried out; he would consult his pocket watch and quickly replace the timepiece into his waistcoat pocket then smartly retreat into the offices to report his findings.

One o' clock

Fairburn rushed out of the offices and began to usher the workmen away from the pithead baths area as the Manager did not want the Mayor to see numerous men cleaning the premises. The afternoon air filled with flashing blue lights as they bounced off the nearby buildings. A big black limousine silently crawled behind a single police car. The Mayoral car pulled up outside the main office buildings, the smiling Mr Jenkins came out to meet the plush vehicle carrying very important passengers.

Iolo tidied up the clutter of paperwork, and left his office for a short walk to the new lifts. He was to lend support to management when the Mayor cut the ribbon, so to speak. The new lifts were locked off so that meant that all workmen and officials had to climb the dreaded steep steps to the pithead baths and main offices.

Iolo finished climbing the last few leg aching steps, suddenly an urgent sounding voice shouted out; Iolo looked up and saw Mr Jenkins gesturing with arms flailing, suggesting that he go over and join the party of bigwigs that were now leaving the main offices and strolling towards the entrance to the gantry that served the new lifts.

Iolo listened as the Mayor made his speech and cut the ceremonial ribbon thus proclaiming the new lifts *open.*

The party slowly made their way down the gantry. The Manager and installation engineer explained to the politely listening audience of council officials and others the pros and cons of building such a project. Iolo felt the hairs of his neck stand up, he shuddered, suddenly stopping to look out of a window. The steep steps below were devoid of struggling gasping miners, all was quiet.

The lift was designed to carry twenty passengers and Mr Jenkins took it upon himself to count the people getting into the one lift.

"Twenty, that's it," he said as he barred the remaining five potential passengers from entering the now crowded lift. Mr Jenkins invited the Mayor to press the down button, Iolo began sweating, and a bead of sweat hung from beneath his wide nose. He eyed the Mayor's long finger poised on the 'down' button. The Mayor stabbed the button sharply. Winch motors in the above motor room began to screech, the lift doors slowly closed. Mr Jenkins stared at Iolo with concerned eyes as the lift slowly descended one hundred feet to the colliery surface. The lift gently landed and the doors opened letting in a flood of sunlight, the relieved passengers vacated the stationary lift in an orderly fashion and assembled on the yard. The visitors stared up into the afternoon sky and marvelled at the modest engineering feat although it took two years to erect. Iolo began making the return trip via the steep steps, Mr Jenkins shouted after him but Iolo turned a deaf ear and began to climb the laborious flights of steps to the pithead baths.

The walk home seemed long and tiring the afternoon sun was low enough in the sky to hurt his tired eyes. Iolo tapped loudly at the front door; Ethel eventually opened it and stared into the haunted face of her husband. He stood motionless in the doorway, Ethel pulled him indoors and led him to the lounge and sat him down. "You had better get to bed, I'll call the doctor," she said. Her eyes then took on a very worried expression and she began to wring her long fingers.

Doctor Philips looked down at his patient, he had known Iolo a number of years and considered him to be a strong character but the doctor had diagnosed severe exhaustion and had administered strong tranquilisers. Doctor Philips spoke quietly to Ethel giving her advice as what to do now. Iolo could hear the droning voices of Ethel and the doctor as he struggled to stave off the effects of the tranquiliser.

Ethel sat in her lounge chair watching the evening news, her eyes became heavy, they batted slowly and then a loud manly scream seemed to fill the house, Ethel shook her tired head and struggled to get her aching body out of the lounge chair. Her legs ached as the top of the stairs seemed further away than she had imagined. The door opened with a quiet squeak, the room seemed very cold and she shivered, Iolo was sitting bolt upright in the bed and staring dead ahead. Curtains billowed in the low light, she strode to the flapping curtains and pulled down the sash window. Iolo hadn't said a single word, he sat staring at the window mouth agape and pale faced.

Ethel wondered about the window, she was certain that she had closed it after bringing Iolo a cup of hot tea earlier in the day. However, Iolo went back to sleep but Ethel was concerned that Iolo was losing his mind. She worried about him incessantly and after all she had as many encounters with the unknown as Iolo had.

Chapter XXX

January 1979

Many weeks had passed since Iolo had taken to his bed. The villagers had gossiped like never before; news of the colliery was consistently being fed to Iolo via Bernard Thomas friend and colleague.

"Do you remember the old twenty six' district?" asked Bernard, he sat on the edge of Iolo's sick- bed and waited for a response.

"Could I ever forget it? Never in a thousand years could I forget that place!" replied Iolo, a faint grin briefly engulfed his now craggy and aging face.

"The surveyors have been busy measuring and marking out for the driving of a gob heading," remarked Bernard, he suddenly noticed a look of mild terror forming in the face of his old butty.

"Where will the gob heading be sited?" asked Iolo with nervousness in his voice.

"When I asked Jack Williams about it he told me it wasn't certain that the drive-age would go ahead but if it did it would start in the old twenty six' gate road and emerge in the tail road at about three hundred and fifty yards from its mouth," explained Bernard, patiently.

"Why would they want to drive a heading through the waste? There's a lot of timber and steel where we worked under bad roof," said Iolo he struggled to remember where he had buried the bodies of Anwen and Maldwyn all those years ago.

"Management want to work the heavily faulted seam to the left of twenty six,' now that we have improved machinery," answered Bernard, quietly, he stared at Iolo who was looking extremely worried.

Iolo eventually left the confines of his sick-bed and began spending his time wandering around the village talking to anyone who would listen to his ramblings. Retired miners were always sitting on the benches that were dotted around the village square, talking about anything that entered their heads. Charlie Dicks now retired sat on such a bench, he sat forearms resting on his thighs, hands clasped and from time to time his bony hunched shoulders would heave as he gasped for a lung-full of clean air. Iolo Pritchard slowly strolled towards the sitting retired miners they eyed him and passed comments accordingly.

"The people you see when you haven't got a gun," quipped Iolo and he grinned broadly. He raised his trouser-legs and sat down beside Charlie Dicks and began a long conversation about the pit and things in general.

The day wore on and the retired miners called to the afternoon-shift and exchanged good-humoured banter with them.

More weeks had passed and Iolo felt fit enough to return to his place of work at the colliery stores. The morning was brightening as the sun was beginning to rise in the east. Iolo responded by raising a hand to shield his eyes from the sun as it peeped over the roof of the pithead baths. Some men who had been doing some overtime passed the time of day with him and remarked that they had not seen him for some time. Suddenly a car came to a sudden halt with squealing brakes. Iolo looked to see the rare smile of Mr Cledwyn Jenkins colliery general Manager. "Nice to see you making a return to work, Iolo," he called out. "Come and see me after you've changed into your working clothes," he added and then drove the remainder of the way to his reserved parking-slot near the main offices.

Iolo knocked loudly on the colliery general Manager's solid wooden office door, "Enter," came a commanding voice, he opened the door and walked in, the old photos of previous Cwm Derw Managers lined both sides of the generous room and seemed to eye the tall aging miner. "Sit down Iolo, I've been waiting for the right opportunity to speak to you, how have you been keeping?" asked the Manager in a polite sort of voice. Iolo looked down at the floor with a thoughtful expression on his lined face, he raised his head and stared at the nicotine stained ceiling the Manager noticed a beginning of a tear in Iolo's eye.

"I...I've had problems since the explosion in sixty-eight this has affected both my wife and me," explained Iolo, fighting back the tears. "A lot has happened since then, it's made an old man of me and I'm finding it hard to carry on," explained Iolo. Mr Jenkins looked at Iolo with saddened eyes.

"Iolo I have asked your union to explore the possibility of you taking early retirement would you consider such an idea?" asked the Manager with a sort of pleading in his eyes.

May 4th 1979

Iolo had accepted early retirement under ill health rules; Ethel was very pleased that he had accepted.

The morning newspaper had arrived and Ethel read out from it." It says here that the Conservative Party won by an overall majority of forty- three seats," She quoted. "Margaret Thatcher is out to tame the unions by the look of it," she quipped.

Iolo continued an interest in the workings of Cwm Derw colliery, and Bernard Thomas kept Iolo up to speed regarding such events as the proposed gob heading which had the possibility of exposing the remains of Anwen Pritchard and her lover Maldwyn Evans.

The Thatcher government was going from strength to strength, the first woman Primeminister in British history was proving to be a formidable leader. The labour party were now effectively the Party opposite.

XXXI

Gob Heading

Due to the management reshuffle of officials, Bernard Thomas had had now left the coalface and was a deputy supervising the driving of the new Gob Heading through old workings, eventually emerging in the tail-road of the old twenty six district, a distance of some two-hundred and twenty yards. The geology to the left of twenty-six district was heavily faulted and management were anxious to exploit the modest reserves of coal that were previously impossible to mine due to the inadequacies of the machines and methodology available in times gone by. Modern machines and methods were now available to the miners of Cwm Derw which enabled miners to exploit coal seams disturbed by geological faults.

The miners employed to drive the new *tunnel* or roadway through the old workings were finding the way forward extremely hard going as the workings were littered with crushed timber and metal girders.
Once a week Bernard Thomas would visit Iolo Pritchard and update him on the politics of the Cwm Derw mine. Iolo would grow more anxious by the week as he was informed of the progress of the advancement of the new Gob Heading where the bodies of Anwen his first wife and her lover Maldwyn Evans were hidden by Iolo in 1967.

The junction of the new gob heading was now going through its final stages. Mr Jenkins colliery general Manager eyed the workmanship with a discerning look about his sharp features. "Not a bad job, boys, I've seen better!" he said as he turned away from the workmen and grinned at Bernard Thomas the deputy assigned to the project.
Once the junction was completed the drive-age workers needed to excavate out from the gob area and then install the conveyor that would transport the muck and stone to the transfer point/junction and then via other conveyors to the pit bottom.

At the Collier's Arms pub, Bernard Thomas leaned on the bar and began a conversation with Iolo Pritchard. He explained the difficulties that his workmen were encountering while driving the new gob heading.

"I never realised how much timber and steel were used when we were securing those falls of ground on twenty sixes, back in the sixties, it's taking us a shift to pull out old steel girders and crushed timber before we can extend the conveyor," he remarked, a serious frown engulfed his face as he spoke.

"Yes, I remember the same thing years and years ago in the old south workings when I was a young miner, I remember coming up against an old tram with three wheels on it, probably easier, quicker and cheaper to bury it than send it out to the pit I expect," remarked Iolo, he smiled faintly and then frowned as he looked up at the clock above the bar. "Quarter past ten, I promised the wife that I would be home at ten," said Iolo, quickly. He swiftly drank the remainder of his beer and left the pub saying his goodbyes as he went through the main doors.

Walking briskly down the dark unlit street Iolo noticed that his house was in darkness. He pushed open the front gate walking up to the door while fishing in a trouser pocket for the small Yale key which was in amongst copious amounts of small change. He opened the door and called to Ethel, a feeble female voice answered and a cold shudder raced up his spine as he felt about the walls for a light-switch. The icy cold house smelled eerie. "Ethel where are you?" he called nervously. No answer, he found a light switch and flicked it furiously, nothing happened, he called out to Ethel once more, no answer, the door to the lounge was shut . Iolo felt for the doorknob and gingerly pushed the creaking door open, the flicker of candlelight met his eyes, slowly his eyes adjusted to the dim candlelight. Sat in a chair below the burning candle on the mantelpiece was Ethel wide eyed and silent, her pale lips quivered in the faint glow as she vainly tried to speak.

"I think the lights have fused," she uttered feebly, Iolo went to her and comforted her.

"I'll have the fuse mended straight away," he said and went to the cwtch (under stairs) for a torch and fuse wire. Iolo had that feeling that the ghost of Anwen had something to do with this terrible darkness that so frightened his wife Ethel.

After a few minutes the Pritchard's household was lit up like a lighthouse no corner was in darkness but the Pritchard's' were afraid to go to their bed as the wrath of Anwen had gripped them like never before.

Ethel peered through the kitchen window her tired reddened eyes hurt as the morning sun steadily climbed in the east. The brightness lit up the kitchen and Iolo lifted his aching head from the kitchen table. "I think we need to go to bed for a couple of hours," suggested Iolo, he gazed at his agonised wife she returned it through half closed eyes and spoke.

"I can't handle any more of this; it's killing us both from the inside out... I've never felt so weak nor tired in my entire life," sobbed Ethel. Iolo took her by the hand and led her upstairs to bed hoping that they could get some well-deserved sleep. The exhausted and troubled couple eventually fell into a deep sleep undisturbed by the antics of ghosts and ghouls.

Hours had passed as Iolo and Ethel slumbered peacefully side by side in their bed. Outside, Bethan Morgan hammered at the door of her mother. Feverishly Bethan fumbled for the spare key that he mother had given her just in case of trouble.

Once inside she scoured the downstairs rooms for signs of her mother or Iolo, desperately calling out their names. Bethan gingerly opened the door of the back bedroom; meekly she called into the quiet and still room. Fearing the worst she swung open the heavy door revealing the slumbering Iolo and Ethel.

Bethan stared down at the tranquil scene not knowing what had caused it. Ethel raised a sleepy eye and closed it with equal ease, a sudden fear gripped her she tried to scream but she thought in her tired mind that it was a nightmare.

Bethan stooped and began to shake her mother by the shoulder. Ethel took on the appearance of a woman possessed and sat up trying to scream, Bethan shouted to her," Mam, wake up, it's three o'clock in the afternoon, what's happening here?" she called.

Iolo began to come around from his deep sleep he stared at his stepdaughter disbelievingly. "What's the matter?" he asked naively.

Bethan could not believe her eyes and ears. She waited for a reasonable excuse.

"We...we had a late night and the lights went out and I was afraid," Ethel blurted.

The weary pair and Bethan sat around the kitchen table drinking from large mugs of strong tea. They were unable to reveal the truth behind the *goings on* as Bethan had called it.

"Me and David have been thinking, there's more going on here than meets the eye." She stared into her half emptied mug of dark brown strong tea and then looked up at her mother and stared her in the eye. Ethel looked away and Iolo felt very uncomfortable in her presence. However, Bethan left the household of her mother and step-father, none the wiser regarding their strange behaviour. The sun was now low in the sky and Bethan could not help but notice the twitching of net curtains as she strode down the street to her home, husband, child, and of course little Iolo bach who seemed to spend more time being looked after by his big sister than of his own parents.

The previous day had passed peacefully enough and the Pritchard's had managed to get some sleep. Ethel managed to pluck up enough courage to dress in front of the long cheval mirror situated in the back bedroom where she had been sleeping.

Today was shopping day in Cwm Derw village and Ethel felt a little uneasy about browsing the local shops.

Today like yesterday was bright and sunny but a little windy as usual. Every shop window seemed to offer a reflection of the worried looking shopper as her imagination took hold. The image of Anwen Pritchard was never far from her mind as she went into shops and people gave her knowing looks and turned away to gossip about her.

On the village square the retired miners congregated and exchanged gossip while lounging on the few benches that were dotted about. Charlie Dicks as usual sat on a bench waiting for the usual one or two old codgers to come and sit with him, suddenly someone tapped him on the shoulder, Charlie turned his tired aching body round to see who it was. "Morning Charlie, got room for a little one have you," said a tall scraggly haired man.

"Hello, big Bob, aye, come and sit by here mun, motioned Charlie tapping the wooden slats with a withering hand, his narrow shoulders heaved and he coughed, spitting coal blackened phlegm onto the grass at the side of the bench. Big Bob and the sly grinning pensioner exchanged their views on the Cwm Derw colliery and of days gone by.

"Aye, I remember a stink about that twenty six' district, it stank of rotten meat, a terrible smell," recalled big Bob. He looked up at the heavens as the sky began to darken and large drops of rain fell about him and old Charlie Dicks. The sky suddenly lit up as a streak of lightning hurtled to earth somewhere in the distance. Big Bob, Charlie Dicks and the other retired miners hobbled to the shops in search of shelter.

Jack Williams stood on the doorstep of the officials-lodge office and studied the dark sky. He remembered the moments just before the underground explosion back in sixty eight, a cold shudder raced up his spine urging him to retreat into the lodge office. He immediately noted the barometer reading and compared it to the records that were made by the mine deputies as they were compelled to do so by an act of parliament. "Hmm, I'll phone the power house," he mumbled to himself.

"Under-Manager here, has the Met office issued a barometer warning at any time to day," he asked.

"Aye, I've just finished informing the deputies, this weather is going to get worse," the powerhouse attendant informed the under-Manager.

Jack Williams felt his stomach turning he was now getting worried and he began phoning the deputies district asking about the gas contents of the general bodies of airways.

Bernard Thomas watched from behind a digging machine, the operator stood up out of the driving seat and stared in utter disbelief at the mysterious objects. He immediately climbed down from his machine and went to inspect the mystifying objects resting ominously on the heap of muck on a mechanical bucket.

Bernard Thomas hurried to the face of the heading and began to handle the odd fragments holding them at arms-length and scanning with his cap-lamp. "They look like old bones… it definitely isn't a fossil but how did bones get down here?" said the deputy to the machine operator. After scratching at the face Bernard uncovered more fragments of bone, a piece of it resembled part of a human skull.

"Fence this lot off, ten yards back, while I inform the under-Manager," ordered Bernard Thomas the deputy in charge of the gob drive-age.

Jack Williams thoughtfully tapped at a large scribble pad with the end of a biro. Suddenly the office phone rang out ominously; slowly he picked it up and the voice of Bernard Thomas shouted out loud and panicky. Jack listened intently, he was expecting the worse but not in the form of the find of 'old bones'. "Have you fenced the area off...?good I'll be with you as soon as I can," he said and began to inform the senior management.

Ethel listened in awe as the women in the queue in the butcher's shop began talking about the finding of skeletal remains 'down the pit' and forensic scientists were being called in to find out who the bones belonged to. In Ethel's mind the bones were of Anwen Pritchard and her lover Maldwyn Evans.

It was only a matter of time before the authorities would work out who committed the murders by using district measurements, records and dates, then searching for missing persons in the relevant records of the time.

Ethel hurried home as fast as her legs would carry her, the image of Anwen Pritchard imprinted on her troubled mind. She hammered at the front door not bothering to look for a door key. Iolo, angrily opened the door not realising that the commotion was caused by Ethel. "Dagnabit, what the hell's going on, Ethel are you out of your mind, mun?" shrieked the maddened Iolo Pritchard.

"The women in the Butcher's shop are talking about the miners... finding skeletons —down the pit," blurted Ethel she pushed pass her bewildered husband and raced to the kitchen sink where she began retching noisily. Iolo sat at the kitchen table unable to speak, the dreaded day of reckoning had come, what could he do? There was no point in running away and where could he go, the authorities would find him no matter where he went. Iolo grabbed the sobbing Ethel and comforted her.

Iolo and Ethel eventually retreated to their bedroom and lay on the bed holding on to each other tightly and in a few agonising minutes a loud deafening; RAT-A-TAT-TAT, it was justice knocking at their door. The Wrath of Anwen was upon them.

The End

Other Books by Gareth J Hughes

Snatchers: (ASIN: B006TJQ4VU)

Would You Believe It? : (ASIN: B00945G0HO)